Running
For The Cross

Running
For The Cross

A HEART DECEIVED

Larry Ivan Vass, DDS, MDiv, PhD

TATE PUBLISHING
AND ENTERPRISES, LLC

Running For The Cross
Copyright © 2014 by Larry Ivan Vass, DDS, MDiv., PhD. All rights reserved.

No part of this publication may be reproduced, stored in a retrieval system or transmitted in any way by any means, electronic, mechanical, photocopy, recording or otherwise without the prior permission of the author except as provided by USA copyright law.

This novel is a work of fiction. Names, descriptions, entities, and incidents included in the story are products of the author's imagination. Any resemblance to actual persons, events, and entities is entirely coincidental.

The opinions expressed by the author are not necessarily those of Tate Publishing, LLC.

Published by Tate Publishing & Enterprises, LLC
127 E. Trade Center Terrace | Mustang, Oklahoma 73064 USA
1.888.361.9473 | www.tatepublishing.com

Tate Publishing is committed to excellence in the publishing industry. The company reflects the philosophy established by the founders, based on Psalm 68:11,
"The Lord gave the word and great was the company of those who published it."

Book design copyright © 2014 by Tate Publishing, LLC. All rights reserved.
Cover design by Junriel Boquecosa
Interior design by Jimmy Sevilleno

Published in the United States of America
ISBN: 978-1-63268-905-4
Fiction / Religious
14.08.22

Mary Meets Her Prince

RUNNING THROUGH THE streets like a wild animal, the young woman had a look of horror on her face. She placed a hand on one wall then another to avoid falling as she stumbled forward over the loose, uneven cobblestones. She glanced repeatedly over her shoulders, searching for whoever or whatever she intuited was pursuing her.

The woman wore a tunic that was dirty and tattered. One of its sleeves was missing; its hem was frayed and ragged. Patches of crimson showed through the smudges, revealing that the garment was once one of quality. She had pulled the tunic up to just above her knees and had cinched it at the waist with a braided leather cord. As she ran through the streets, the tie trailed on the ground behind her like a wilted tail.

More than half of the maiden's legs and exposed arm was covered by cuts and bruises. Her disheveled coal-black hair, styled by dust and sweat and by the wind and the rain, was twisted and mussed into wet clumps of tangles and snarls. Some of her hair had even been wrenched out by people who had felt threatened by her bizarre behavior or scared by her unruly appearance.

Her hazel eyes were speckled with islands of green, and in spite of being sunken deep within their sockets, they showed to be wide and wild. Pure unabated fright and unrelenting torture crossed her face like the roads on a map. Her eyes darted hither and yon; she saw all and yet saw nothing. An ebony dye commonly used by women to enhance the size of their eyes ran in streaks over her prominent cheekbones onto a strong square jaw. Underneath, her delicate thin neck appeared rusty from the buildup of dirt.

More and more bruises and cuts appeared on her frail frame each time she tripped and fell. She seemed to be oblivious to the pain; not once did she cry out. Drool collected as froth at the corners of her mouth and cascaded down either side of her chin, leaving trails in the dirt like snail trails on dank rocks.

She clawed at the walls of the houses that lined the alleyways as she ran past, screaming at the top of her lungs, "Leave me alone! Stop hurting me!" Between the outbursts she sometimes made sounds like that of a pig grunting, sometimes like a dog growling, and sometimes even a wolf howling. Other times she swore at the top of her lungs, "What have I done to deserve this? I hate you, Jehovah!" Occasionally she would stop and wave her arms wildly in the air above her head, as if fighting off a swarm of bees. Then she'd drop to her knees and growl or grunt or bark. She would crawl a little, get to her feet and stumble forward a little, and then run like a decathlon competitor.

Seven demonic spirits had taken up residence in this young woman. Why? No one could explain it, but passersby certainly knew to stay out of her way.

This young woman's mother and father had died when she was only eight years old. An only child, she had been raised by her nearest relative, an uncle by the name of Haggadi. He was a very well-to-do businessman and had no problem taking in his niece. However, his wife had taken no interest in the girl; she ignored her completely. From the time she had come into their home, Haggadi's two daughters had refused to share with her or to allow her to take part in any of their activities. They even refused to include her when their friends came to visit. Haggadi's four sons had teased her unmercifully about being a girl without a mother and a father, and therefore without hope. They had abused her both verbally and sexually, but she had always managed to wiggle free before she was ever violated totally.

Violation seemed to be her lot. At seventeen years of age, she had no betrothed, no husband, no friends, and no real family. She had had a successful business selling cloth to and making clothes for the merchant's wives in her hometown of Magdala, and her business had sustained her until one day, the seven evil spirits had taken possession of her and had driven her into the realm of insanity. Instead of attending to her only means of support, she had begun to run the streets, cursing people with whom she had once done business. Many times she acted like a swine, an animal that the Jews hated and shied away from. Since losing her home on the city wall, she had roamed and plundered the streets and ate with the dogs.

The citizens of Magdala who had known this woman and dealt with her on a professional level knew her as Mary, but now they called her *Ma'ac*, a Hebrew word meaning "vile person." All her life, Mary had scratched and clawed, worked and saved, and had done all she could do to improve her lot and take care of herself. She had depended on no one and had made sure her name went untarnished; but now, now she lived with the animals, sounded like the animals, and behaved generally like them—wild, ferocious, and unruly.

After falling down once more, Ma'ac scrambled to her feet and snapped at the air around her like a dog that was trying to catch some annoying insect, some mysterious something that no one else could see. She screamed obscenities so loudly that passersby held their hands over their ears and hugged the walls of the houses that lined the avenues through which they passed. They felt it necessary to stay as far away as possible from this creature, this God-abandoned "thing." The scene repeated itself over and over as Ma'ac made her way toward the gate that led to outside the city. As this poor creature struggled to exit through the gate, she ran headlong into a holy man and the four men who followed him. The Holy Man grabbed Ma'ac by her shoulders to keep her from falling onto the cobblestone street, but she shrieked loudly and rudely and tried to pull herself free from his grasp. Her glazed eyes became wider and wilder. She barked at the Holy Man like a mad canine, and from down deep inside her came hollow, gruff sounds that the followers of the holy man perceived to be words saying, "We know you, Jesus! And we know that it is not your time. Why do you bother us? Leave us be!"

The Holy Man's disciples were startled by the voices. They huddled together like frightened sheep. They cupped their hands around their mouths and whispered to their Teacher, "Were those words the words of this loathsome creature, Rabbi? How did she know your name?"

One of the four known as Peter said to his master, "The voice that came from inside that hideous creature just spoke your name."

The Holy Man blinked not an eye, nor did he look surprised. He turned to his followers and commented with a laugh. "See, even the demons know who I am! If they recognize me, why do you think the people who should know me do not?"

Peter scratched his head and replied, "I don't know, Master!"

Ma'ac wiggled and squirmed and kicked until she freed herself from Jesus's grasp and then ran headlong through the city gate into the olive groves beyond. The Rabbi called to her. "Wait, Mary, wait!" He made a move to chase after her but was restrained momentarily by Peter, a man who was larger than life and a head taller than Jesus.

Holding his mentor firmly, Peter said, "Rabbi, why trouble yourself with one such as that?"

His hot breath poured over his teacher's face like the heat coming from a rock under the sun. Jesus's frustration welled up. He put both his hands on Peter's chest and pushed him away, as if he would do him harm. Peter staggered backward. One of the other disciples who walked with Jesus grabbed him before he hit the ground.

"She is a wild woman with whom you need not concern yourself, Jesus!" Peter roared from the clutches of his companion. "What good would it possibly do to try and help the likes of her? She is obviously not in her right mind. Besides, you have more important things to attend to today than to bother with her!"

"The likes of her!" the Rabbi screamed through clenched teeth. "She is the one who is in need of my help. A physician does not come into the house of the well but into the house of the sick. Do *you* need a physician today, Peter?"

"No, of course not, Rabbi," Peter replied. "But I thought…"

"Well, that's the problem Peter," Jesus retorted angrily. "You don't think or you think incorrectly. The voice coming from that woman was not her own. It was the voice of a number of evil spirits that have taken possession of her. She is a 'sick' person who is in need of a doctor. Who can heal her? Can you heal her, Peter?"

Peter looked down at the ground and replied sheepishly, "Well, of course not, Rabbi. I have seen you heal the diseased, give sight to the blind, and make the lame to walk. You are the great physician, not me."

"Indeed," Jesus said. "Indeed. She needs a doctor, and I am that doctor. Have I not told you before that I have come into the world to heal the sick, give life to the dead, grant forgiveness to the sinner, bring hope to the hopeless, and to save the lost? You say I should not bother with the 'likes of her!' Where is your compassion, man? Where is your heart? Where is your brain for that matter?" Jesus reprimanded.

He turned to his followers and continued, "Remember what I have told you. I have come to do the will of the Father, and that, men, is what I will always do, just as I have always done, even before the foundation of the world."

Ashamed, the disciples hung their heads and acknowledged that yet once again, they had not been thinking on a high-enough plane. They still thought like earthly creatures and had not yet fully grasped the reality of what their pedagogy had been teaching them since they had left everything behind to follow him.

Jesus knew to where the possessed young woman had fled, but he let her go. He knew that the Father had worked all things out providentially and that he would encounter her again before leaving Magdala. Jesus led his men into the center of the city and went straight to the synagogue to talk with the elders. As they walked, the disciples whispered among themselves about the many things their teacher had told them that day. They even marveled about the fact that he knew the possessed woman's name, and they were equally amazed that the voices coming from deep within her knew who Jesus was. Jesus knew what they were discussing so secretively, but he decided not to say anything.

After Jesus finished speaking in the synagogue, the resident teachers were mystified and astonished at what he had to say. Jesus and his men withdrew and stood outside. They nodded and said shalom to the bewildered Jews as they filed out of their place of worship.

"I just love it, Lord," said one of Jesus' followers they called Andrew. "I love the look on their faces when you read and teach the Scriptures and indicate that they are written about you. I can't tell you enough what it means to me to be your disciple. To have been called by you and allowed to be your student is just more than I could ever have imagined or dreamed of."

"I'm happy you feel that way, Andrew," Jesus said. "For there will come a day when you will be tested and have to suffer for my name's sake."

"I'm ready for any eventuality, Lord," Andrew boasted.

"You may think that way now, Andrew," Jesus responded, "but I can assure you that there will come a time when you will face death for my name's sake."

That seemed to quell his enthusiasm. No one spoke again regarding how brave they thought they were. Jesus walked toward the district of the city where rooms to let were available. His disciples quickly followed after him. They looked at one another quizzically about the words their teacher had just spoken to Andrew concerning his martyrdom. Not knowing at this moment what fate lay ahead for each of them, they still were willing to follow this man called Jesus. They knew and understood that he alone had the gift of eternal life, and that, in and of itself, was worth anything and everything that they would ever have to face.

The next day just after daybreak, after they had already broken bread together, Jesus and his disciples rose up to leave the city of Magdala. As they approached the city gate, Ma'ac again came charging into Jesus and his four followers. This time, however, Peter grabbed her by both arms and, with determination not to let her escape again, held her firmly. She kicked and screamed and wiggled and tried to bite Peter's arms; all the while, the seven voices deep down inside her swore obscenities and begged at the same time to be left alone.

"Let us alone, you cretin," they chimed. "Stop bothering us."

Then in voices that changed from gruff growls to voices of softer pleading, they begged, "Don't harm us, Jesus. Let us go to someone else if you must have her." The voices changed their tone abruptly and said harshly, "You know it's not your time! Why bother us now? You don't need this creature! We do!"

"Silence!" Jesus commanded sternly. "Speak no more!"

Instantly, the voices from the demonized woman fell silent. Like everything that Jesus said or did, all things great and small, all of nature, to include the demons, obeyed him without question. He then stood directly in front of the possessed woman and spoke gently. "Peace be unto you, Mary. Do not be afraid."

Ma'ac stopped her screaming and flailing about and hung limply in the grasp of Peter's large hands. Her eyes went from wide and wild to soft and serene. Not wanting to frighten her, Jesus whispered softly, "The power that speaks to you is greater than the power that now indwells you. You have nothing to fear. From this moment forward, the demons will no longer indwell you or bother you. Your sins are forgiven."

Jesus stepped back and spoke with a voice of authority. He commanded, "Demons, leave this woman!" At that very moment, a box turtle came out of the grass by the side of the road. Jesus pointed to it and pronounced, "That is your new home for now, demons."

The woman slumped to the ground and involuntarily opened her mouth. A rush of visible wind with a brownish sheer tail, a smell of putrefaction, and screeching voices decrying obscenities flew from her mouth across the road into the box turtle. Momentarily, the turtle meandered slowly from its resting place. As it crossed the road, a cacophony of voices could be heard complaining, "It's crowded in here! Don't touch me! Can't we go any faster? Hey, turtle, we're talking to you! Can't you hear us? Oh, this is going to be no fun at all!"

The four disciples laughed at what they observed. Screeching, complaining, and cursing emanating from such a gentle creature as a box turtle were indeed a funny thing to see and hear.

Jesus rolled his eyes and said, "I guess moving from deluxe spacious quarters to those that are cramped might be uncomfortable. Oh well!"

While his disciples laughed, an almost imperceptible smile crept across Jesus' face. Kneeling before the young woman on the ground, he took her hands in his and gently urged her to raise her head. Tears began to overflow the rims of her eyes and run down her cheeks. She cried uncontrollably and fell into Jesus' arms. Her shoulders heaved up and down as she gasped for each breath. She made Jesus' robe wet with her tears.

The Rabbi patiently let her cry her eyes out and, with the utmost sensitivity, dropped her hands from his, took her narrow shoulders in his large hands, and pushed her away so that he could look at her eye to eye. He brushed the tangled hair back and took her face in his hands. Wiping the tears underneath her eyes across her face with both his thumbs, he said comfortingly, "Mary, Mary, do not cry! You are free! You have been set free from the bondage of Satan. You have been set free from the bondage of sin. I have forgiven your trespasses, Mary, and have placed you into the family, the family of God."

Before he could utter another word, Mary broke down again into repentant sobs, sobs that rang out with rejoicing, sobs that revealed repentance, sobs that displayed thanksgiving, sobs that uttered a kind of praise and a kind of reverence that heretofore she had never had the opportunity or a situation for which to cry.

She finally regained enough composure to say, "Thank you, sir. I shall be eternally grateful. Your kindness has overwhelmed me. I feel…I feel totally different. I know that the spirits have departed from me, but, sir, I not only feel different inside, but I feel different in my vision. I see things quite differently than before."

The woman known previously as Ma'ac knelt down and started kissing Jesus' hands. Peter and Andrew put their hands on the top of her shoulders and pulled her back to a seated position. They informed her that it was inappropriate to show such affection to a holy man. Jesus quickly intervened. He pulled the men's hands from her, reached down, and lifted the woman back onto her feet. Placing his own arm around her waist and pulling her close to him, Jesus rebuked them both, saying, "Would you keep the children from their Father? Do not prevent them from coming unto me. The Father loves the Son, and the Son loves the Father and loves all those whom the Father has given to him. This woman I love and have loved from the beginning of time. If she showers me with her love and affection, do not stop her, or anyone else. They come to me out of love because I have loved them first."

Peter reminded Jesus. "She is an unclean woman. Until this very moment, she was filled with seven evil spirits. No doubt you have exorcised the spirits from her and made her whole, but she is from Magdala, and you know that the women of Magdala have a reputation of being loose and free."

Jesus rebuked Peter yet again, saying, "Enough, Peter, enough! What she was makes no difference. You should know that. She stands before me now forgiven."

He paused momentarily, lowered his eyes and his voice, and said softly, "Like you, like all of you, she has my righteousness imputed to her, so that you all are covered and my Father can then look upon you, something that he could not do until now. This woman is no woman of ill repute just because she's from Magdala. She resisted the devil to the point that he realized that he could not win her soul, so he sent his demons to possess her, thinking that he would then have her. Possession is not her sin, nor is her sin the sin of fornication. I am really surprised at you, Peter. I thought certainly, you of all people would understand. All have sinned and fallen short of the glory of God. There are none righteous—no, not one. But somehow, Peter, you put qualifications on people being my followers, my disciples, my very own. But I tell you the truth: if it were not for the grace and mercy of my Father, no one would be saved, not one person would see the kingdom of heaven. He draws the ones he has chosen before the foundation of the world, and I do his will. When my time has come, I will pay the sin debt for all that the Father has given to me, and I will lose none, except the one that was meant to be lost to fulfill Scripture."

Lessons for Peter were never-ending. It would be only a matter of minutes before class would be back in session. The tall, lanky fisherman had been admonished once again. He felt that he would never be able to be like Jesus, no matter how hard he tried. He loved the man, but he certainly could mess up! Where was his discernment? When would he be able to think in terms of the kingdom? When would he stop being such a fool?

Peter hung his head and said quietly, "I'm sorry, Jesus. I just wasn't thinking."

"I know, Peter, I know," the Lord said softly. Jesus shook his head and walked over to the big rough leader of his pack, reached up, and placed his arm around his shoulders and said, "You're my man, Peter. You're my rock. There will be many times that you will fall, but you will rise up again. There will even come a time when you will deny me, but you will come back and you, along with my other disciples, will be the twelve foundations for the New Jerusalem."

Peter started to speak, but Jesus placed his finger to his lips and said, "Not now, Peter, not now. Instead of saying a word, Peter, I wish for you to pray, especially for this young woman. I want you to give thanks for her deliverance. Pray for a hedge of protection to be placed around her, and pray for her growth and discernment. Okay, Peter? Will you do that for me?"

"Of course, Lord," Peter answered humbly. "You know I will do anything for you. I will do anything you ask of me."

Jesus stooped down and picked up the staff that he had dropped to the ground when he had collided with Mary of Magdala. He turned to his four disciples and announced their departure.

Mary quickly blocked their way and nervously asked, "What about me? What am I to do now? I have no place to live, no work. The people who were once my customers will certainly not return to me, especially after I have harangued them, cursed at them, and have failed to deliver their goods for which they had paid a deposit. What am I to do?"

Jesus looked at her with empathy and said, "Well, you certainly can't stay with us. We are five itinerates who have no place to call our own. We travel from place to place teaching, preaching, and healing. Besides, you must return the money given to you as interest or else deliver the goods." He stopped abruptly and thought. "However, I know that we cannot leave you here. Go first and return the money and come with us this day to

Capernaum and I will introduce you to my mother. I know that she will help you."

"Thank you, my Lord," said Mary. "Thank you. I will be no trouble to you. You'll see. But I'm not sure I know your name. Did those spirits call you Jesus?"

"Yes," the Teacher replied. "My name is Jesus."

"Thank you, Jesus," Mary cooed. "Thank you for ridding me of those terrible demons, and thank you for making me feel different, different from how I have ever felt in my entire life. I don't know what it is, but I feel alive for the first time."

She started to spin and circle around Jesus and his men. Waving her hands in the air as she danced, she announced, "I feel absolutely as light as a cloud. Nothing is weighing me down, nothing is making me feel guilty for being an orphan, nothing is making me feel that I am not worthy of people's affections, nothing, absolutely nothing, has ever caused me to want to know my Creator more than I want to know him now. Thank you, Jesus, thank you."

Mary said these words to the One who had released these feelings within her. She just had not grasped the fact that this man was indeed the Creator, God incarnate. All she knew was that she was alive, really alive, and somehow this man had made her feel this way. And she felt love for him, a love that she had never felt before—a love that confused her, a love that overwhelmed her, a love that was indescribable, a love that filled her with longing, a love that overcame the resentment that she had felt for men because of the abuse she had received at the hands of her cousins. This Jesus was something else. He had shown her gentleness, he had shown her compassion, and he had shown her a love that had taken possession of her heart, possession of her being, possession of her thoughts. Was this the man that her mother had envisioned for her when she was just a small child? Was this the prince that she had always dreamed of, fantasized about, hoped that she would someday meet and at that day be carried away to safety, away from all the hurt, away from all the conflict in her soul, away from the tormenting of not only her soul by demons but of her psyche as well by cousins who hated her on the one hand and wanted her body on the other? Her heart burned within her and her stomach was filled with butterflies. She felt so confused! Was this the one? Was this the man who would love her unconditionally with passion and with abandonment? Mary was so happy that she was being allowed to travel with this man who so obviously loved her that she never noticed that the four disciples gave her disapproving looks. And so Mary's journey began.

Meeting the Mother of My Prince

I REMEMBER IT as if it were yesterday. Jesus, his disciples, and I were on our way to Capernaum where I was to meet the mother of this man who had cast out seven demons from me, a man who had literally saved my life. The sun was unusually forbearing. The heat of the sand had reached a temperature that could cause the feet to blister. It was always hard for me to understand how we could be wearing three and four layers of clothes and yet somehow remain cool enough to withstand the heat bearing down upon us. Our heads, our arms, and our legs were completely covered; only our eyes could be seen peering out through a narrow slit left in the headdress that covered our faces. It was almost the sixth hour and there was not one cloud in the sky. Surely it was the bluest blue I had ever seen. There was no air stirring; the heat was simply oppressive.

As we walked along chattering and laughing about the commotion we had witnessed going on inside the box turtle, a messenger came toward us from the east. He approached us and yelled, "Jesus! Is that you?"

Before Jesus could answer, the man continued, "You are a sight for sore eyes, Jesus. You are the very one I seek. I have a message for you."

It turns out that this man was one of Jesus's neighbors during the years he had grown up in Nazareth. The messenger recognized Jesus from his stature and his gate.

Jesus went up to the diminutive fellow, wrapped his long arms around him, and gave the man a kiss on each cheek. He pushed back from the little man and said with honesty and sincerity, "Simeon, old friend, you too are certainly a welcome sight. How are you?" He dropped one arm from around his friend's shoulder and said, "Why, I haven't seen you in years, not since Mother moved to Capernaum. How long has it been, Simeon, how long?"

Simeon breathed in deeply to calm his heavy breathing and answered, "Jesus, I am well, albeit a little tired and out of breath, as you can see, but I am well. You know, perhaps fifteen years have passed since we have seen each other, maybe more. I have moved my family just recently to Capernaum as well. As a matter of fact, I live not too far from your mother, your brothers, and your sisters."

"Really!" Jesus exclaimed with delight. "That's wonderful, Simeon. I have always held you and your family in the highest regard. I think it is just exceptional news that you are living close to my mother. Oh! Forgive me, Simeon," Jesus said a little red-faced. "Allow me to introduce you to my friends. These are the sons of Jona of Bethsiada, Andrew and his brother Simon, who we call Peter. And this is Phillip of Bethsiada and his friend, Nathanael."

They removed the coverings from their faces and greeted one another with a kiss and the greeting. "Shalom."

Then Jesus introduced me. I can tell you that I was shaking in my sandals. I was scared to death that Jesus would mention in what wretched condition he had found me, but he didn't. Instead, he put his arm around my shoulder and pulled me out from behind Simon Peter where I had been hiding and said, "And this is my newest friend, Mary." He didn't even tell Simeon that I was from that immoral city of Magdala. He simply said that I was his newest friend. Can you imagine being called a friend of a man who has the power to cast out demons? For the first time in my life since I had become an adult, I felt and acted shy. I said hello to Simeon without ever looking up from the ground. I don't know what had come over me.

When we had finished exchanging greetings, Simeon gave Jesus the message he had been instructed to bring to him. "Your mother asked me to come this way to find you so that I might give you this message. Your cousin Nathan is getting married in three days in Cana. You, and of course your friends, have been invited to come. Naturally, we don't know the hour when the guests will be asked to come, but rumor has it, it will be around the ninth hour. Anyway, your mother asked me to make sure that you not only received your invitation but that you would come as well."

Jesus smiled and said, "That sounds just like my mother. If there's a wedding to go to, she will make sure that her children are there. Simeon, are you going now to Cana or back to Capernaum?"

"Well, actually, Jesus," Simeon responded, "I have to return to Capernaum for at least a day. Then my wife and I will go over to Cana for the wedding feast."

"Good," Jesus said. "Please tell my mother that I and my friends will be coming to the wedding. We will go directly to Cana from here and then afterward to Capernaum."

We walked toward Capernaum together before parting ways. Simeon said that he would see us in Cana, but for now, he headed on toward his home.

Jesus, his disciples, and I went on to Cana to attend the wedding. Nathan's bride was so kind to me. She took me into her quarters and allowed me to wash and straighten out my hair. I was quite unkempt. I was introduced to everyone there as Jesus's friend. I could feel that my face never ceased to glow.

As Simeon had thought the bridegroom called for the people to come to the wedding midafternoon. What a great time we all had dancing and eating and drinking the special wine provided. Ultimately, the celebration had gone on for so long that all the wine had been consumed and the bridegroom was on the verge of being embarrassed.

Mary, the mother of Jesus (who I just loved the moment I was introduced to her), had come to the wedding with Jesus' siblings. She was so small; it was a wonder that she could have given birth to the strapping men that she bore. Her big brown eyes were the most inviting eyes I had ever seen (outside of her firstborn son's of course), and her smile could melt the heart. The tunic she wore was a sort of drab brown, but the orange scarf she wore around her tiny waist brought it to life. She came over to where Jesus was seated with his four followers and me and pulled him away to speak with him in private. We could see that she was asking him to do something.

From where I was seated, I could hear Jesus say most lovingly to his mother, "Woman, how is that a concern of mine? My hour is not yet come."

I wondered what he meant by those words, but then I heard his mother say, "They are out of wine, Jesus. Please don't let your cousin be embarrassed! You know that the guests have taken off from their work for an entire week and have brought gifts to the bride and groom. They expect the food and wine to keep coming. By custom and by law, they could bring suit against Nathan and his father for failing to meet the requirements of this important tradition."

It should have been evident to his mother that Jesus did not intend to refuse to provide additional wine, just to delay it a little. It was obvious to me that he spoke as he did to allay her anxiety and to prevent her from being solicitous about her request. Jesus was not yet ready to interfere, but when that time came, he would certainly furnish a supply of good wine.

After the discussion with her son, Mary told the servants, "Whatever he tells you to do, do it."

I watched intently to see what this man, this Prophet of God, was going to do. Nearby were six large earthen jars for the purpose of washing the hands before and after eating, and for the formal washing of vessels. Because of the dust, even the furniture had to be cleaned off at times using this water. Jesus quietly instructed the servants to fill all the jars with water to the brim so that there could be no appearance that wine could have been added to the top or that his disciples had anything to do with the miracle he was about to perform. Without any magic wands being waved over the water and without some magic words being spoken, the miracle was immediately wrought when Jesus, after simply willing the water to be turned into wine, said to the servants, "Draw out some wine now and give it to the governor of the feast."

Pointing to a man standing at the head table, Jesus indicated, "That's the man."

The servants did as he had instructed them, and when the governor of the feast tasted the water that had been turned into wine by Jesus, he called the bridegroom to his table and said to him, "I've been to and presided over many weddings in my time and know that every man at the beginning serves the best wine he has. After all the men have drunk to satiety and destroyed the keenness of their taste, then the inferior wine is brought out. But you, sir, have kept the best pure juice of the grape until now. My compliments I give to you, young man." The governor of the wedding raised his goblet and toasted the bridegroom and his bride, wishing them happiness, long life, good health, and many children.

The servants did not say a word about the fact that Jesus had turned the water into fine wine, nor did his disciples mention it to anyone, not even to me. But they certainly whispered back and forth to one another about this miracle. Jesus' disciples had witnessed their Teacher exorcise evil spirits from me and tell me that my sins were forgiven. Now they had seen him turn plain water into the finest of wines.

Just as these two had accomplished, henceforth, Jesus' miracles would always serve a purpose. This miracle along with the exorcising of demons from me and forgiving me of my trespasses resulted in some manifestation of his glory. I knew it would certainly strengthen and confirm his disciples' faith in him, as it did mine. They witnessed the miracle and it satisfied them that Jesus was the one the prophets of old had testified about—the Messiah. Before this, they had believed the testimony of a man called John the Baptist, and from their conversations with Jesus, now they saw that he was invested with almighty power, and their faith was being established more and more.

By accepting the invitation to the wedding for himself, his disciples, and me, Jesus had made it very clear to his followers that the institution of marriage is honorable, and that he, if sought, would not refuse his presence or his blessing. Of course, on such an occasion, his presence and approbation should be sought. No pact entered into on earth is more important. None affects so much our comfort in this world. Perhaps none will so deeply affect our destiny in the world to come. Entering into a marriage contract should therefore be done in the fear of God.

In the very beginning of his ministry, Jesus worked a miracle in public to show his benevolence. Perhaps there could not have been a more appropriate beginning to a "new" life in which he would go about Israel doing what was good. From this time forward Jesus seized every opportunity to perform miracles, give a sign at a marriage feast as well as heal the sick and help the poor. He displayed the character which he would always sustain, that of a benefactor of mankind.

The disciples were talking among themselves in a corner of the courtyard away from the wedding party, away from those people who were engaged in dancing and celebrating the marriage. Still unhappy that I had been allowed to tag along with them, Jesus' disciples stopped their whispering when I approached. They eyed me with an air of mistrust, if not disgust. Peter, the self-appointed spokesman for the group, asked me curtly, "Is there something that you want?"

I felt flush from embarrassment. I looked down at the ground and answered in a subdued voice, "I'm so grateful to you and the others for allowing me to come to Cana with you. I realize that it was a great inconvenience, but I still give you my heartfelt thanks and of course to Jesus for expelling those awful spirits that had taken over my life. I'm not sure what he meant when he said that my sins were forgiven and that now I was a daughter of the King, but I do know that somehow I am different. I feel ashamed of the things that I have done, and I know that I must follow him."

Peter responded harshly to me, "Well, you can't! You heard what the Master said earlier, 'Foxes have holes and birds of the air have nests, but the Son of Man has nowhere to lay his head.' Neither he nor we have a place to call our own. We move around. He teaches us as we travel about the countryside. As things come up or as we observe something he preaches about, he instructs us and tells us about God, his Father. I confess, I'm not sure what all that means, but I'm learning."

They must have realized that I was embarrassed. I didn't understand why Peter had such contempt for me and why he treated me with such loathing. Regardless of how he felt about me, there was no doubt in my mind that I must follow this man called Jesus. I had concluded that I must do that whether I would be allowed to stay in their camp or not. Besides, being itinerate meant that they would need resources. Having been on my own with no one to care for me or for me to care about, I had squirreled away a considerable amount of money, and I had already decided that I was going to use it on the man who had set me free. Neither Peter nor anyone else was going to keep me away from the man I loved. I may have felt embarrassed to be confronted the way I was by Peter, but he was not my father, my brother, or my keeper. To be sure, he certainly was not my master. This man called Jesus, however, was.

I walked away from Peter and his friends to stand with Jesus' mother. No one could have been kinder or more wonderful to me. She had invited me to stay with her in Capernaum. As of yet I had made no commitment to her. Her son, who had set me free from demons and free from the guilt of sin, had not only captured my imagination, he had also captured my heart. I knew that I loved him with all my heart, and no matter what, I must be near him.

Standing there with Jesus' mother, Mary, I felt such a strange kinship with her. I knew that I belonged to her son. I felt like he loved me, but he also displayed a similar love to his four companions. Oh, if I only knew his heart. Jesus' mother must have intuitively known what I was feeling; out of the blue, she began to tell me a story.

"Before I was wed, the angel Gabriel appeared to me when I was betrothed to my husband, Joseph. Gabriel spoke to me saying, 'Hail to you who are highly favored. The *Lord* is with you. Blessed are you among women.'"

"Gabriel the archangel spoke to you? You saw him, and he actually spoke to you?" I queried incredulously.

The look on my face must have betrayed what I was thinking. *This woman's son cast out demons and turns water into wine, and she sees and talks to the head angel.*

"I know you must be terribly confused by what I have just said," Mary said lovingly. "Needless to say, I was terribly confused as well. But regardless, he did speak to me. I was exceedingly troubled and understandably frightened, but the angel said to me, 'Don't be troubled or frightened, Mary, for you have found favor with God. I have been sent to give you the news that you shall conceive in your womb and bring forth a son. You shall call his name Jesus. He will be great and shall be called the Son of the Most High. The Lord God shall give unto him the throne of his father David. He shall reign over the house of Jacob forever and of his kingdom there shall be no end.'

"Then I said to the angel, 'Son of the Most High, his father David, reign over the house of Jacob...what are you talking about? What does any of this have to do with me, and really, how can this be, seeing that never in my life have I ever slept with a man?'

"The angel had compassion for my confusion. He responded, 'God the Holy Spirit shall come upon you, the power of the Most High shall overshadow you, and that Holy One which you shall bear shall be called the Son of God. Furthermore, God has removed the barrenness from your cousin Elizabeth, the wife of the priest Zechariah, and in spite of her old age, she has already conceived. She is now in her sixth month. Remember, Mary, nothing is impossible with God.'

"I went down on one knee, bowed my head, and said to the angel, 'Behold the maidservant of the Lord, if this is the will of God, then let it happen to me according to all that you have said.'

"I looked up and Gabriel was gone. He left me to ponder all that he had said. In a few days, I made arrangements for travel and journeyed to see my cousin Elizabeth who lived in a city of Judah in the hill country. As soon as I was shown into Zechariah's house by their housekeeper, no sooner had I said, 'Peace be with you,' than the baby in Elizabeth's womb made quite a commotion. She just knew that she was filled with the Holy Spirit.

"Elizabeth's eyes widened in amazement. She was so overcome that she blurted out, 'Blessed are you among women, Mary, and blessed is the fruit of your womb. How is it that the mother of my Lord should come to visit me? For as soon as I heard your greeting, the baby in my womb leaped for joy. So I say, 'Blessed is she who believed that there will be a fulfillment of those things which were told to her from the Lord.'"

"I can tell you for a certainty, Mary, this mother of Jesus became very reflective. How could this all be happening to me? I asked.

I guess I was filled with the Spirit at the time for I responded in a song to Elizabeth, 'My soul exalts the Lord, and my spirit has rejoiced in God, my Savior. He has regarded the lowly estate of his maidservant, for behold, from this time forward, all generations shall call me blessed. For he that is mighty has done great things to me. Holy is his name. His mercy will be on all who fear him from generation to generation. He has shown strength with his arm. He has scattered the proud in the imagination of their hearts. He has put down the mighty from their thrones and exalted those that are lowly. He has filled the hungry with good things. He has sent away the rich empty-handed. He has helped his beloved Israel in his mercy. And he has spoken in times past to our fathers, to Abraham, and to his seed forever.'

"I said these things, Mary, and yet was totally amazed at what I had said. To this day, I cannot explain the words or the wisdom that came out of my mouth.

"I stayed with my cousin Elizabeth for about three months and then returned to my home in Nazareth. I didn't see my cousin Elizabeth or her son, John, again for years."

"Oh, I am truly blessed to know you, Mary, mother of Jesus," I responded. I went down on my knees before her to kiss her hand, but she grabbed me and pulled me back to my feet, saying, "Do not bow before me or any other. I am a mere mortal who has been blessed exceedingly to bear this son, the Son of God. He and he alone is to be worshipped and no one else. Do you understand me, my child?"

"Yes, I understand, Mary," I answered bewildered. "I am sorry."

"You need not apologize," she added. "You didn't know, and how could you possibly understand? I've been Jesus' mother for thirty years and had a visitation from God's own messenger, and I certainly don't understand it all. I live by faith, and that is what you must do as well. That's all we can do, Mary of Magdala, that's all we can do, live by faith."

I didn't know what else to say, so I simply agreed with her.

When the wedding festivities had ended, Jesus told his followers to pack up; they were going to escort his mother, brothers, sisters, and me back to Capernaum. It was a little less than two weeks until Passover would be observed in Jerusalem, and they could take a breather there at his mother's home before going up to the celebration. Every male among the Jews was required to appear at the feast, and in obedience to the law, Jesus was going as well.

Peter thought that Jesus and the others would go straight from the wedding in Cana to Jerusalem. It came to him, however, that since many families go up to Jerusalem together to celebrate Passover, that after a few days of rest at the home of Jesus' mother, not only his followers, but all of Jesus' family (including myself) would be traveling together. It seemed that I just might be part of the group after all, for a little while at least.

He Scared Me When He Cleansed the Temple

AFTER THREE DAYS of relaxation and good food at the home of Jesus' mother, his brothers, sisters, his mother Mary, the disciples, and I set out as a caravan heading south along the western shore of the Sea of Galilee. When we reached the southern tip of the sea, instead of crossing over the River Jordan to travel to Jerusalem through Decapolis, Jesus announced that we would be traveling on the western side of the river through Samaria. Going through Samaria was something that Jews just did not do, for they hated the Samaritans, who in turn hated the Jews. Even though it was easier to travel between Galilee and Jerusalem through the land of the Samaritans, the hatred between the two nations caused the Jews to cross over to the eastern side of the River Jordan at either Bethabara in the south or at the junction of the Jordan and Yarmouk Rivers in the north and travel through rougher terrain just to avoid any contact with the local people.

The Samaritans were hated and despised because they were Jews who had intermarried with Gentiles during the Assyrian captivity. In spite of God's law to the nation of Israel calling for one temple, the one in Jerusalem, the Samaritans had built their own temple on Mount Gerizim during the time Judea was under Persian control.

Jesus wanted to show his followers, as well as his family, that Samaritans were just as much their brothers or neighbors as were the Jews. Even though his ministry seemed to have officially started at the wedding when he had turned the vats of water into fine table wine, he had lived his thirty years declaring, "Love everybody as you love yourselves." He certainly was not going to break that example now to appease anyone. Even Peter knew that there would be no argument; if Jesus said we were going through Samaria, we were going through Samaria. We thus continued on the west bank of the River Jordan all the way to Jerusalem for Passover.

Travelers to Jerusalem for Passover arrived a day or two early to set up tents or construct lean-to shelters like the ones the children of Israel constructed and lived in while wandering in the wilderness after they were delivered up out of the land of Egypt. Leaving his family members to prepare these shelters, Jesus and his disciples went into the city. He went right into the temple to teach. I followed at a distance so as not to be discovered; of course I've realized that Jesus knew all along that I was there. I slipped in behind one of the massive columns that lined the courtyard of the temple and watched as Jesus walked about, looking at all the things that were there. Merchants were selling sheep, goats, and doves and exchanging foreign currency to aid travelers in purchasing lambs and doves needed for their offer of sacrifice, and help them by exchanging their money into money that could be used in the temple. Instead of finding them sitting outside the walls of the temple, Jesus found them set up inside the temple courtyard.

The animals were housed in open pens and tied at stakes with twisted rushes. Cages stuffed to the brim with doves were stacked five and six high in the center of the open space. They emitted a cacophony of cooing that was in direct competition with the shouts of, "Doves, doves, get your doves here for only twenty mites. There are none like them in all of Jerusalem. They have already been blessed by the priests! Get your doves before the cages go empty!"

The sun bore down upon the courtyard producing a stench that filled the air. The smell permeated the visitors' nostrils and brought tears to their eyes. The changers of money sat at their foreign exchange booths and chattered to one another and to their customers. They sounded like monkeys frightened by a jungle cat. They were ready to exchange Roman coins into the money accepted at the temple. This year, as every year, the temple tax of half shekel in specie, by way of poll for the service of the tabernacle, could be paid.

When Jesus entered the courtyard, his wrath was kindled within him because of the great regard he had for the pure worship of his Father. He found the situation utterly intolerable. I remember Jesus saying, as we walked along the road to Capernaum, one great design of his coming was to reform the abuses that had crept into worship, and to bring man to a proper regard for the glory of God.

I could see the veins in Jesus' temples and in his neck begin to stick out like overfilled waterskins. The color in his face went from bronze to crimson. The intense look in his eyes frightened me. I didn't know what he was going to do, but I felt sure that it was going to spell trouble. He crouched down on the ground and picked up some rushes (those reeds that were spread on the ground for bedding and some that were twisted into cords for tying the cattle) and made a scourge. I knew then that he was going to use them to eject the goats and the sheep, along with their keepers. He was about to reveal the spiritual nature of who he was and why he was there. As a consequence, he was about to experience the first open symptoms of antagonism from the rulers of the Jewish people.

I placed my hand over my mouth to keep from crying out when I realized what he was about to do. Before I could scream to him, 'No, Jesus! Don't do this. They will hurt you,' Peter and James, who had come up behind me, grabbed both my arms and held me firmly in their grasp. The three of us seemed to remain frozen in time, as if we were watching Jesus move in slow motion. We witnessed him pull his prayer shawl from around his neck and toss it to the ground as if it were disposable. In the manner of a sheep herder twirling his tether high in the air, he swung the cords over his head, hooped and hollered, and drove the animals past those in attendance out of the courtyard into the open. They stampeded down the flight of stairs that led up to and down from the temple mount. As the animals fled, their keepers followed in hot pursuit, trying to keep them from scattering too far.

Expressing the combined indignation of his authority and his impulse to carry it out, Jesus threw the twisted cords of rush to the ground, marched over to the handlers of exchange, and proceeded to empty their money boxes and overturn their tables onto the large flat stones that covered the floor of the courtyard. The "image of Caesar" clanked on the stones and rolled in all directions. To those that sold doves, the sacrifices for the poor, Jesus used discretion to guide and govern his zeal, but he screamed to the ones that sold them, "Take these things out of here. Do not make my Father's house a house of merchandise!"

With their hands and purses over their heads, the merchants scrambled from the temple courtyard with their cages filled with the "birds of love" in tow. I realized, as did the others who had heard Jesus that day, that when he called God his Father, he was intimating that he was the Messiah, of whom it was said, "He shall build a house for my name. I will be his Father and he will be my Son."

I actually started to laugh at the scene of the men chasing after their goats and sheep. The money changers crawled around on all fours to retrieve their coins off the stone squares, and others hurried to carry their cages filled with doves to outside the temple. As I giggled, Peter and James looked at each other as if the same thought had entered their minds at the exact same moment. They remembered and mouthed together, "It is written in the Psalms, 'The zeal of your house has eaten me up.'"

I stopped my giggling and looked from one to the other and realized that they had just quoted something profound. How could something written by a psalmist hundreds of years earlier be written about this man, Jesus? And though the scene was funny, I understood that what Jesus had just done had great significance.

I asked Peter and James, if it was wrong to be selling the goats and sheep and doves, and was it wrong for the money changers to be doing what they were doing?

James explained to me that there was nothing wrong with the actual merchandise, but to have brought it into that most sacred place was a profanation, which Jesus just could not endure. The goats, sheep, and doves were not for common use but for the convenience of the tens of thousands of countrymen who had come from every country in the known world who could not bring their sacrifices in kind along with them. The market had been formerly located by the pool of Bethesda but was later admitted into the temple by the chief priests for filthy lucre. I had no doubt that the rents for standing there and for certifying that the animals were without blemish would be considerable revenue for them.

When he was a youth with no authority of his own, Jesus was a son in his own house. Now, he was *a Son over his own house*. As *heir* in the flesh of his Father's rights, as the proper representative, Jesus could not allow his "house" to be violated and desecrated.

Jesus had made no formal public appearance until he had come here to the temple. His presence and preaching there were for the glory of the temple as it stood now, and was to exceed the glory of the first temple in former days. The prophet Malachi had predicted that God would send his messenger, John the Baptist, cousin of Jesus, who would never preach in the temple but proclaim, "The *Lord*, whom you seek, will suddenly come to the temple." This was the time and place the Messiah was to be expected, but no one was looking for him or even cared. It was business as usual. The law prevailed and the temple was now. Buy and sell, sell and buy, transact business, for who could possibly know when God would act on his word. After all, it had been hundreds of years and there had been many who had claimed messiahship. No one had come to throw out these Romans who inhabited and ruled over their land. What good would it do them to have a self-righteous young man come in and start trying to reestablish the temple of former times? Who did he think he was? Did he really believe himself to be the messiah?

This question begs an answer: "How was it that those engaged in the temple traffic so readily yielded to Jesus of Nazareth that they left their gains and their property and fled from the temple at the command of one as obscure as he?"

The time had come for the reformation, and Jesus had come as the great reformer. To do his work, he first had to purge the leaven in the temple of what was amiss, teach them to do well, and then to keep the feast.

Jesus' righteous indignation came as a response to the profaning of the temple, because it was the *house of God*, not a house of merchandise. Exchanging merchandise was a good thing for the welcome distant traveler, just not in the temple. It defiled that which was dedicated to the honor and glory of God. It was a sacrilege because it robbed God. It debased that which was solemn. And it disturbed and distracted those services in which men were to be most solemn, serious, and intent. The zeal Jesus had for his Father's house consumed him.

It might be said that the vendors' consciences reproved them for their impiety, and they could not set up the appearance of self-defense. It was customary in the nation to cherish a profound regard for the authority of a prophet; and the appearance and manner of Jesus, so fearless, so decided, so authoritative, led them to suppose that he was a prophet. They were afraid to resist him. It is not improbable that many of those in the temple that day considered him to be the Messiah. Besides, on all occasions, Jesus had a most marvelous power over men. None could resist him. There was something in his manner that produced awe and caused men to tremble in his presence. At this particular time and in this particular place, Jesus had the manner of a prophet, the authority of God, and the testimony of their own consciences; and they could not, therefore, resist the authority by which he spoke.

Certainly, Jesus had cleansed the temple for now, but likely, all would soon forget these most solemn reproofs and return to their evil practices. No sacredness of time or place would guard them from sin. Not even the sacredness of the temple, the presence of God, or the awful ceremonials of religion would deter them from their unholy traffic. When possible, wicked men will always turn religion into gain. Not the sanctuary, not the Sabbath, not the most awful and sacred scenes would deter them from their schemes of profit.

The use of the court in the temple was particularly an affront to the Gentiles because the exchange of merchandise took place in the Court of the Gentiles, the nearest point to the temple they could reach for their worship. The noise of a marketplace would certainly disrupt, if not curtail, any semblance of worship. What must have been their feelings toward earnest men among them when they observed the buying, selling, and trading in the court where it was intended to be a house of prayer for all nations? The Gentiles were admitted to the Court of the Gentiles so that they might become attracted to the Jews' religion and worship Jehovah. Because the holiness of the place advanced the market and promoted the sale of its commodities, the business of religion was made subservient to secular interests. The world and its traffic and pleasures had penetrated even to the inner sanctuary where the noise and the clamor of it all tended to drown out the voices of praise and prayer, crushing down the aspirations of devotion and worship.

Above it all, silence and order were produced where noise and confusion had formerly prevailed. This was accomplished when Jesus drove out the merchandisers with his own arm, without resistance from any of his enemies, either the market people themselves or the chief priests that had issued them their licenses and who had the temple force at their command and their disposal. The corruption in the marketplace was just too evident to be justified or defended. As the reformer, Jesus was protected by the consciences of those that were in the wrong. Those engaged in the traffic readily yielded to Jesus and fled from the Court of the Gentiles at his command. Their consciences reproved their impiety and left them with no self-defense. Besides, the appearance and manner of Jesus that was shown in his fearlessness and his authority left the Jewish leaders with no other option but to believe that he meant to assert his claim as Divine Son and Messiah, one they would fear to resist. Right there in the temple, under the watchful eye of God, these men bought and sold for profit for which their consciences should have reproved them and for which they knew that God would disapprove. Deep-rooted was their passion for money, and deep was the depravity that demonstrated no fear of God, his day of rest, his place of worship, or for his law.

Holding their purple robes of honor up above their knees and running as quickly to Jesus as their legs would carry them, coming face-to-face with the Son of God, the breathless officials in the temple demanded of him, "What do you think you are doing? What gives you the authority to do these things? If you have that authority, show us a sign."

Jesus's face was still crimson red, and his breathing was labored from the adrenalin that coursed through his veins. The dark brown hair that he usually kept pushed back out of his face now covered his eyes that were ablaze with anger and righteous indignation.

"A sign?" he bellowed. "You children of the Most High God always demand a sign!"

In an effort to slow his rapid breathing, Jesus bent over for a moment, grabbing hold of both his knees. Momentarily, he straightened up and said more calmly, "You wouldn't recognize a sign if it rose up and bit you from behind like a viper, but here is your sign: destroy this temple and in three days I will raise raise it up."

The officials of the temple became absolutely hysterical. They doubled over in uncontrollable laughter. "You must be a lunatic! This temple took forty-six years to build. Assuming the temple were to ever be torn down again, will you raise it up in three days?"

"Oh! This is too much," one of the officials said through his laughter. "You cannot be serious, young man! First, who would dare touch the temple again, and secondly, I'm not sure even God himself could do what you say!"

The fire within Jesus blazed to almost out of control! *What blasphemy you speak*, he thought, but he kept his composure. He was speaking of the temple of his body, but he knew that because of the scales that covered their eyes, they could not possibly see or understand just what he truly meant.

Many people would see the miracles that Jesus would perform while he was in Jerusalem during the days of the Passover feast and would believe in his name, but he would not commit his fate to their hands, for he knew what was in man. He knew what was in their hearts.

Not understanding what Jesus meant and not wanting to risk being seen as fools, the leaders in the temple allowed Jesus to leave. He walked over to where Peter, James, and I stood beside one of the large columns. During the commotion, two other disciples had joined us and waited to see if Jesus were going to provoke the crowd or the leaders to violence. As he approached,

Jesus could hear the argument among his followers. Half wanted to leave immediately and the other half wanted to stay and see what other reactions they could provoke.

I pulled free from Peter and James and rushed to Jesus as he came near and offered him a cool drink from the waterskin that was attached to the sash around my waist. He was beginning to cool off somewhat, and the water was a welcome refreshment. He took the waterskin from my trembling hand and raised it to his lips. Rapidly swallowing one gulp after another, he let the cool, wet liquid run over his chin down onto his neck. He took the waterskin away from his mouth and said, "Ahhhh! That was good. Thank you, Mary, I needed that."

I felt flush and looked down at the ground. Then I said shyly, "It was my pleasure, my Lord, for I am your servant."

I think Jesus understood that my meaning of being a servant was different from being a servant of him as my God, but he let it pass. Then he asked me, "Why are your hands trembling?"

Not looking up to meet his eyes, I simply responded, "Just the excitement, I guess."

As I stood before Jesus, my heart pounded so loudly that I was afraid he would be able to hear its beat as well. Thoughts of love coursed the convolutions of my brain as swiftly as a fallen branch cascades over a waterfall. Jesus must have felt it prudent to abandon this conversation for now, so he said nothing more.

Nathaniel broke the tension of the moment when he said, "We had better get back to the tents where your mother and siblings are, Jesus, before they hear of what you did this day and come looking for you out of concern for your safety."

"Perhaps you're right, Nathaniel," Jesus replied. "Perhaps, you're right. Let's all go back together and see what my mother has cooked up for us to eat this last night before Passover."

We were all eager to partake of Mary's cooking. She was absolutely an artist at turning a lamb's leg into a roasted culinary delight or making onions, barley, and herbs into a tasty hearty stew. Everyone knew that to savor the results of her labor was always a delight.

Leaving the Temple Mount behind, I ventured forward to take my place at Jesus's side. As we descended the high ground into the Kidron Valley below, I looked up into Jesus's face for some approving glance, but he took no notice. I stuck close to his side anyway while Peter, James, Phillip, and Nathanael walked along behind. This was not normal. Peter and James had always been the ones to walk closest to Jesus, not some woman like me who, less than a week ago, had run through the streets of Magdala as a possessed, disheveled wild woman. The natural order of things had been upset, but I loved this man. He had saved my life, and I knew that he loved me too. He just didn't know how to show it, but I knew he would.

Jesus Reveals Himself, and I Am Rejected

BY THE MIDDLE of the week of Passover, what Jesus had done in the temple had spread throughout all Jerusalem. Jesus went daily and taught in the temple. He quoted passages from Isaiah and verses from the Psalms, making claims that they spoke directly about him. The common people that listened to him were impressed by his knowledge and a few actually believed him and became his followers.

Even before he cleaned out the courtyard of his Father's house, Jesus's reputation had already preceded him. Prior to coming to Jerusalem for the Passover, Jesus, his mother, brothers and sisters, his disciples, and I had gone first to Nazareth. There had been no doubt that he had a purpose in taking that detour before going up to Jerusalem.

When Jesus had come to his birthplace and childhood home of Nazareth, he went into the synagogue to worship. He sat with the rest of the men who had come and participated in the prayers (both public and private), listened to a sermon by one of the rabbis, and when the call was given for someone to come forward and read from the Torah, Jesus stood up, walked up to the front of the room, and took the scroll from the leader.

Once Jesus had received the scroll, he turned to face the crowd of worshipers in the long, narrow room. Peter said that Jesus stood there, facing them for what seemed an eternity before he began to read. He could hear the men toward the back of the chamber whispering to one another, saying. "Isn't that Mary's and Joseph's boy? Why I haven't seen him around here in ages, not since he and a couple of his brothers, I think their names were James and Judas, would come here and listen to the sermons as if their very lives depended on hearing the words being spoken. Come to think of it, it was really the oldest boy, Jesus, who did all the listening. James and Judas seemed to always be punching and teasing each other and complaining about one touching the other."

Then he overheard others saying, "That Jesus has certainly matured. I've never seen him go forward to read from the Torah before. He sure looks different."

Since they knew he had been a resident of Nazareth and was the son of Joseph the carpenter who had died in his sleep three years earlier, the rabbi, without question, handed Jesus the scroll of Isaiah the prophet to read.

Jesus smiled a minuscule smile, unrolled the scroll, and perused the text until he came to that section in Isaiah where it was written, and where he read, "The Spirit of the Lord is upon me, because He has anointed me to preach the gospel to the poor.

He has sent me to heal the broken-hearted, to preach deliverance to the captives and recovery of sight to the blind, to set at liberty those that are oppressed, and to preach the acceptable year of the Lord. I have come to preach the gospel to you."

(Although Jesus was God-incarnate during his earthly life and ministry, he still recognized his dependence upon the ministry of the Holy Spirit. This was particularly necessary in view of his humiliation in the Incarnation. So intimate was the relationship between him and the Holy Spirit that he has to be viewed as being endued with the power of the Holy Spirit.)

After reading two verses from Isaiah, Jesus left off reading the end since it dealt with "the day of vengeance of our God," which related not to the Messiah's first but his second coming. He made his point, however. By reading a few lines effectively, he called the whole promise-laden context to his hearers' attention.

Jesus rerolled the scroll, handed it back to the attendant of the synagogue who looked after the scrolls, and sat down in the seat of the one who would teach. He did not return to the seat that he had occupied before the reading. All eyes in the synagogue became fixed upon him, and the cacophony of sounds that had bounced off the walls before the reading now had become stone-dead silent. It was as if everyone held their breath collectively. No one dared move out of fear that attention would be brought to them. Ultimately, the silence was broken when Jesus said to them, "Today, this Scripture is fulfilled in your hearing." (In other words, the one the prophets said would come to preach has come.)

Everyone in the synagogue who had been listening to Jesus looked around at one another in astonishment. They could not but speak well of him and be in wonder at the gracious silk-like words that had flowed past his lips, and they whispered to one another up and down the rows, "Is not this Joseph's boy?" They knew Joseph; they did not know anything about Joseph that could have caused his son to be as special as they were noting this man to be.

Knowing their bewilderment, Jesus said something that was unconscionable. "No doubt you will quote this proverb to me, 'Physician, heal yourself! Whatever we have heard that you did in Capernaum, we want you to do also here in your hometown as well.'"

Now that they had identified him as a very special person and had spoken well of him, Jesus knew that they were going to want him to do some miracles there to demonstrate his supernatural powers. Then he said something else that was very strange. "I tell you the truth, no prophet is accepted in his own country. And I tell you another truth: many widows were in Israel in the days of Elijah when there fell no rain for three and a half years that resulted in great famine throughout all the land. But God sent the prophet Elijah to none of them. He did, however, send him to Zarephath, a city of Sidon, to a woman who was a widow. In Israel in the time of Elisha the prophet, there were many people who were diseased with leprosy and none of them were cured of their disease except Naaman the Syrian."

I'm sure everyone there was thinking, *What kind of answer was that? Naaman was not a Jew, he was a Gentile. What was Jesus saying to them?*

He was saying that God had not determined for him to heal everybody. God would decide what widow received healing and God would determine what leper received healing. It was not up to them; it was up to him. They might expect him to do in their town what was done in Capernaum, but God does not work that way. God picks and chooses what he does, not us.

The absolute clincher of how those in the synagogue really felt was manifest. When they finished hearing the things that Jesus had said, they were filled with indignation and wrath. The faces of the attendees of the synagogue (those sticklers for keeping the law) turned a crimson red in the dimly lit room. The veins on their necks and foreheads stuck out like giant night crawlers stretched out on the grass on a damp summer night, and the pitch of their voices reached into the stratosphere. They rose up in anger against Jesus. Some of them grabbed him by his arms, some by his legs, and they carried him bodily out through the gate of the city of Nazareth to the edge of the cliffs upon which their city was built. Even though their intent was to cast him over the edge that he might plunge headlong to his death, not one had taken notice that Jesus had allowed them to carry him without one iota of resistance. When they set him on his feet at the edge of the bluff, by dint of his imposing presence, Jesus was able to stare his opponents down and simply walk away untouched.

By the time Jesus and his disciples had returned to the camp just outside the city, it was two hours before the start of another day. As they came near, they could smell the fragrant aroma that drifted up into the air from the lamb that was being boiled in a ceramic pot on an open fire. The boiling water that had been anointed with dry sherry had herbs of saffron, parsley, and oregano; salt and fresh ground pepper; sprigs of mint; and a dash of barley flour for thickening. A roll of unleavened barley dough was turning to a golden brown on an iron griddle; and earthen bowls of vinegar, bitter herbs, and olive oil for dipping had already been set on a bench that was used for a table when traveling. Grapes, pomegranates, olives, and goat cheese were set out for fillers, and a large flask of half red wine and half water and enough wooden goblets for each person was placed at strategic places. The wonderful aromas came on the air, tempting the hungry entourage. Peter quickened his steps so that he could be the first to take a fragment of barley bread to dip into the fresh olive oil and bitter herbs that his hunger might be satisfied just a little. But to his chagrin, Jesus's mother smacked his hand and said, "What are you doing, Peter? Wait until everyone can be seated and a prayer has been offered to God before you take a portion. You know better than that. Besides, everything is not yet ready."

Peter let go of the piece of barley bread that he had in his hand but showed no remorse in acting the pig. James and John snickered at the childlike scene in which Peter played the lead, but it was not an uncommon scene. Peter often acted immature, often speaking out of turn without first considering what he was going to say and how what he said would affect those around him.

It wasn't long until Jesus's mother announced that the meal was ready and that the table was set. We all were famished and quickly took our places. Unlike taking a meal inside, instead of reclining, we sat cross-legged on twisted straw mats placed on the ground before short benches. Everyone was seated except Jesus. Standing at the head of the table, he took a piece of bread and a cup of wine, held them up over his head, and gave thanks to God for the food and asked blessings upon all who were present. Without trying to be too obvious, I orchestrated the seating so that when Jesus took his seat, it was beside me.

I confess my heart burns for him. I don't know how, but I must be with him.

As we sat eating our food, Jesus's disciples described what took place at the synagogue. John told us how angry the attendees had become when Jesus said that the Scripture he read from Isaiah was about him, that he had come to fulfill God's Word. James added that he heard the men in the back asking how the son of Joseph the carpenter could possibly know so much theology and think that he was the Messiah. With his mouth full of bread and cheese, Peter jumped in and pictured how those in the synagogue had turned into a mob and had whisked Jesus away to the edge of a cliff with the intent of throwing him over.

Mother Mary and I both gasped at the thought!

"You must be more careful, son," Jesus's mother admonished. "You must know those words will evoke anger, especially in the Pharisees. They think so highly of themselves anyway. According to them, there is no one in all Israel or Judea who knows more than they do, and they don't think the Messiah is anywhere close to appearing."

I couldn't help myself. I had to add my two mites. "Jesus, they could have killed you! Why do you do such things? You are lucky to have come out of that situation alive."

Jesus interrupted me, "There's no such thing as luck, Mary. They cannot take my life until I lay it down of my own will."

Hindering Jesus from speaking further about laying down his life, I jumped up and screamed, "You're just a man, Jesus! God has undoubtedly gifted you with supernatural powers, but if you keep agitating them, they will kill you!"

I stormed away from the group and marched a good distance to be by myself. I wanted Jesus to come after me, but he did not. He stayed with his precious men, men that hung on his every word, men that kissed his feet.

Dropping to my knees, I covered my face and cried aloud, "Why can't he love me like I love him? Does Jesus love and cherish God so that he will actually give up his life to promote him? God, are you so selfish that you would let him? Oh please, God, if you are truly all-knowing and know all about us, change Jesus's heart. Make him love me like I love him. Please, God, please!"

A Lesson for Nicodemus and an Admonition for Me

Toward the end of the week of Passover celebration, a man came out to our encampment outside the city wall. As he approached our campfire, we could see in the light of the fire that he was clothed in the traditional dress of a Pharisee. It was very obvious that Peter was not fond of these leaders of the Jews for he jumped up at the approach of the stranger and put his hand to his belt, close to the handle of the short sword that he kept hidden underneath his cloak.

"Can we help you in some way, Pharisee?" Peter asked curtly.

The man knew instantly from the sound of Peter's voice that he was in hostile territory, so he slowed his approach and answered meekly, "I seek Jesus of Nazareth."

Jesus came to the man's defense. Quickly positioning himself between the outsider and Peter, he said, "Shalom! God be your protector and bless you richly."

"Thank you, and shalom to you and your household," the stranger said. "My name is Nicodemus. I am a ruler of the Jews, a member of the Sanhedrin. I came hoping to speak with the man they call Jesus."

"I am he," Jesus responded. "How may I serve you?"

In the manner of a small boy, Nicodemus shuffled his feet in the sand, kicked up a small cloud of dust, and finally answered, "If it be possible, Jesus, I was wondering, er…I would love to have a few minutes of your time to discuss some things about which I have questions."

Recognizing the man's embarrassment, Jesus answered, "Of course, Nicodemus. Come with me to the side here so that we might have some privacy."

"Thank you, Rabbi," Nicodemus responded. "I feel honored to have an audience with you."

They walked away from the campfire where we had all been talking about the events of the week in Jerusalem and sat down under a large olive tree that was growing wild just outside our camp. It was about a hundred yards from the grove that was near the harvest. I had heard of this man called Nicodemus; he was a man of integrity, distinction, and power. I wondered why he would want to have a private conversation with Jesus. My curiosity got the better of me, so I concocted the story that I was tired and was going to retire. Moving away from the fire and walking in the direction of my tent, I darted around to the backside. I quickly made my way to within earshot of Jesus and Nicodemus and crouched down in the shadows to listen.

Nicodemus spoke first. "Rabbi, we know that you are a teacher sent from God for no man can do the signs you do except God be with him. I am convinced that you are a godly man, and I come to you by night because you are so busy and preoccupied during the day with your teaching as I am with the work of the Sanhedrin. I thought this would give us more time for me to inquire more fully about this doctrine that you are teaching. I desire to know more about it."

It certainly was unusual for a man of rank, of power, and of great wealth such as Nicodemus to come to inquire of any man, especially one with the reputation that had preceded Jesus. Yet it would be certain that the most favorable opportunity for teaching such a man the nature of personal religion would be when they were alone. In the midst of their colleagues or their companions or engaged in business transactions, they might refuse to listen or may even cavil. However, when alone, they would hear the voice of reason and persuasion and be willing to converse on the great subjects that concern men and what would become of them after death.

Without asking Nicodemus what it was he wanted to talk to him about, Jesus responded, "Verily, verily I say to you, except a man be born again, be born from above, he cannot see the kingdom of God."

Even though my understanding was limited and nothing like that of Nicodemus, it seemed to me that Jesus was telling him that the Jewish dependence on being sons of Abraham was no longer good enough. There must be the work of God above in a person's life. No longer would just having children be sufficient for God's blessing. He was telling him that it was necessary to have a new beginning.

Nicodemus removed the covering of his head and scratched the back of his neck. His response to Jesus was most peculiar. "How is it possible for a man to be born when he is old, Rabbi? Can he enter a second time into his mother's womb and come out a new babe?"

I could see the smile that crossed Jesus's face; however, it wasn't the smile of delight for he strongly urged, "Verily, verily I say unto you, except a man be born of water and of the

Spirit, he cannot enter into the kingdom of God. That which is born of the flesh is flesh, and that which is born of the Spirit is spirit. Nicodemus, you may object to this doctrine because of your lack of understanding, but don't marvel that I say that you must be born again, for the wind blows where it wishes and you hear the sound of it when it rustles the leaves and the branches of the trees. You cannot tell from whence it came or where it goes, so is everyone that is born of the Spirit. Sinful men become holy, the thoughtless become serious, the licentious become pure, the vicious become moral and religious, the prayerless prayerful, and the rebellious and obstinate become meek, mild, and gentle. When we see such changes, we should have no more doubt that they are produced by an agent mightier than ourselves as when we observe the trees move, or when we see the waves of the ocean lap over one another, or the cooling effects of a summer evening breeze. When these things happen, we attribute it to the wind that we don't see, and in spite of the fact that we do not understand how it all works, we can understand that the proper evidence of one's conversion is the effect it has on one's life. Just as God has the power to bring down a mighty oak with a single blast of wind, so he has the power over the most hardened sinner's heart to change it."

It was clear to me that Jesus was telling Nicodemus that it was the duty of everyone not only to love the Savior but to make an acknowledgment of that love by being baptized, by devoting himself to his service. But Jesus made it perfectly clear that Nicodemus should not suppose that was all it meant, so he added that it was necessary that he should be born of the Spirit also. There was no doubt in my mind that Jesus clearly intended that the heart must be changed by the agency of the Holy Spirit, that the love of sin must be abandoned, that one must repent of sin and turn to God, that one must renounce all their evil propensities and give themselves to a life of prayer and holiness, of meekness, purity, and benevolence. This was the way, the only and appropriate way of entering into the kingdom of the Messiah in the here and the hereafter. To show the necessity of this change, Jesus drew Nicodemus's attention to the natural condition of mankind. Jesus told him that being born of the flesh, which is man's nature, would not be the answer to any valuable purpose; he would still have the same passions for sins that he had before. Therefore another change would be necessary. A person in his flesh nature—which is corrupt, defiled, and sinful—partakes of the nature of parents. As the parents are corrupt and sinful, so will be their offspring; as the parents are wholly corrupt by nature, so their children will also be.

Jesus said to his visitor, "Due to the flesh, Nicodemus, man's nature is always corrupt, and the works of that flesh are manifested as adultery, fornication, uncleanness, licentiousness, idolatry, witchcraft, hatred, contentions, jealousies, wrath, selfish ambitions, dissentions, heresies, envy, murder, drunkenness, reveling, and the like. But when a man is born of the Spirit, there will be fruit as a result of that as well. And that fruit is love, joy, peace, long-suffering, gentleness, faith, meekness, and self-control. All men are by nature sinful and none are renewed but by the Spirit of God. If man did the work himself, it would still be carnal, sinful, and impure. The effect of the new birth is to make men holy. No one can have the evidence of the rebirth that is not holy, but as he becomes pure in this life, there will be evidence that he is born of the Spirit."

Still unwilling to admit the doctrine had validity unless he understood it, and being an example of one that stumbled at one of the most basic doctrines of religion, Nicodemus ran his fingers through his hair as a sign of embarrassment. He pursed his lips, shook his head, and looked totally befuddled. After staring at the ground for a few minutes, he asked Jesus, "How can these things be?"

His facial expression and the tone of his voice became more serious. Castigating Nicodemus, Jesus answered, "Are you not a teacher of Israel and yet you don't know these things? This is not new. These things are clearly taught in the Torah. Verily, verily I say to you, if the wind cools and refreshes me in the summertime, if it brings down the mighty oak to lie prostrate upon the ground or stirs the sea into a foam, if it utterly destroys my crops or blows down my house, it doesn't really matter how it does it, and so it is with the Spirit. If the Spirit renews a man's heart, brings his pride into submission, subdues his sin nature, and brings comfort to his weary soul, it matters little how he does all this. It is sufficient to his soul to know that it is ultimately done so that he might have a taste of the blessings that flow from the renewing and sanctifying grace of God. We speak about the things that we know and testify to the things that we have seen, but you don't accept our witness. If when I tell you earthly things you do not believe, how in the world do you expect to believe the things that I say when I tell you about heavenly things, things pertaining to the government of God and his doings in the heavens, things that are removed from human view and cannot be subjected to human sight, the more profound and inscrutable things pertaining to the redemption of men? There is much that man cannot understand yet. The feebleness of his understanding and the corruption of his heart are the real causes why one understands the doctrines of religion so little.

"No man has ascended to heaven except the One that came down from heaven, even me, Nicodemus, the Son of man, who is in Heaven. To speak of those things requires intimate acquaintance with them, demands that we have seen them, and as no one has ascended into heaven and returned, so no one is qualified to speak on these things but the One who came down from heaven, and that's me. That's me, Nicodemus! Do you understand that the Son of man is bodily in your presence, conversing with you, yet I declare to you that at this very moment I am also in heaven?

"I might say this to you Nicodemus that when worldly minded men are placed into positions of authority in religious matters, when they seek those offices for the sake of reputation, it is no wonder that the plain truths of the Scriptures are foreign to them. There have been many, and there still are those, who are in the ministry itself, and yet the doctrines of the gospel to them are obscure. No man can understand God's truths fully unless he humbles himself and places his trust in God. The easiest way to comprehend these truths is to give one's heart to God and to live to his glory. In this manner, a child may have more real understanding about the way of salvation than those teachers and preachers to Israel who declare that they know the truth. Don't you understand, Nicodemus, that just as Moses lifted up the serpent in the wilderness, even so I, the Son of man, must be lifted up? Moses was a 'type,' an illustration. You know the Scriptures! The people in the wilderness were bitten by fiery flying serpents for which there was no cure. Moses was instructed by God to make an image of the serpent and place it in the sight and presence of the people that they might see it and be healed by their belief. I use this truth to illustrate my work. Men are sinners, and there is no cure by human means for the iniquities of the soul. As the people who were bitten might look on the brass image of the serpent and be healed, so might sinners look to the Savior who is lifted up high on the cross to be cured of the moral maladies of their nature. Just as with those people in the wilderness, there is no other way that either group can be benefited. The bite of the serpent was deadly and could be healed only by looking on the brazen serpent high and lifted up. Sin is deadly in its nature and can only be removed by looking at the cross and putting your trust in its effect. One was used to save the life, the other the soul, the one to save from the temporal, the other from eternal death. It is proper, necessary, and indispensable if men are to be saved, Nicodemus. Whosoever believes in me, all who feel that they are sinners, that they have no righteousness of their own and are willing by the regeneration of the Holy Spirit of their hearts to look to me as their only Savior, should not perish but have eternal life."

My heart was beating so hard within my chest at these profound words of Jesus that I thought it surely would explode. I grew faint at the sound of such marvelous words and knew that this Man of God who spoke to Nicodemus had the truth within him. I feared that both men would be able to hear the thumping of my heart for the sound of its beat within my own ears was so loud that it was deafening. The pounding was so persistent that my head began to ache. I slid down the side of the support beam of the tent behind where I had hidden and held my hand over my mouth. As I tried to recover from the holy words that had come flooding into my mind, I thought to myself, *What kind of man is this that speaks such wisdom to a learned man like Nicodemus? I am so confused! I knew that he was a man of God when he was able to order the demons to leave me, but he now talks as a teacher to one of the Jewish teachers! What am I to think? What am I to do?* I got up from my knees and peered around the corner of the tent. Breathing as shallow as possible, I listened intently to each word that went between them.

Jesus shifted his weight where he sat and continued to instruct Nicodemus. "You know, Nicodemus, God hates sin, but he so loved the world that he created and all that is in it that he gives his only begotten Son, that whosoever believes in his Son should not perish but have everlasting life. God did not send his Son into the world to condemn the world, not to pronounce judgment on the world, but that the world through him might be saved. He that believes on him has confidence in him, relies on him, and trusts in his merits and promises, for salvation, and is not condemned. He that doesn't believe, Nicodemus, is condemned already because he did not believe in the name of the only begotten Son of God. To believe in me is to feel and act according to Truth. God pardons sin and delivers his elect from deserved punishment because of the belief that his children have in him. I will die in your stead, Nicodemus. I will suffer for you, and by my sufferings, your sins will be expiated, which is consistent that God should forgive. But for all those who do not believe, whether the gospel has come to them or not, by nature, all men are condemned already by conscience, by law, and by the judgment of God. This condemnation comes from God's disapproval of their character with a feeling of disapprobation. God disapproves of man's conduct and will judge according to Truth. Woe to that man whose conduct God does not approve for there is but one way by which men can be freed from condemnation. Without my gospel, all men are condemned, and those who hear and do not believe are still under condemnation, not having embraced the only way by which they can be delivered from it. Those to whom the gospel comes and those who still reject what they hear will have their guilt heightened by rejecting the offer of mercy and will trample underfoot the blood of the Son of God.

"This is the cause of the condemnation: the Light, the Messiah, the Christ has come into the world, and men have loved the darkness more than they have loved the light. Why? Because their deeds, ignorance, iniquity, error, and superstition are evil. Men love darkness more than they love the light when they are better pleased with their error than the truth, more with sin than holiness, more with Baal than me. Men who do evil commonly choose to do their evil in the darkness to escape detection. Those who are wicked prefer false doctrines and error to the truth. Those who think this way try to convince others that they have great zeal for God. But everyone who practices evil hates the light. Nor will they come to the light lest their deeds should be exposed. Therefore they hate the Gospel for it condemns their conduct, and their consciences would trouble them if it were enlightened.

"Everyone who practices truth comes to the light that their deeds may be made manifest. The sinner acts from falsehood and error. The good man acts according to truth. The sinner believes the lie that God will not punish or that there is no God or that there is no eternity or no hell, but the man who follows me believes all these and acts because he knows they are true. The one who follows me will search for truth and light that he may have evidence that his actions are right."

There was a long silence. Jesus said not another word but slowly rose to his feet, as did the inquirer. After Jesus had taken the hand of Nicodemus to help him up, Nicodemus said, "I wish to speak to you further."

"And I wish to talk with you more," Jesus said. "It would please me greatly."

The two men gave each other a holy kiss, and Nicodemus departed. Jesus watched Nicodemus until he disappeared from sight.

"Mary! Come to me, please," he commanded.

I was horror-stricken. Jesus had seen me. I crawled out from behind the tent and stood in front of him. I said, "Here am I, my Lord."

"Mary, Mary," he said softly. "You have got to stop eavesdropping on my private conversations. Nicodemus came to talk with me, not you."

"I'm sorry, my Lord," I answered. "It's just that you have such words of wisdom and I know so little that I want to hear every word that you speak. I'm not being nosey as much as I simply desire to learn of you. I am truly sorry, Rabboni."

"I know, Mary," Jesus said kindly. "I know. You are truly a delight to me. You desire so much to learn." He put his arm around my shoulder and walked me back to where the others sat around the campfire. Peter saw us come from around the other side of the tent and gave us a stern look, but Jesus ignored him.

My knees grew weak when he touched me, and my mind whirled round and round like a dreidle. I knew not how I was going to capture his heart, but capture it I must, for a fire blazed within me that was getting more and more out of control. My body shivered with excitement and nervousness. I actually had trouble walking as we rejoined the others by the fire. That's when I thought to myself, *If he only knew how much I love and need him, he would not be so cavalier with me.*

The Woman at the Well in Sychar

AS THE FESTIVITIES of Passover had come to an end, we packed all our belongings and started back toward Capernaum. But at Bethabara, Jesus made the announcement that he and his followers would not be going on to Capernaum but would tarry in the land of Judea where he intended to preach and his disciples would baptize.

"But, Jesus," his mother begged, "why can't you come home for a little while? I miss you so much."

Jesus responded firmly yet with compassion, "Woman, how many times have we had this same conversation? You know that I must be about my Father's business. My Father sent Gabriel unto you that you would know and understand what I am about."

Mary gave her son a big hug but clung to him much too long for his comfort. He pulled free of her grasp, took both her hands in his, and proceeded to kiss the fingers on both her hands.

Oh, how I wish that were me! I thought. *Oh, that he might show me that same affection. My God, am I wrong to feel this way? He says that he is your Son. He proclaims so many things that I don't understand, and yet the love I have for him in my heart is so strong that much of the time it feels like a giant pain that will not go away. Dare I feel this passion that burns within me? Please help me, God, to understand these newly found feelings, these newly discovered yearnings, these passions that flood my soul unchecked, unwanted, yet real and unbridled! Oh, he is coming to me. Please, Jesus, take me in your arms, hold me, squeeze me, and let me know that you love me too.*

Jesus put his arm around me like a man would hug his sister and said, "Mary Magdalene, my mother has indeed opened her home to you that you might dwell with her. I can't tell you how pleased I am that you will be staying with her. My disciples and I will dwell here in Judea for a while, and I want to express my thanks to you for sharing your savings with us. It means a lot when someone's heart has been touched by our ministry to the point that they are willing to help us in what we are attempting to accomplish. God bless you, Mary. My Father and I love you."

He gave me a peck on the cheek and handed me over to the care of his mother and his siblings. I could still feel his arm around my shoulder. I imagined that it was still there and that he was squeezing me harder and harder. My fantasy was broken when he asked, "Mary, did you hear me? Did you hear what I've been saying?"

Startled back to reality, I answered, "Of course, I heard you. I was...I was just thinking, that's all." Then without thinking, I began to plead, "Can't I come with you?"

"No, Mary," he answered, "not this time. But you are indeed my disciple as these men are, and you shall come with us soon."

Childishly, I asked, "When?"

"Soon, Mary, soon," he chuckled.

"You promise?" I implored.

"Yes, Mary, I promise," he answered with hands outstretched. "That is what I said, and when I say something, Mary, you can count on it for my words are true."

My face went flush. *Why did I question him? What is wrong with me?* Finally coming to myself, I said, "I know that every word you utter is true, my Lord. It's just that it has been a long time since I could take what a man says as truth."

He flashed a reassuring smile and said, "I know, Mary. Your trust has been violated. I know this, but I am the Truth."

It wasn't the words he spoke as much as the reassuring way in which he said them. My fears were instantly alleviated, and I knew that I could trust him.

"Now, Mary, please go with my mother back to Capernaum. Make sure that she arrives safely. Okay?"

I knew that my going back to Capernaum with Jesus's mother would have nothing to do with guaranteeing her safety. His brothers would be the ones to see to that. But somehow, he made me feel that I did indeed have purpose and value. There was nothing I could do but say, "Of course I will take care of your mother."

Jesus's disciples had grown to twelve. They separated out the things they would have need of from our burden and said goodbye to us. We went on to Capernaum and they stayed behind to minister in Judea.

Jesus and his disciples made their way along the rough fifty-three-mile trek that led from Jerusalem northeast to Aenon, the city of fountains near Salim to where Jesus's cousin, John, had been preaching and, because of the abundance of water, had been baptizing for the remission of sins. When Jesus and his followers arrived in Aenon, they became observers to a dispute over purification that had arisen between John's disciples, who had been baptized by him, and the Jews that had come out to either hear him speak or spy on his activities. And these Jews asked John, "Rabbi, who was the One with you whom you baptized in the River Jordan, the One of whom you bear witness? Were you aware of the fact that he and his men are also baptizing and that because of his popularity, many are flocking to him? We fear that you may be forsaken and your followers may be diminished in numbers and influence."

John was certainly a character. He is a mere five feet four inches, and he shuffled from side to side as he walked, probably because his legs were so bowed. Below the knees, his legs remained bare, and he covered his torso with some sort of preserved hide of a long-haired creature, possibly a desert bear. The garment was cinched around the waist with a wide leather band that was tied together in the back. He wore no sandals upon his feet but walked on short pieces of wood that were held in place by pieces of animal skins that were wrapped around his feet and were tied around his ankles with leather straps. His coal-black hair stuck out in all directions and went well past his broad shoulders. His beard was equally long in front. He ate what God provided him in the desert, mainly locust and wild honey.

It was apparent to John what these troublemakers were up to; they were trying to divide and conquer, so he answered them, "A man can receive nothing except it be given to him from God. You yourselves have heard me say that I am not the Christ but that I have been sent before him to prepare for his coming. Don't you see that he who has the bride is the Bridegroom? I am not he. I am the friend of the Bridegroom who stands and hears him and greatly rejoices when I hear his voice, knowing that my joy therefore is truly fulfilled. He must increase in his ministry and I must decrease. We now have concurrent ministries, but I will continue only for a season. I tell you the truth that the One who comes from above is above all, whereas the one on earth is of the earth and speaks of the earth. But he that comes from heaven is above all things. Remember, the spirit of the gospel teaches us to rejoice that sinners turn to the Messiah and become his disciples."

John didn't succumb to their feelings or sympathize with their love of party. He arrived on the scene to prepare the way of the Lord to honor Jesus, not to build his own sect, his own following. He rejoiced in the success of the Messiah and had already begun to teach his followers to rejoice in it as well. After all, all his successes were from God, and all the successes of Jesus were from God as well. Since all success came from the same source, no one should be envious.

Then John reminded those who were interrogating him that he had already answered the question before about who he was. He had told the scribes and the Pharisees that came to him when he was baptizing in the River Jordan that he was not the Christ and that he was not Elijah but was "the voice of one crying in the wilderness." He was preparing for the coming of the Lord.

Then he said, "I came not to start a separate peculiar sect but to prepare the way that the Messiah might do his work, that the people might be prepared for his coming, and that he might have the success with which he has already met. Therefore rejoice! Being not envious of his success is the clearest proof of the greatness of my words and the success of it as well. It is absolutely necessary that his doctrine should continue to spread until it extends throughout all the earth. My ministry is short-lived. It simply points men to him, and when that has been accomplished, my work is done. I am like the morning star that shines brightly for a while, but when the sun comes, the star disappears in the sun's rising beams. I am honored for having been allowed to point sinners to him."

Then John said to those that confronted him, "What I have seen and what I have heard I bear witness to. Though God's doctrine is pure, plain, and sublime, though multitudes—drawn by various motives—have come out to hear, yet few have become disciples. Those that have received my testimony and fully believed its doctrine, and have yielded their hearts to its influence, pledged their veracity to its truth. Though Jesus is God as well as man, God the Father has anointed him as our Mediator and endowed him with the influences of his Spirit, not in a small degree, but fully and completely so as to be completely qualified for his great work. God loves the Son eminently above all the prophets and all his other messengers and has given all things into his hand. Those that believe on the Son possess that which is a recovery from spiritual death and will result in eternal life in heaven. Here, life begins: the first breathings and pantings of the soul for immortality. Yet it is life, though at first faint, eternal in its nature, that shall be matured in full and shall reach the perfect bliss of heaven. But let me say, he that does not believe in the Son shall neither enjoy true life or happiness here or in the life to come. He shall never enter into heaven for the wrath of God, his very anger that burns because of the sin of man, abides on him."

Jesus and his disciples heard all that John had to say when he replied to the Pharisees about Jesus making (and his men baptizing) more disciples than he (for Jesus himself did not baptize). They were extremely unhappy that John and indeed Jesus had introduced a new religious rite into Jewish life without having consulted them first. They felt that they had the market cornered and had all authority to regulate the rites and ceremonies of religion. No Jewish man (or woman for that matter) had a need to be baptized. It was only the Gentiles who had decided to convert to Judaism that needed to be baptized, for they were unclean. No Jewish person had ever needed to be baptized in the past. They certainly did not need it now. They had not authorized it.

Knowing that John was certainly capable of taking care of himself, and realizing that the envy and malice of the Pharisees was growing so rapidly that his life was in danger, Jesus and his disciples left Judea for Galilee. Of course Jesus did not fear death, nor did he shrink from suffering; yet he did not place himself, or his disciples, into dangerous situations needlessly.

To bypass the hated inhabitants of Samaria, the land that lies between the Jordan River on the east and the Mediterranean Sea on the west and between Galilee on the north and Judea to the south, legalistic Jews would take a circuitous route from Jerusalem to Galilee by way of Jericho. They would cross the Jordan River to the east side, go north through Perea, and finally recross the Jordan into Galilee. Jerusalem, which lies in the hill country twenty-six hundred feet above sea level, is fifteen miles from Jericho, which sits on the edge of the Dead Sea. Jericho is twelve hundred feet below sea level; therefore it is almost a four-thousand-foot drop from Jerusalem. When Jesus said that he was going down to Jericho, that's exactly what he did.

The Samaritans were hated and despised because they were Jews who had intermarried with Gentiles during the Assyrian captivity. In spite of God's law to the nation of Israel calling for one temple (the temple in Jerusalem), around the time when Persia, under Artaxerxes, ruled Israel, the Samaritans had built a temple on Mount Gerizim. When Jesus left Jerusalem, he headed north toward Ephraim instead of northeast toward Jericho. Since his chosen route would take him and his followers through Samaria, Peter, as usual, spoke first and said, "My Lord, I don't want to seem impertinent, but it appears that you have chosen the wrong route." He turned and pointed to the dirt road behind them and said, "We needed to turn right at the crossroads back there."

Impertinent! Peter was questioning the choice made by the Son of God, and he had said it out loud, "You have chosen the wrong route."

Jesus just shook his head, smiled up at the goofy disciple, and said, "I need to go through Samaria, Peter."

Waving his hands in the air as if in indecision, Peter replied, "Hey, whatever you decide, Lord. It's just everyone who is not a Samaritan crosses the Jordan first. But if you say you need to go through Samaria, then, heh! We all need to go through Samaria, right, men?"

He was out on a limb all by himself. No one answered and no one else made a comment, confirming that if it were Jesus's choice, it was a given.

They walked in silence for a while. As they traversed the western slope of the foothills, winds from off the Mediterranean Sea rushed headlong into their faces and carried away the clouds of dust kicked up by their feet. Jesus had made up his mind to go to a certain place in Samaria, and no one was about to turn or dissuade him. He and his followers came within sight of a city of Samaria called Sychar that sat between Mount Ebal and Mount Gerizim, not too far from the plot of land where Jacob (later called Israel) had bought for a hundred pieces of silver and had given to his son Joseph. It was here that the bones of Joseph were buried after they had been brought up out of the land of Egypt. Sychar was one of the oldest cities in Palestine, a part of the tribe of Ephraim. This was the same place that Joshua, just before his death, had gathered his people together to renew their covenant with God.

It was nearing midday when Jesus and his followers came to a well within a half mile of the city. The well, known as Jacob's well, was set on the right of the road where it bends from the plain of Makhneh into the pass of Schchem. Wearied by the travel and by a week's worth of itinerate preaching and healing, Jesus sat down by the side of the well under the shade to rest. Since it had been many hours since they had eaten, Jesus's disciples left him by the well and went into the city to buy what they needed for their noonday meal. It was nearing the height of the heat of the day.

Jesus's followers hardly had disappeared from sight than a lone Samaritan woman came to the well to draw water. Still sitting in the shade of the well, Jesus leaned against its cool rock wall and watched her as she approached. She appeared tall and willowy with her hair hanging in ringlets down her back. Her tunic was shorter at the bottom and lower at the top than most modest women would have worn. It was cinched around the waist with multiple strands of different-colored sashes that accentuated her hourglass figure. You could tell that she was once a real beauty, but now her skin was drawn and leather-like. Her cheekbones were covered with red rouge, and her eyes were entirely encircled with a black dye.

When she got to the well, she fastened one end of a hemp rope to the wooden pulley just above the orifice of the well and tied the other end to the bale of her bucket. She dropped the bucket into the well and waited until she could feel it begin to sink. After much labor, she pulled the bucketful of water back to the top of the well and rested it on the wall. Jesus got to his feet and said to her, "Give me some water to drink, please."

The young woman placed her hand over her heart and jumped back in a start! She dropped her bucket, spilling all the water onto the ground. She let out a shriek that could have been heard back in the city. Gasping for air, she screamed at Jesus, "Have you lost your mind? You scared me half to death! Why were you hiding?"

"I am so sorry," Jesus said, half laughing. "It never occurred to me that I would frighten you by my speaking. I wasn't hiding, just resting in the shade of the well."

"Well, I didn't see you!" the woman said exasperated. "You could have caused my heart to stop. What is wrong with you? I come here every day at noon to draw my water. I guess my mind was lost in thought. When you spoke to me, you frightened me."

Jesus repeated himself and said, "Again, I am truly sorry for having frightened you. I still would like that drink."

Placing her hands on her hips and wobbling her head, she said to Jesus defiantly, "Do you have any idea what labor it is for a woman to draw water from a well that is nearly a hundred feet deep? All the water that I had drawn has made mud in the dust. Besides, how is it that you, being a Jew, ask for a drink from me, a woman of Samaria? Jews have no dealings with us."

Jesus smiled at her and replied passionately, "If you knew the gift of God and who it is that says to you, 'Give me a drink,' you would have asked me, and I would have given you living water."

In saying this to the Samaritan woman, Jesus was referring to himself as the gift of God to the world, given to save men and women from eternal death. He was giving her the opportunity to seek after salvation. He was telling her that he was the Messiah. However, she had no idea what favorable an opportunity was being afforded to her by God to gain knowledge of him.

Neither did she understand exactly what *living water* was all about. Jews used the expression *living water* to denote springs or fountains or running streams as opposed to dead or stagnant water. Jesus was using the phrase to denote his doctrine, his grace, his religion.

Not yet grasping Jesus's design, the young woman brushed the dangling strands of auburn hair from her face, eyed Jesus very carefully before making her reply, and then said sharply, "Sir, you have nothing with which to draw water, and indeed, the well is very, very deep. So I guess I have to ask you, from where do you intend to draw your living water? Do you claim to be wiser or better able to find water than our father Jacob who gave us this well, who drank from it himself along with his children and livestock?"

To find water in this region and to furnish a good well was, doubtless, a matter of a signal skill and success. If the Samaritan woman had had any proper anxiety about her soul, she would have at least suspected that what Jesus said was meant to direct her thoughts to spiritual matters.

Despite the fact the Samaritans were composed of remnants of ten of the twelve tribes of Israel, and of the people sent from Chaldea, still they considered themselves descendants of Jacob. Since Jacob, his children, and his livestock had drunk from the well, it must be pure and wholesome, honored, and certainly as valuable as any Jesus could provide. Like people over all the earth, this woman loved to speak of those things that their ancestors had done and boast of their titles and their honors even if these were no better than what was before them.

A smile appeared on Jesus's face once again. He did not answer her question directly or say he was greater than Jacob, but he rendered an answer that might lead her to believe that he was. Jesus said to the woman, "Yes, this water is good. However, whoever drinks this water shall thirst again."

Jesus walked around to the woman's side of the well and sat down upon its wall and continued his discourse face-to-face. Doubtless referring to his own grace, his spirit, and to the benefits that come into the soul when one embraces his gospel, Jesus said to the woman from Sychar, "But let me tell you that whoever drinks the water that I give to them shall never thirst again, but the water I give them will be in them a fountain of water springing up unto everlasting life."

This was certainly a striking image. Because of the vast deserts, water in this part of the world came at a premium. By nature, the human soul could be compared to such a desert. It was thirsting for happiness and satisfaction, for rest, and for peace and yet could not find it. If one were satisfied by the grace of Jesus the Christ, he would not desire the pleasures and amusements of this world. Whoever drank of the waters that Jesus had to offer, whoever partook of his Gospel would be forever satisfied with its pure and rich joys that were unspeakable. Not like some stagnant pool or some deep well, the water that Christ offered would spring up like a fountain—like an everlasting fountain that would never run dry, that would flow season after season, in heat and in cold, in all kinds of weather, whether foul or fair or whether wet or dry. And best of all, it was not temporary like the supply of our natural desires. It would never change in its nature like a natural fountain or a spring of water, flowing over abundantly one minute only to be dry or dusty the next. This supply of living waters would continue to live on forever; its end would be everlasting life.

It seemed so strange to think that the woman yet did not understand what Jesus was driving at. Was she playing games, or was she like so many sinners, not understanding because her sin covered her eyes with scales of misunderstanding?

Becoming self-conscious, the young woman pulled her shawl together to cover her exposed cleavage and said to Jesus, "Sir, give to me this water that I might quench my thirst forever, that I thirst not again or have to come here to draw water ever again."

Jesus looked at the ground and shook his head in a manner that could hardly be perceived. As was his manner, he took the lead so as to make her perceive that he was the Christ. He looked up into her face, eye to eye, and instructed her to do something that she did not understand. "I tell you what, go and call your husband and tell him to come here. I would like to meet and talk with him as well."

She did not understand Jesus's instructions but he proceeded regardless to show her that he was acquainted with her life and with her sins. He intended to make her look at her own state and her own sinfulness, to come to the understanding that she was a sinner in need of a savior. Though having never met her before this encounter, by showing the young woman that he knew her life, Jesus meant to convince her that he was qualified to show her the way to salvation, and to cause her to admit that he was the Messiah.

Even though she had no idea what Jesus was up to by this time she suspected that he might be a prophet. Embarrassed, cheeks glowing red, she made a weak attempt to evade the subject. Meekly, she answered, "Sir, I have no husband."

Jesus knew that she had spoken the truth, for he said to her, "You have well said, 'I have no husband,' for is it not the truth that you have had five husbands, two of which died and the other three divorced you on account of your conduct, and the one with whom you now live is not your husband?"

A question that would have brought out anger in some people brought out surprise and anguish in this woman. Her face turned a deeper shade of red as a result of her embarrassment of having her sordid past brought to her attention. It turned colors as well because this man whom she had never met before knew all about her. At this very moment, she wanted to run away from the probing questions and the penetrating eyes. She desired to blend into the surroundings to avoid having her immoral behavior exposed; but this man knew who she was. He knew all about her. There was no running away.

The harlot realized Jesus knew that she had left her last husband without a divorce and her marriage to this man was unlawful. In fact, she was simply living with a man in open sin, with no form of marriage covenant at all.

The woman at the well said to Jesus, "I perceive that you are one who has been sent from God, a prophet who understands life, not one who foretells future events, but one who knows the human heart and certainly knows all about life. You have definitely confirmed to me that you have come from above."

Perhaps wanting to divert the conversation that was hitting too close to home, or wanting to settle a dispute that had raged for years between the Samaritans and the Jews, the woman at the well purposed this question, "Our fathers worshiped on this mountain, and yet you Jews say that Jerusalem is the only place where God's people ought to present their worship to him. Is this the truth or not?"

Nothing is more common than for a sinner to wrangle a conversation into a new area or into a new direction when it begins to hit too close to home and bear too hard upon their consciences. It is a common matter to redirect the conversation to something that is speculative about religion, as if to show that they are willing to engage in a religious conversation. They do not want to seem opposed to it but want to show that they are willing to talk about the external things of religion, not the things that pertain to the salvation of their very souls.

As she had professed to believe that Jesus was a prophet, he felt that it only right to require her to put her faith in what he was about to tell her. So Jesus said to the woman at the well, "Woman, believe what I am about to tell you. The time is near when the solemn public worship of God will not be confined to one place. Up until now, there has been a running dispute over whether worship should be held at the temple in Jerusalem or at the temple built on Mount Gerizim. The time is coming and now is when that controversy will be much less important than you have ever supposed. The old covenant is about to pass away, and the rites peculiar to the Jews are close to ceasing. The worship of God that has for so long been confined to a single location is soon to be celebrated everywhere. Despite the fact that you were given the five books of Moses, you rejected the prophets and practiced your worship of God in comparative ignorance and corruption and joined the worship of idols to that of the true and living God. The Jews know what they worship because God had commanded them, because they worshiped in a place appointed by God, and they did it in accordance with the directions and teachings of the prophets. You must realize that salvation is of the Jews because they have the true religion and the true form of worship, and the Messiah , who will bring salvation, is to proceed from them.

"But I tell you, madam, that the hour comes, and now is when the old covenant will pass away and a new one will commence. There will be so much light that God may be acceptably worshiped in any location by all who are truly and sincerely his followers. These will be the ones who worship him with the heart and not merely with form. In contrast to those who worship through rites and ceremonies and in opposition to the pomp that is brought on by external worship, the true worshipers of God will do so with the heart, the soul, and the mind. These are the ones that worship God with a sincere mind, with the simple offering of a prayer of gratitude. And where the heart is offered, it is offered to God with the sincere desire to glorify him without yielding to all the pomp and circumstance and in truth, not yielding to the medium of shadows and types, not by means of sacrifices or bloody offerings, but in the manner represented or typified by all these. The true way of direct access to the Father is through his Son. The reason why this kind of worship will take place is that God seeks it and desires it. God is a spirit, and that is another reason that men should worship him, worship him in spirit and in truth. You understand that God is without a body, that he is not material or composed of parts. He is incorporeal, he is invisible and in every place, pure and holy. And since God is a spirit, he dwells not in temples made with hands, neither is he worshiped with men's hands as though he needed anything, seeing that he gives to all life and breath and all things. Therefore he seeks worship that is pure, holy, and spiritual, an offering of the soul rather than a formal offering of the body, the homage of the heart rather than that of the lips."

The woman at the well squirmed like a worm hanging by its own silk thread over the flames of an open fire. As the Samaritans acknowledged the five books of Moses, so they anticipated the coming of the Messiah. There was no question about this to anyone who lived on the west side of the Jordan. To avoid the flames from completely consuming her, the Samaritan woman said to Jesus, "I know that Messiah comes and that he is called the Christ. I also know that when he comes, he will tell us all things."

Since Jesus had decided her question posed to him in favor of the Jews, the woman at the well was not satisfied with this answer, and said that the Messiah would tell them all that they needed to know, including the answer to her question. Perhaps the Samaritans were expecting to see the arrival of the Messiah sooner than later.

Then in the manner only Jesus possessed, he surprised the squirming adulteress with the words, "The One who speaks to you now is he. I am the Great I Am. I am the Messiah you have been waiting for."

What an amazing statement! For the very first time ever, Jesus unequivocally professed who he was, and he professed it to a woman who lived a life in total sin. To have made this announcement to the Jews would have elicited envy and opposition, but here in Samaria, nothing would be apprehended. Since the woman appeared to express hesitancy to listen to this man whom she believed to be a prophet, but had expressed her willingness to listen to the Messiah when he came, Jesus openly declared himself to be the Christ, that he would work his work of salvation of her soul.

This woman could not help but now understand the nature of religion—the pure, spiritual, active, ever-budding fountain that leads to worship of a pure and holy God, where the heart is offered, and where the hopes of a humble spirit are breathed out for the justification of the sinner that salvation will occur.

The shock of Jesus's declaration left her stone-faced and speechless. Fortuitously, at this moment came Jesus's disciples who marveled that he was engaged in conversation with a woman—and a woman of Samaria at that. But out of their respect and reverence for Jesus, not one of them dared to ask him the reason for his conduct or even to render any appearance of reproving.

With her mind greatly excited, when the woman at the well heard the men approaching, she dropped her bucket and its rope to the ground and ran past them toward the city.

Peter spoke first as usual and asked, "Where is she going in such a hurry, Rabbi?"

Jesus responded, "She's on her way back to the city to tell all those who will listen to her that she met the Messiah."

"Met the Messiah?" Peter questioned. "You told her who you are? She is a Samaritan and a woman, and for the very first time ever that I am aware of, you tell a Samaritan woman who you are?"

"You have a problem with that, Peter?" Jesus asked.

"Of course I don't, Master," Peter answered. "I am just surprised, that's all. What do you think she's going to say?"

"Well," Jesus answered, "I can tell you exactly what she is now saying to the people in Sychar. She has just entered through the city gate and has run into some of her male acquaintances and is saying to them, 'Come and see a man who has told me all things that I ever did.' Then she says, 'Could this be the Christ?

Is not this satisfactory proof that he is who he says he is?' And, Peter, those men and that woman are on their way here even as we speak."

At this time, knowing that the men of the city were coming to see and speak with Jesus, his disciples encouraged him to eat before they arrived.

But Jesus said to them, "I have food to eat of which you are unaware."

Being slow to understand, his disciples said to one another, "What? Has someone else brought him something to eat? Did that Samaritan woman give him food?"

Jesus just shook his head and said to them, "My food is to do the will of him that sent me and to finish his work. My great object, the great design of my life, is to do the will of God."

(Jesus and his disciples had come to this appointed place weary and thirsty. But an opportunity of doing good—of doing the Father's will—presented itself, and Jesus forgot about his physical desires and his physical needs. He forgot about his hunger; he forgot about his fatigue. He found comfort and joy in doing what is good and what is right, in seeking to save a soul. His mind had become so absorbed in doing the will of God that he rose above his fatigue, his hardship, his wants, and he forgot all other things. He bore all with pleasure in seeing the work of his Father: the salvation of men. Jesus came to provide that. He came to apply salvation to the heart through his teaching, by his example, and by his death on a cross for the expiation for the elect's sin. There is no doubt that if he were diligent in doing his work for our welfare, then we should be diligent also in regard to not only our salvation but also in seeking salvation of others).

Jesus spoke a proverb that at first sounded strange to his disciples: "Men say that the common time from sowing the seed to the harvest in Judea is about four months, so that the husbandman is compelled to wait a considerable period before being able to realize a crop. He has encouragement in his sowing the seed.

He expects fruit from his labors, and his labor is lightened by that expectation, but the harvest is not immediate."

Before speaking another word, Jesus looked beyond his men who stood listening intently to his every word, pointed to the multitudes who were coming from Sychar to see him because of the testimony of the woman at the well, and said, "Behold I say to you, lift up your eyes and look on the fields, for they are white, all ready to harvest. But I tell you the truth: the long wait for harvest is not so with my preaching. The seed has already sprung up. Scarce was it sown before it produced an abundant harvest. The Gospel was just preached to a single woman, and do you see how effectual it is? Many of the Samaritans come out to hear it also. There is therefore more encouragement to labor in this field than a farmer has to sow his grain. This wicked and ignorant people were ones who appeared most likely not to be affected but have heard the voice of their Savior, have turned to God, and have come in multitudes to me to learn the way of life. Let this be a lesson to you. You know not how much good may be done by conversation with even just one individual, but look how my conversation with a woman resulted in a deep interest felt throughout the city of Sychar. Under the hand of the Holy Spirit, a single person may be the means of leading many to the Savior. It may have crossed your minds that it was esteemed improper for me to have had a conversation with this woman alone, that she was an abandoned character, and perhaps there would have been little hope of doing her good, but I tell you that it was I who sought out to have a conversation with this woman in order that I might bring about her conversion by giving her the truth. Just remember, he that reaps receives wages and gathers fruit unto life eternal, and that both he that sows and he that reaps may rejoice together. Your preaching will not go unrewarded. And herein is that true saying of old: 'One sows and another reaps.' The seed, long buried, may spring up into an abundant harvest. I am commissioning you to preach the Gospel. You have not toiled in preparing the way for the great harvest, which is now ready to be gathered in. Other men labored: the prophets, who long labored to prepare the way for my coming; the teachers among the Jews who have read and explained the law and taught the people; John the Baptist, who came to prepare the way; and finally, myself, who by my ministry teach the people and prepare them for the success, which is to attend the preaching of my heralds. You are to sow the seed in the morning and in the evening. You are not to withhold your hand, for you know not whether it shall prosper, this or that, and so you go forth bearing precious seed, though weeping, knowing that you shall come again rejoicing, bringing in the sheaves."

That day, many of the Samaritans of that city received faith to believe in Jesus for salvation, all because of what an immoral woman of their city said, "He told me all that I ever did."

From a single conversation with an individual little likely to yield results, according to our way of thinking, in circumstances that had been prearranged by God himself and in a place outside the Jewish land, many believed on the basis of the testimony of the woman, many more came to hear for themselves, and many believed because they heard Jesus speak for themselves.

So when the Samaritans had come to Jesus, they surrounded him on all sides, asking untold questions. They urged him to stay with them so that they could inquire of him further, and he agreed.

At first they believed because of the woman's testimony, but to the people of this culture, this was not adequate. They would have to hear for themselves. Jesus's acceptance of the woman in her new role showed that he did not share a condescending attitude toward women as did men of his time; however, many more believed in him because of his own words.

After Jesus had stayed with them in their city of Sychar for two days, preaching and his disciples baptizing, he and his men moved on to Cana in Galilee where he had previously turned the water into wine at the marriage feast of his cousin.

Jesus Heals a Lame Man on the Sabbath

AFTER JESUS AND his disciples had come back to Cana, he sent word to his mother that he was back in the area. I cannot tell you how elated I was to hear that my Jesus had returned. In his absence, I had busied myself filling orders for the women back in Magdala. I had taken their money for deposits toward future work, and after my healing by the most remarkable man, I took the time to complete those orders and recapture the reputation that I had once enjoyed. I was known as the top seamstress and cloth dealer in the area.

Jesus's mother had been an absolute dear to me, treating me as if I were one of her very own daughters. Judas and James, her two sons that remained at home, became big brothers to me. They protected me, kidded me, and treated me with unprecedented kindness, the likes of which I had never heretofore experienced.

Even now, the way they treated me brings tears to my eyes whenever I think about it. I know in my heart that those new "big brothers" of mine sensed the feelings I had for their older sibling. They never once treated me as if they would like to know me better. They kept their affections in check, as if I were being held in reserve for Jesus.

One morning, Jesus appeared in the doorway of his mother's house. I was seated cross-legged upon a straw mat in the corner of the front room, stitching a hem into a full-length tunic, while the mother of Jesus sat opposite me, brushing out her long black hair that was highlighted with many strands of silver. When I saw the light that came in through the door become partially blocked, I looked up. Even though I could not see his face because of the bright morning light, there was no doubt who it was. I could hardly contain myself. The sight of Jesus standing there with the rays of light from the morning sun creating a halo of light around his head was almost more than I could handle. The brightness of the halo blinded me momentarily, but I could just see in my mind's eye that smile of his spreading from ear to ear across his sun-drenched face. The mere sight of him set to flight a thousand butterflies in my stomach. This man could set loose such passion in me that I often found it hard to breathe. My chest heaved up and down rapidly. Before his mother ever had a chance to move, I jumped to my feet. Spilling all my sewing materials onto the floor, I ran to Jesus and threw my arms around his neck. Crooning like some crazed dove, I smothered him with my affection and cried out with glee, "Jesus, you're home. I'm so glad to see you." Catching myself, I added, "We are all so glad to see you."

Taking hold of both my wrists, this man for whom my heart ached, gently pulled down my arms that were locked like a vise grip around his neck and responded with his usual calmness, "I am glad to see all of you as well. And how are you, Mary of Magdala? My, you certainly have changed. You look wonderful, happy, and content."

"Thank you for asking, Jesus," I said excitedly. "I do well, and I am indeed happy. Thank you again for delivering me from the grips of those demons and for bringing me here to Capernaum, and for letting me stay with your mother, and for…"

"Whoa! Whoa! Slow down," Jesus said. "Take a breath. I am sure that my mother enjoys having you here with her. I have no doubts that you are a comfort and a blessing to her."

"Yes, she is," his mother chimed in. By now, she had gotten to her feet and had come to where her son and I stood.

Jesus took both her hands in his and kissed the palm of each tenderly. "Hello, Mother," he said. "And how is my favorite woman?"

Her answer was drowned out by the thoughts running through my brain. I thought to myself, *How I wish he would have taken my hands in his like that and would have kissed my hands. Does he not see that I love him with all my heart? Oh, Jesus, please see me! See me! I love you so!*

I must have appeared dazed. Jesus had placed his hand on my shoulder and was shaking me back to reality. "Mary? Mary?" he said. "Are you all right? You seemed for a moment not to be here with us."

"Oh! I am so very sorry, Jesus and Mother Mary," I quickly answered. "I was just thinking…I was contemplating…I was just wondering what I might go out and gather to help with lunch preparations. That's it! I know that you and your disciples must be famished."

"Well, the truth is, Mary—"

"The truth is, Mary of Magdala," Peter said, interrupting our conversation as he stepped into the room, "the truth is that we are indeed famished. As a matter of fact, I could eat a whole lamb all by myself."

Everyone laughed. Peter certainly was as entertaining as he was predictable. No one ever felt the need to speak as much as he. Presently, the rest of Jesus's disciples came into the room where we had a chance to catch up on all the things that had happened in Sychar. While the others talked and laughed and exchanged all manner of cordialities, without thinking, I allowed my mind to wonder off to Sychar. How wonderful it would have been to have had Jesus all to myself for a while like the woman at the well. I thought, *How lucky she was to have been able to talk with Jesus at length, without interruption.*

Finally, the mother of Jesus said to me, "Mary, why don't you and I go and prepare for these hungry men a lunch that they will not soon forget?"

Her words brought me back to reality and I answered, "That sounds like a marvelous idea, Mother Mary. I will go and gather some wood for the fire."

"Excellent," she said, "and I will get the barley and the buckwheat. Judas, would you please milk the goat, and, James, please gather some eggs and some honey? This is going to be a glorious day. I feel it in my bones."

After four days of rest and relaxation at his mother's home, even though rest for Jesus was still a busy time of teaching his disciples, he said that he and his followers must go back up to Jerusalem for the feast. It had been only fifty days since Passover, but Jewish men needed to return to celebrate the feast of Pentecost. Jesus acted as though he would rather I stay with his mother here in Capernaum, but he also knew that I was not a relative and could do as I pleased. I indeed insisted that I tag along. "Besides," I said, "I can be of benefit to you with my money."

It was hard for him to argue with that, so he, his men, and I packed our things into packs we could carry on our backs and set out on foot for Jerusalem. The trek was laced with danger from possible attacks of would-be thieves, from attacks by wild animals, and from desert storms that could pop up out of nowhere. But in spite of all possible occurrences, we arrived safe and sound to Jerusalem at midafternoon.

We were about to enter the city by the Sheep Gate on the north side of the temple when Jesus, who was in the front, raised his hand, signaling for us to stop. We stood for a few minutes watching a great multitude of sick people who had been made weak and feeble by long-standing diseases. Either they lay by themselves or huddled together in masses under the five covered porches used for shelter and walkways in inclement weather. There must have been a hundred or more afflicted people lying in the shelter of the porches. Some were barely able to move because of their crippled conditions. Some had withered hands from years of suffering with different forms of palsy. Some had only one eye; still others had no eyesight at all. Whatever their ailments, they were all weak and feeble. Unable to maintain any measure of hygiene, the smell that drifted on the air from them urinating and defecating on themselves caused passersby to hold their breath and others to heave as they picked up their pace to quickly move beyond the area. Noticeably absent were those who were afflicted with skin diseases. They were the unclean and therefore were not allowed by law to be in the midst of those without skin eruptions.

The porches surrounded a pool (by the gate), which was called in Hebrew *Bethesda* (meaning the house of mercy); and at this pool—when the waters at a certain time were stirred up, supposedly by a visiting angel—those who entered the troubled waters first were made well from their diseases.

But Jesus had his eye on a man that he knew had been there for thirty-eight years. The man lay on a straw pallet a few feet from the edge of the pool. He was clothed in rotting filthy rags and he held his hand out continuously to beg for alms from each and every person that happened to pass his way. Both his feet were gnarled from palsy and completely turned around. His hair was waist-length, and his graying beard hung to the middle of his chest. His bronze-colored skin was blackened from the filth that covered his body from head to toe.

Taking no notice of the squalor, Jesus walked over to this poor fellow lying upon the straw pallet and said to him, "Do you want to be made whole?"

We all gasped at such a question! After all, the man had been lying by this same healing pool for more than half his life and Jesus wanted to know if he wanted to be made whole. What kind of question was that? It's not like the man wandered all over the city; he had lain by this pool for thirty-eight years. He had lain on that same straw pallet asking for alms to keep him alive in hopes that someone might help him into the waters of the pool when the angel came and stirred them up. But alas! The impotent man never was able to elicit help for his cause.

The crippled man looked as surprised at Jesus's question as the rest of us. After shaking his head in almost disbelief, he answered Jesus and said, "Sir, when the water is stirred up, I have no friend to help me into the pool. When I attempt to crawl into the railing water, others step down into it before me and are healed."

"Well," Jesus said, "that no longer will be your excuse. I say to you, rise up, take up your bed as proof that you have truly been made whole, and walk."

Never was a sinner more helpless than this man, but God gave him the strength to do his will. Immediately, the man's feet started to ungnarl and turn around to face forward. The man's feet appeared as if they had become normal, and he was rendered well. Being wobbly at first, the man struggled to his feet, picked up the straw pallet upon which he had reclined for thirty-eight years, and walked about, showing that his once-twisted feet were now straight. One should not infer that a sinner should delay repentance as if waiting for God but simply to understand that the man had no power to heal himself.

When the man picked up his bed to carry it, he completely forgot that it was the Sabbath and the law of the Torah forbade one from carrying a burden on the Sabbath. He was so overjoyed and so overwhelmed that he literally clicked his heels together and jumped squarely into the center of the pool. This simple gesture was done to show everyone that in spite of having no one to help him for all those years, he now didn't need anyone else; he had Jesus.

Being very legalistic in the observation of the external duties of religion, when the Pharisees saw the man carrying his bed on the Sabbath, they admonished him, "It is the Sabbath. It is not lawful for you to carry your bed."

The healed man reasoned that if Jesus had the power to work such an incredible miracle, he certainly had the right to explain the law, and if he had conferred so great a favor on him, he had a right to expect obedience. So he answered them, saying, "He that made me whole said to me, 'Take up your bed and walk.'"

Instead of looking at the miracle wrought and at the man's statement of the manner in which he had been healed, they looked only at what they thought to be a violation of the law, and so they asked him, "What man is it that said unto you, 'Take up your bed and walk?'"

A great source of disagreement among men is that they look only at the points in which they differ and are unwilling to listen to the reasons why others do not believe as they do.

Then the man who had been healed by Jesus set one end of his bed upon the ground, scratched his lice-infested head with his other hand, and said, "Amazingly, I don't even know who it was that healed me. He didn't tell me his name. He withdrew so quickly and blended into the crowd there by the pool I never really saw the man after my feet became straight and I could walk again."

"If you see that man again, you need to point him out to us," said the Pharisees. "Do you understand?"

"Yes, I understand you," answered the jubilant man. For the first time in over thirty-eight years, he turned and walked away under his own power.

Later that day, the healed man went to the temple, a privilege of which he had long been deprived, to seek the sanctuary of God and give him thanks for his mercy. He ran into Jesus, who said to him, "Well, I see that you have been made whole. I tell you to sin no more lest a worse thing come unto you."

It seemed to me that Jesus was implying to this man that his infirmity was caused by sin, perhaps by vice in his youth. His crime or dissipation had brought on him this long and distressing affliction, and Jesus was letting him know that he knew all about his indiscretions and was taking the opportunity to warn him not to repeat them. He was telling the healed man that he had a priceless experience, and if he continued sinning, it would be worse. He should learn to avoid the very appearance of evil, shun the places of temptation, not mingle again with his old companions, and he should touch not, taste not, and handle not.

When the two parted, the man went straight to the leaders of the Jews and told them that it was Jesus who had healed him. That's when they came after Jesus. They opposed him and attempted to ruin his character, destroy his popularity, and hold him up before the people as a violator of the law of God. Without making inquiry of whether he was the Messiah or not, they assumed that he had to be in the wrong and should be punished. They therefore sought to put him to death as a directive in the law of Moses. Even though Jesus had restored an infirm man to health, something they would have done for an animal they might have owned, yet they sought his life because he had done it for a sick human being on the Sabbath. These leaders of the Jews had such zeal for their laws (that had been added to the laws of God by man) that they hated and persecuted him who did good, who loved revivals of religion and the spread of the Gospel because he did not do according to some matter of form which had been established by man. Jesus hated hypocrisy, and there was nothing that he set himself against any more than those who proclaimed that all goodness was found in *forms,* and all piety in the *shibboleths* of a particular party or group.

Jesus saw the fire in their eyes and said, "My Father has never ceased to work on the Sabbath, and I work. He makes the sun to rise. He moves the stars in heaven. He causes the grass, the trees and the flowers to grow. He created the world in six days and ceased the work of creation, but he has never ceased to govern it nor failed to carry out his providence on the Sabbath. As God does what is good on the Sabbath, as he is not bound by the law, which requires his creatures to rest on that day, so I do the same for the Son of Man is Lord of the Sabbath."

The leaders of the Jews became infuriated at what they considered to be blasphemy spoken by Jesus because he was equating himself with God. Since he had applied deity to himself and applied the Yahwistic "I Am" to himself, and his claim to be equal with God in nature, the Jews instructed their followers to lay hold of him, but Jesus spoke, and they hesitated.

"Verily, verily, I say to you, the Son can do nothing independent of the Father but does what he sees the Father do, for things whatsoever he does, these also the Son does likewise."

In other words, having stated the extent of his authority, Jesus proceeded to show its source and nature and to prove to them that what he had said was true, that he does nothing without the appointment of the Father and nothing contrary to him. Even though my own eyes had been enlightened by the Holy Spirit when Jesus forgave my sins and had accepted me into the family of God, I could see how the Pharisees and Sadducees would take an affront to this. The scales had not been removed from their eyes, and in spite of the miracles that he had wrought, they just could not accept Jesus as the Christ. His reputation had spread throughout Judea and Galilee for exorcising demons, healing the lame, healing all sorts of diseases, and giving sight to the blind. But somehow the Jewish authorities could not imagine that he was the one spoken of by Isaiah, the one who had fulfilled the prophecies of being a Nazarene (a branch), being born in a manger in Bethlehem and being called out of Egypt, or the fulfillment of the prophecy in Daniel of being born at the exact time as history prophesied. Even at the time when John the Baptizer baptized Jesus in the River Jordan, God spoke from heaven, saying, "This is my beloved Son, with whom I am well pleased." Now tell me, how anyone could not grasp it when God himself spoke and said, "This is my Son." Of course these leaders of the Jews may not have been present, but what transpired there surely would have been spread abroad. I find it incredible that every time the Jewish leaders told their minions to seize Jesus, they seemed to be frozen in place whenever he opened his mouth to speak.

Then Jesus said, "The Father loves the Son and makes him acquainted with all things that he himself does. He conceals nothing from him. God shows him all that he does. The Son is obviously possessed of omniscience, for to no finite mind could be imparted a knowledge of all the works of God. But he will direct the Son to do greater works than healing an impotent man and commanding him to carry his bed on the Sabbath day, and when he does, you will marvel. For as the Father raises the dead and gives life and judges the world, even so the Son gives life to whom he will. The Son has the power to renew persons, and the renewing of the heart is as much the result of his will as the raising of the dead. But you must understand that the Father judges no man but has committed all judgment into the hands of the Son. The Son, having the power to judge the world, has the ability to search the heart and omniscience to understand the motives of all actions."

I literally stood to the side with Peter, James, and John and marveled at the words that flowed like honey from the mouth of this man to whom I had secretly pledged my heart. I knew that he was a prophet come from God and had the power of exorcism and of healing, but here he was talking about raising the dead and giving life eternal and judging the world. I kept thinking, *Could this be true?* I know he had said to me after driving out the seven demons that had taken possession of me, "Your sins are forgiven;" but can this be real? Is this man with whom I have fallen in love the Son of God? I looked up into the face of Peter for some kind of answer, but all I got from him was an expression of pure joy and delight. I looked from him to James and from James to John and found the same funny little cockeyed smile. I said to Peter, "What is he…?" But before I could get out another word, he put his finger to his lips and shushed me! I turned to John, who was closer to my age, and caught his eye, but he shook his head for me to be quiet. *Would no one answer me and tell me who this Jesus really was?* For now, all I could do was listen to his conversation with men who would kill him.

Then I heard Jesus say, "All men should honor, esteem, and revere the Son, even as they honor, esteem, and revere the Father. As I have declared unto you I have the power and authority equal with God so that you should honor me when you recognize this in me. He that honors not the Son honors not the Father who sent him. I tell you the truth: he that receives my word into his heart and believes in him that sent me to redeem the elect has everlasting life and shall not come to judgment but has passed from spiritual death unto eternal life. I tell you the truth: the time is coming and now is taking place when the spiritual dead, either the ones walking about on the earth or the ones lying in the grave, shall hear the voice of the Son of God and they shall inherit eternal life. As the Father is the source of all life and derives his life from no other source than himself, so he has appointed his Son to have life in himself and has given to him authority and power to execute judgment also, because he is the Son of man."

My ears were burning from new information that came pouring in. It was hard to assimilate it all. If this were true for me, even though the Pharisees were students of the law, it would certainly be hard for them because of their deeply entrenched beliefs. They were looking for a king to come who would run out the Roman occupiers, not a suffering servant who would turn the other cheek to those who would take the advantage to strike it. Jesus stood his ground, but the ground was a miniscule island surrounded by crocodiles, and the crocodiles were baring their teeth. For every breath he took, it seemed as though they would pounce upon him; but whenever he spoke again, it was like a hand being put into the faces of his enemies. They were stopped cold in their tracks. Jesus continued to admonish them, seemingly taking no heed to his life being threatened.

"Marvel not at what I say now, for the hour is approaching in which all the dead of every age and nation, even though their bodies may have turned to dust and perished from human view, will hear the voice of God. He sees them where they are, will reassemble their remains and raise them to life, and will command them to appear before him. They shall come out of their graves, those who are righteous. They who have by their works shown to be the friends of Christ will be raised up to the full enjoyment and perpetual security of life eternal where they shall never see death ever again. But those who have done evil and those who have done wickedly in the sight of God will be raised to judgment and everlasting punishment and destruction."

I don't know about the others who heard Jesus speak these words, but when I heard them, I shivered and felt a cold that went straight to the bone. His comments were severe and cutting; there was no mincing of words. He intended to bring them to a state of alarm for the time was wasting away. The kingdom of heaven was at hand. It was now and they needed to wake up and recognize the presence of God. Even though I knew that I was a member of the family of God, having been told that I was forgiven of my sins by the very Son of God, I still felt terror strike into my very being. Was this terror for those who were dead in their sins and lost, or was it for me not really being sure that my salvation was secure? I reasoned that my feelings must be for the others for I loved this man and knew for a certainty that he loved me equally as well. And even though I knew that he loved me, it wasn't just the romantic type of love that I felt in my heart for him. That definitely was a disappointment for me, but I felt certain that someday, he would share similar feelings for me.

I wanted so much for Jesus to leave with us and leave these angry men behind. I could see that rage was just seething inside them, churning like a vat of maggots. Their hatred grew with every word he spoke, and with each passing moment, one could see their hands trembling for the want of seizing him. Their restraint was about to shatter like a wooden barrel thrown against a rock. Fear for my loved one gripped me, and tears started streaming down my cheeks. As if clawing the wind, with outstretched arms, I reached out to him and cried aloud, "Jesus, please!"

Before I had a chance to speak another word, Peter put his hand over my mouth and pulled me back with his massive arm around my chest. He quieted me and admonished me to not interfere. "Jesus knows what he's doing," he reproved me. "You will just have to trust him. What he is doing is needful. He has to drive them to the point of either acknowledging him for who he is or denying him altogether."

I looked at Peter first then at the others with pleading eyes. Without saying a word, I was begging them to get Jesus out of here. I just knew the Pharisees were going to kill him.

Not flinching, Jesus glanced with a determined look my way, but continued his dissertation to those unbelieving angry men.

"Without the concurrence and the authority of God, I can do nothing. Such is the union between us that I do nothing independent of him. Whatever I do, I do according to the will of the Father. I speak to the world those things that I have heard from him and have been taught by him. From those things that the Father has shown unto me and knowing his will and wishes I judge, and my judgment is righteous. And because I have no selfish bias, I came not to elevate myself, but I came to do the will of the Father who sent me."

Already agitated, the crowd shouted and scoffed at him, "You say you came not to magnify yourself? What do you call it when you call God your Father? Do you really think that *you* will judge *us*? You better first judge yourself for the blasphemy you speak!"

Jesus was unfazed. He raised his voice even higher to be heard over the screams and the shouts. "If I provide no other evidence than my own testimony about myself, my witness would not be worthy of belief, but God bears witness of me, and I know that his witness of me is true."

"Blasphemer, heretic!" came shouts from the crowd. The pitch of their voices had gone up by several decibels. "We are not going to allow you to speak to us in this manner. Seize him!" a voice shouted from the middle of the crowd.

Before they could make their move, Jesus continued unshaken. "You questioned John the Baptist who bore witness of me. That should have satisfied you. He is an eminent man and many of you believed him. He is candid, unambitious, sincere, and his evidence is presented impartially. But *I* adduce evidence of a higher order. I do not depend on proof of who I am from the testimony of men, nor do I pride myself on the commendations or flattery of men.

"You sent to make inquiry, and he gave you a satisfactory answer. Had you believed him, you would have believed in the Messiah and been saved. You knew that John was a burning and a shining light, and you were willing for a short time to rejoice in his doctrine and to admit that he was a distinguished prophet until he bore witness of me, Jesus of Nazareth. Then your king Herod had him thrown into prison.

"But I have greater witnesses than that of John. The miracles of healing the sick and raising the dead, the works that the Father has committed to me to do until my tasks have been completed bear witness to the fact that the Father sent me. The Father himself, who has sent me, has born witness of me. It has not been your practice to fully obey God, nor have you been disposed to listen to his commands or his declarations at any time, nor have you seen his form. This has been the uniform characteristic of Israel for all times. You have disregarded and perverted the testimony of God just as your fathers did, and you do not have his word abiding in you. Whom he did send you refused to believe. God foretold that the Messiah would come, and he has given abundant evidence that I am he. This is certainly proof that you do not regard the word of God.

"You anxiously search the books of the Torah for by studying them, you think you can obtain eternal life. These same Scriptures bear witness of me. They predict my coming, and they tell the manner of the life I am to live and the death that I am to die. Although the Scriptures bear witness that I am the Messiah, although you professedly search them to learn the way to obtain eternal life, and although the works that I do prove it, yet you will not allow yourselves to come unto me that you might have life to the fullest here and in the hereafter. I do not say these things because I desire accolades from men but to account for the fact that you do not believe on me."

A Pharisee at the back of the crowd yelled, "Why do you allow this man to blaspheme the name and character of God? Is he greater than Moses or Father Abraham? Is he greater than the prophets and the law given to us by God?"

Jesus moved to a higher step leading up into the synagogue and yelled back to the man at the rear of the crowd. "This I know, you do not have the love of God in your heart. I have come by the authority of God, but you do not accept me for who I am. Someone else, a false teacher, can come and set himself up as the Messiah and do nothing to prove that he has a divine commission and you will follow and obey him as a teacher. How can you possibly believe when you are studious of praise and live for pride, ambition, and vain glory?

"Had the Messiah come as you had wanted him to come, with pomp and circumstance and power, you would have considered it an honor to follow him. As it is, you despise and reject me. A man cannot believe what I say while he is wholly under the influence of ambition. The two are incompatible. A man cannot open the lid of a trunk if he stands on top of the trunk and attempts to raise his own weight and the lid at the same time, but if he gets off and then opens it, he will discover the treasure inside.

It simply requires him to come outside himself, to lay aside his pride and his ambition. The honor that comes from men is their praise, flattery, and commendation. The honor that comes from God, however, is his approbation for doing his will. If you seek after God's honor, you will come to me for I am the Way, the Life, and the Truth.

"Do not think that I intend to follow your example and accuse you to the Father of breaking his law. There is one that accuses you, even Moses, in whom you trust. He wrote of the coming Messiah and commanded the people to hear him. Because they did not do it, they disregarded his command. Don't forget, Moses was divinely commissioned and therefore should have been obeyed by the people, but they disregarded him, so his command reproved them for being disobedient and rebellious. If they, as you, had believed Moses, you would have believed me for he wrote of me. If you don't give credence to what he has written, which you profess to believe, how shall you believe my words?"

That was all that needed to be said! The crowd rushed forward and grabbed Jesus by the arms and by the legs with the intent of carrying him to outside the city wall and casting him over the edge of the bluff upon which Jerusalem was built.

I tried to run to rescue my Lord, but it was as if I went into slow motion while everything else continued on in real time. I "rushed" forward and stretched out my hand, thinking that I could pull Jesus free from the grasp of the throng that had now deteriorated into a mob. Then time stood still. My forward motion became frozen. Not only could I not reach Jesus, but I also could not move - at all. I saw him glace over his shoulder at me and give me a tiny smile, a most peculiar smile, a knowing smile, a confident smile, a smile that melted my heart, a smile that said, *Don't you worry now, my Father is in charge here. Things are totally under his control.*

I cannot tell you how it happened or when it happened. I was there, and I thought my eyes were wide open. But in a moment, a mere twinkling of an eye, there was no longer a screaming mob, screaming for Jesus's blood. There were no more steps leading up to a synagogue. There was no more Pool of Bethesda, no more crippled man, no more people in distress, only Jesus, twelve disciples, and me sailing over the Sea of Galilee.

Jesus just sat there in the rear of the boat, calm, serene, and demure. The sea was very rough with black swells five to six feet in height. Some of the disciples worked feverishly to keep the sail just at the right angle with the wind; others bailed water that washed over the sides. James manned the rudder, and I sat shrouded in a blanket made of sheepskin on a crossbeam not more than two feet from Jesus. I looked around as if eyeing the inside of the boat for the first time. Finally, I asked, "Jesus, how did we get out of Jerusalem and into this boat?"

He raised his head and fixed a penetrating gaze upon me. Without changing his expression, he said just above a whisper, "God is in charge of all things, and my time has not yet come."

"Well," I said, "God may be in control, but it certainly seemed that at any moment back there, you could have been torn to shreds and thrown over the cliff outside the city wall."

He smiled at me and then responded, "My life will never be lost as you say for my life is mine to give. And I will not give my life until I have accomplished all that the Father has given me to do. I came down to earth to do my Father's will. When that has been finished, then I will lay down my life for my sheep."

"Lay down your life for sheep? I don't understand all that you say, Jesus. All I know is that I love you and I am scared to death that you are going to incite these people to take your life, *before that time you talk about!*"

"Mary, Mary," Jesus said softly. "You fret too much. You do not yet understand who I really am. I love you, Mary, as I love Peter and James and John and all the rest of my disciples. Just as the Father loves me, I love those that believe in me and love me and have been looking for my coming."

"How can you say that you love me just as you do your disciples? That was not a love pat you gave me when you touched me and held me that day in Magdala, when you chased those demons out from me. I felt your love. I know better. You may be fooling yourself, but you cannot fool me!"

I could feel my face grow hot from the anger that arose in me and also from the embarrassment that I felt by his rejection. I jumped to my feet and moved to the front of the boat, not taking notice that the sea had completely calmed. I could see from the corner of my eye that he was shaking his head. As a woman, I knew that the love he said he had for me was not the same as the love he felt for everyone who were his. It would take time, but I would show him that his love for me was different.

Fish and Chips Feed Five Thousand

AFTER LANDING IN Gergesa the following day, Jesus said to me, "Mary, I desire to be alone with my men for a little while for instruction. Would you please wait here with the boat while we go up into the mountain?"

I could not say anything except, "Of course, I'll stay here," all the while thinking, *Of course I'll stay here while you and your boys go off and leave me. I'm not very happy with you right now anyway.*

After Jesus and his disciples had been gone for a while into the mountain, praying, I could see a great multitude of people coming along the seacoast toward where I sat with the boat. I knew intuitively that they were coming seeking Jesus. At that moment, Jesus and his disciples came up to the boat. Seeing the great crowd coming to him, he turned to his disciple Phillip and asked him a very strange question, "Where shall we buy bread that these folks may eat?"

I think that Jesus asked Phillip this question to test him, to determine if he had the faith to believe that Jesus had the power to supply their needs. He already knew what he would have to do to feed these people.

Phillip frowned, and with a questioning look, he answered Jesus, "You know, Lord, that we have in the purse approximately two hundred days' wages with which to buy supplies. Two hundred denarii of bread is certainly not enough to make sure that everyone in this crowd has at least a morsel to eat. I know that you have a big heart, Rabboni, but there is not enough. We must consider what we will have for tomorrow."

Another of his disciples, Simon's brother, Andrew, came up to them and somewhat sarcastically said, "There is a lad here who has five loaves of barley bread and two small dried fish. Maybe you can feed this multitude with them, but what is that among so many?"

Andrew and Phillip held on to each other, waiting to see if Jesus would enter into laughter with them. They thought Jesus might enjoy a good joke and surely would appreciate the humor as well.

But Jesus didn't see the humor in what they had said for his concern was for the welfare of these people and for the reasons for which they had come out to see him. Without changing his expression, Jesus said to his comic followers, "Direct all the people to sit down on the grassy slopes."

Having realized that their attempt at humor was wasted, they shouted instructions to the estimated five thousand men (plus women and children) to sit down on the grass. Jesus took the barley loaves and the fishes from the lad's basket, held them high above his head, gave thanks, and prayed to God for his blessing upon the meal. Then he handed the bread and the fishes to his disciples, who in turn distributed the food to all the people that sat upon the ground.

I watched this entire event take place from the bow of the boat in which I sat. It was incredible! I could hardly believe my eyes! As the food was distributed to the hungry people sitting upon the grassy slopes, the baskets were never empty, and all had enough to satisfy their hunger. John brought me a piece of barley bread and a large piece of dried perch. Then he served Jesus. The rest of the disciples sat down and ate from the baskets from which they had just served.

When everyone had his fill, Jesus said to his disciples, "Gather up the fragments that remain that nothing be lost."

Though he obviously had power to provide any quantity of food he wanted, Jesus was also teaching his followers that the bounties of providence are not to be wasted. Even though he had an infinite supply at his disposal, and though he was Lord of all, he was modeling the example of good stewardship. Just as the loaves and the fishes created by Jesus were his gift, all that we have, including the very air we breathe, is a gift from God and should not be squandered.

The disciples gathered the leftover fragments and filled to the brim the twelve baskets from which they had distributed the food to the thousands who had come out seeking Jesus. Their hunger being satisfied, the men had risen to their feet and had gathered themselves together into small bands and had begun talking about what they had just witnessed. The sound of their talk escalated. Then those same men, realizing the miracle that Jesus had just done, said, "Truly this must be the Messiah who is to come into the world."

Jesus perceived that these men were satisfied by the miracle and that they believed he was the Messiah; however, he knew that they were about to come and take him by force, to make him king. They supposed that the Messiah was to be a temporal prince. They could see that Jesus was unassuming, retiring, unambitious, and indisposed to assume the head of office. They had decided that they would proclaim him as the long-expected king and pressure him to assume the character and title of an earthly king. I suppose they thought they understood what was right better than he did. They sought grandeur and power, but Jesus sought retirement and displayed profound humility. Hunger was common in Israel, and a Messiah who could multiply food was the One most people were ready to follow.

Before they had a chance to take him by force, Jesus told his disciples to send me on to Capernaum and for them to take the boat out into open sea. He would meet up with us all later. After he had seen John and me start walking toward the north and his other disciples take the boat out, Jesus quietly moved past the crowd and went up into a mountain to pray.

⸻

When the sun had bid the day farewell and the night had wrapped itself in a blanket of cold air, Jesus's men set sail out into open water where the sea had awakened from a calm sleep. The wind and the sea responded with crashing waves, causing the men in the boat to become exceedingly apprehensive.

After they had taken the sail down to prevent it from being torn apart, Jesus's disciples rowed out about three miles into the sea and were fighting desperately to prevent being capsized or overfilled with water.

In the midst of his prayer time, about two hours before daybreak, Jesus knew that his disciples were in trouble. He left the refuge that he had in the mountains and went down to the edge of the waters. He could perceive his men beginning to cry out for his help. There were no more boats tied at the docks except those that required a full crew to manage. Jesus simply walked on the water to reach his frightened men.

The nearly exhausted disciples had been rowing for hours, and when they looked out and saw Jesus walking on the sea, they didn't recognize that it was he, but were utterly terrified. The frigid night air and the charging waves had made them wet and cold, but they became chilled to the bone when they thought they were seeing an apparition. Pointing to the figure walking on the water, they fearfully cried out, "It's a ghost!"

Jesus quickly spoke to them to calm their fears, "Be of good cheer, men, it is I Am. Be not afraid."

His disciples were literally shaking in their sandals. Peter was the first to regain his composure, and in his characteristically impulsive manner, with a voice that shook from its very foundations, he cried out, "Lord, if it is truly you, bid me come unto you on the water."

Jesus knew Peter so well, he answered, "Come."

It was amazing! It was life changing! Peter stepped over the side of the boat and actually started walking on top of the water toward Jesus. However, when he felt the wind and the water spray on his neck, he realized that they were yet violent. Failing to keep his eyes on Jesus, Peter began to sink. The amazing thing was that even though he began to sink, he did so almost in slow motion. By the time he had sunk up to his waist, he cried out, "Lord, save me!"

Without hesitation, Jesus immediately stretched out his hand and grabbed Peter's forearm. Instead of raising him up forthwith, he made the comment, "O you of little faith. Why did you doubt, Peter? We could have walked all the way to shore together!"

Peter knew that he had missed an incredible opportunity, but now was not the time to analyze his failures. Fear gripped him tighter than Jesus's grip upon his arm.

"Please save me, Lord, I pray. Please save me!"

Jesus pulled him up out of the turbulent water and placed Peter into the boat. Immediately, the wind ceased to howl and the sea became still and calm. The surface of the water at once became like polished brass.

The disciples were astonished to see that all was calm, all was still. Without hesitation, they went down on their knees in the bottom of the boat and began to worship Jesus, saying, "Of a truth, you are the Son of God."

Jesus did not try to stop them. He knew for certain that they finally had captured the vision, that he was the Messiah who had been prophesized to come. He accepted their worship.

Eating His Flesh
and Drinking His Blood

THE FOLLOWING DAY, the people that had been fed with the loaves and fishes stood on the shore where Jesus's boat had been tied and realized that he and the boat were gone. They had seen Jesus go off into the mountain to pray, but when they searched the area, he was not there. Many of the people got into other boats that were nearby and set sail to Capernaum in search of him.

After their vessels had reached the shore in Capernaum and after they had found Jesus on the other side of the sea, they asked him, "Rabbi, when did you come over here?"

Knowing what was their design, Jesus answered, "Truly, truly, I say to you, you seek me not because you saw the signs but because you ate the food and were filled. To seek me because you have seen the miracles and were convinced by them that I am the Messiah would be proper, but to follow me simply because your wants were met is mere selfishness of the worst kind. Do not manifest anxiety over food that perishes but unto everlasting life, which the Son of man shall give unto you for he has been sealed by God the Father. You should seek after those things that can supply your spiritual wants, those things that support and nourish and strengthen the soul. You should seek after the doctrines of the Gospel that are to a weak and guilty soul what needful food is to the weary and decaying body."

Jesus stopped talking to the crowd that had found him and walked into Capernaum to the synagogue. The masses were on his heel and stopped only when he entered the building, whereupon he sat down in the seat of the teacher.

The shutters on the synagogue remained open almost year-round so that those that remained on the outside could hear the teacher as well as those that filled the hall.

Then the Jewish leaders said to Jesus, "What works shall we work that will be acceptable to God?"

"I do not say that there is no work to be done," Jesus answered. "The work of God is that you believe in him who the Father has sent—that is, believe in the Messiah. This is the work that sinners are to do, and doing this, you will be saved for Christ is the end of the law for righteousness to every one that believes."

There were other Jews, rulers of the synagogue, who had not seen the miracle of the loaves and fishes but had come along with the crowd that had followed Jesus across to the other side of the sea. They asked Jesus, "What sign do you show us that we may see and believe? What work do you work? Our fathers who were led by Moses ate manna in the desert as it is written in a Psalm, 'He gave them bread from Heaven to eat.'"

It was obvious that Jesus was becoming a little more than frustrated with those who continually sought after some sign or miracle as proof of who he claimed to be. He answered those that asked for a sign and said, "Most assuredly I say to you, Moses gave you not that bread from heaven, but my Father gave you the *true bread* from heaven, for the bread of God is he who comes down from heaven and gives life unto the world. Moses gave you food for the body, but he did not give the food that would preserve the soul from death. God has given in me the *true bread* from heaven, which is fitted to man and of far more value than any supply for your temporal wants. It is not false, deceitful, or perishing. Just as bread supports life, so my doctrine supports, preserves, and saves the soul from death.

"Furthermore, I say to you, I am the Bread of Life, the bread that gives support to spiritual life. He that comes to me shall never hunger, and he that believes on me shall never thirst.

"But I said to you, not in so many words but in substance, that you also have seen me and the full proof of my divine mission, yet you believe not. Every individual that the Father has given to me shall come to me, and everyone that comes to me in a proper manner, feeling that he is a lost and ruined sinner, in no manner or at no time, will I cast out.

"I came down from heaven for a specific purpose: not to do my will, but the will of my Father who sent me. And I will be faithful to the trust. This is the Father's will that sent me, that of all that he has given to me I should lose none, but should raise him up again at the last day, the Day of Judgment. Even though those who believe in me will die and their bodies deteriorate, they will not be destroyed. Even when they are in the grave, I will watch over them and keep them to the resurrection of the just. And this is the will of him that sent me that everyone who sees the Son and believes on him may have everlasting life, and I will raise him up at the last day."

Evidently, Jesus was telling the inquisitors that it was not sufficient just to see him and hear him, but it was also necessary to believe in him. Many of the people had seen him, but few had believed in him. Believing in him would be the evidence that the person had been given to him by the Father, and this would be conclusive evidence that he would be saved. Jesus was teaching man to strive to enter heaven as if he could do the work himself, all the while realizing salvation depends on God for he alone seeks the lost and does all the work for salvation.

The Jews then grumbled at Jesus because he had said, "I am the Bread which came down from heaven." They asked one another, "Is not this Jesus the son of Joseph whose father and mother we know? How is it then that he says, 'I came down from heaven?'"

They knew his mother and father, and there was nothing they were aware of that would indicate their son Jesus was divine. Many of them had seen Jesus as a child and then as a young man growing up in Nazareth and going up to Jerusalem with Mary and Joseph, his brothers, and his sisters to celebrate the feasts there. How could he claim that God was his Father when they all knew that Joseph was his father?

When Jesus perceived that they questioned everything among themselves, he said to reprove their murmurings, "I do not deny that these things appear difficult, and hence if any man believes, it is proof that God has inclined his heart. But stop grumbling among yourselves! No man can come to me except when the Father who has sent me draws him, and when they have come, I will raise him up at the last day. In changing the heart of a sinner, God enlightens the mind. He inclines the will and influences the soul by motives by just views of his law, by his love, his commands, by his threatening, by a desire of happiness, a consciousness of danger, and by the Holy Spirit applying truth to the mind and urging him to yield himself to the Savior.

"It is written in the Prophet Isaiah, 'And they shall be all taught of God.' Every man therefore that has heard and has learned of the Father comes unto me. Not that any man has seen the Father save he who is from God. He has seen the Father.

"Truly, truly, I say to you, he that believes on me has everlasting life for I am that Bread of Life. Your fathers ate manna in the wilderness and since have died."

Then he pointed to himself and said, "But I am the Bread that comes down from heaven that a man may eat thereof and never die. I am the Living Bread that came down from heaven. If any man eats of this bread, he shall live forever, and the bread that I will give is my flesh, which I will give for the life of the world. My body will be offered as a sacrifice for sin."

What Jesus was telling these people was that sinners might, by his atoning sacrifice, be recovered from spiritual death and be brought to eternal life. When he had said to the people that his flesh had been given for the life of the world, he was telling them that his sacrifice was full, free, ample, and designed for all men.

But the Jews present started to quarrel among themselves, saying, "How is it possible for a man to give us his flesh to eat? Isn't this the falsehood spread about us by the infidels who say that we kill and eat our young? We cannot stand for this blasphemy! We must stop this foolish man now before wind of what he is saying reaches the ears of the Romans!"

Jesus knew what they murmured, so he said to them, "Truly, truly, I say to you, except you eat the flesh of the Son of man and drink his blood, you have no life in you."

Because they missed his point, this was indeed a hard saying for them to hear and receive for the Jews were forbidden to drink blood.

There he stood, a living man, his body still alive, blood coursing through his veins, and the question became, *How could it be believed that his body could be eaten and his blood be drunk?* The plain truth was that his body and his blood would be offered in sacrifice for sin. He would procure pardon and life for many that they who would partake of that, or would have an interest in that, should obtain eternal life. Because the subject of their discourse had been talking about eating and drinking—and the fact that the Jews prided themselves so much on the point that their fathers had eaten manna, and because Jesus had said that he was the Bread of Life—it was natural and easy to carry out the figure and say that bread must be eaten in order to be of any avail in supporting and saving man.

The gathering in the synagogue was quickly becoming a mob. They shook their fingers in the face of Jesus and shouted obscenities in his ears. They stuck out their lips and gnashed their teeth and tore their outer vests to show their disapproval of and aversion to the words spoken by the Son of God. One of the leaders of the synagogue pushed his way to the front of the horde of men that advanced toward Jesus, and not knowing that he stood face-to-face with his judge, he spat in Jesus's face.

Not batting an eyelash, Jesus continued with what he had been saying. "Whosoever eats my flesh and drinks my blood has eternal life, and I will raise him up at the last day, for my flesh is food indeed and my blood is drink indeed, for it is these that give life to the soul."

The men pressing in upon Jesus put their hands over their ears and screamed, "Stop this blasphemy or you'll pay with your life. Grab him! We'll put an end to this nonsense! You glutton and wine-bibber! How dare you tell us that you are the Son of God when you hang around with the dregs of our towns! Be silent or we will silence you!"

Jesus backed up not one step; he stood his ground. The angry mob pushed in all around him, screaming and yelling their curses, and even though they reached out with their hands to seize him, not one finger touched him. It was as though there was an invisible shield that prevented every single one of the would-be attackers from being able to lay hands on him.

Not hesitating one little bit, Jesus continued, "I tell you that the one who eats my flesh and drinks my blood is truly and intimately connected with me. To abide in me is to remain in the belief that my doctrine is true. Then I will dwell in the believer by my Spirit and my doctrine. It can be said that I dwell in man when my Spirit comes to live in the believer of my doctrine."

The noise of the synagogue attendees had grown so loud that Jesus had to shout to be heard. "When my temper, my meekness, my humility, and my love pervade your hearts, when you receive my doctrine and your lives are influenced by it, when you are supported by the consolations of the gospel, it may be said then that I abide in you."

"You don't dwell in me now, you blasphemer, and you never will," shouted a voice from the rabble.

Someone else in the crowd screamed, "If we have to drink your blood to be part of you, then that certainly won't be long in coming, you counterfeit! You think that you are the teacher? We're going to teach you a thing or two."

Jesus's face became flush and his voice became higher than normal. His demeanor had gone from a calm Giver of Truth to one who had become frustrated. He had come from heaven to do his Father's will, had given up his equality with his Father, and had taken on the humility of a servant to bring his people the good news of the Gospel, to bring salvation to the lost and the dead, those chosen by God before the foundation of the world, and to show God to the world.

Jesus pointed toward heaven and declared, "As the living Father has sent me and I live by the Father, so he that eats me, even he shall live because of me. I am that Bread that came down from heaven, not as your fathers ate manna and now are dead, but he that eats of this Bread shall live forever, not on earth, but in the enjoyments of a better world."

When Jesus had finished speaking these hard sayings, there was an ever-increasing uproar among the men who were professed learners and who had been listening to his words. They stood in clusters, wagging their tongues, shaking their heads, and pointing their fingers in the direction of where Jesus had stood up. Some spoke out loudly, "These are offensive, disagreeable sayings! Who can understand or tolerate them?"

These were more sophisticated words spoken than those of the common rabble rousers pushing in upon Jesus, but they were just as precipitous and emotion evoking. There was no miscommunication here! They had no difficulty in understanding at what

Jesus was driving! The problem lay with the fact that the doctrine that he delivered was opposed to their prejudices. What Jesus said seemed to be absurd, and they therefore rejected it. They wanted to know who could hear it, listen to such doctrine, or believe it.

The offensive doctrines that Jesus taught appeared to have included that he was superior to Moses, that God would save only those he had chosen to save, that he had said he was the Bread that had come down from heaven and it was necessary to partake of that Bread. Additionally, atonement had to be made, and they would be saved by that. It appeared from the crowd's reaction to his words that many would rather draw back to perdition rather than trust in Christ for their salvation.

Word reached Jesus's mother and me that he was back in Capernaum, back in the synagogue, teaching something concerning manna and bread. As soon as these sweet words of his return reached my ears, I dropped the sewing with which I had occupied myself and ran from the house and headed for the synagogue. My heart started to race even before I began to run. Jesus was constantly on my mind. When someone would just mention his name, I found myself having trouble breathing. I would become giddy and imagine his giant smile being just for me.

As I ran close to the walls of the buildings through the streets of Capernaum on my way to be with Jesus, I kept saying to myself, *I don't know why I love him so. It scares me half to death. When I look into his eyes, I become numb. I lose all sense of direction. I don't know if I love him because he "saved" me from the possession of demons or because he makes me absolutely giddy. When I hear his name, my chest burns as if I had indigestion. My vision becomes narrow as if I were looking into a tunnel for I can only see him. When I am near him, my legs become so weak that I can hardly stand.*

As I ran, I kept praying, *Father God, please open his eyes to the love I have for him! Please make him see!*

As soon as I came within sight of the synagogue, I knew that Jesus had said something that stirred up the crowds, something that had caused them to want to do him harm. I could hear yelling and screaming and obscenities being carried on the midday air.

I ran headlong into Peter and John, who were standing just in earshot of the entrance to the synagogue. With eyes wide open to the possible dangers emanating via the doorway, I asked, "Peter, what in the world is going on here?"

"The Master has just been telling the crowds that all they want is manna like their forefathers, but that he is more than mere bread. He is the Bread that has come down from heaven and that if they freely partake of him, it will be a sign that they will be among the chosen of God to be saved. Some have become very angry, Mary. I fear that he may have gone too far this time!"

I don't know what I thought I could do, but I rushed past Peter and John. Peter grabbed me by the arm, but I pulled free before he could establish a firm grip. Words came from my mouth before I even knew that I was speaking. "Jesus!" I screamed, "Jesus, what are you doing? They don't care about you! I do. I care!"

I ran smashing into the backs of men standing in the doorway of the synagogue. They were not moved. They didn't even flinch. I was repelled as if I were a bug flying headlong into a stone wall. Their attention was so focused on Jesus that a bull could have charged into them and they would have taken no notice.

At this very moment, I could hear Jesus yell in a loud voice, "Are you offended at what I have just said? You take offense because I said that I came down from heaven?"

Instead of explaining that statement away, he proceeded to put forth another doctrine just as offensive to them, that he would reascend to heaven. "What if you should see the Son of man ascend up where he was before?"

Since he was telling them that he would ascend to heaven, it should have been clear that he could not have intended literally that they should eat his flesh. Then he said something that was again provocative.

Referring to the doctrine, which he had been teaching in opposition to their notions and desires, Jesus said, "My doctrine is spiritual. It is fitted to quicken and nourish the soul. It is from heaven. Your views are from earth and may be called fleshly, as pertaining only to the support of the body. You place a great value on the doctrine that Moses fed the body, yet that did not permanently profit anything, for your fathers are dead. You seek also for food from me, but your desires are gross and worldly. The words that I speak to you are spiritual, and they bring life but, for what you strive, it will not avail to the real wants of man. My words are not to be understood literally as if you were really to eat my flesh, but they are to be understood as showing the need of that provision for the soul of man, which God has made by my coming into the world."

Jesus obviously understood the heart. He understood the secret principles and motives of men. He seemed to possess some kind of omniscience for he appeared to know within himself about what these men murmured out of earshot.

Then he said something very peculiar. "There are some among you that believe not in me or in the words that I speak. I have known from the beginning who would believe and who would betray me, but I tell you this: no man can come unto me except it is given unto him by my Father."

I thought then and there that this was the end. The faces of those hearing Jesus's words turned purple from the rage that boiled inside them, and they scowled like ravenous wolves as they circled about him. I knew any moment they would have seized and killed him if it were not for the miracle that appeared out of nowhere. Suddenly, at the side of Jesus appeared a man dressed in pure white linen with a glow about him like moonbeams bouncing off a lifeless body of water. He looked Jesus squarely in the face, and without a word passing between them, they moved together through the angry mob to the outside of the building where Jesus's disciples and I stood. By the time Jesus reached us, the figure I had seen with him was nowhere to be seen. I stared at Jesus with a questioning look, but he would not make eye contact with me. Instead, he and his disciples and I walked briskly down the street away from the synagogue to the outside of the city.

Jesus stopped abruptly. To try them and test their choice, Jesus posed this question to his twelve disciples: "Many of these listeners will walk with me no more. Will you whom I have chosen, on whom I have bestowed apostleship, and who have seen the evidences of my messiahship also depart and slip away?"

With his characteristic ardor and promptness, Simon Peter answered Jesus with firm conviction, "Lord, to whom shall we go? You only have the words that lead to eternal life. Speaking for all of us, Lord, we have no doubts. We believe that you are that Christ, the Son of the living God."

It was one of Peter's noblest confessions, the instinctive promptings of a pious and upright heart. Peter realized that there was no one else who could teach them. The scribes and the Pharisees and the Sadducees were corrupt and totally unable to instruct them as to what was right. In spite of the fact that Jesus's doctrines were strange and mysterious, they were the only ones that could teach them and save their souls eternally. Though sometimes difficult to understand, they should not be rejected out of hand. Poor, lost sinners had nowhere else to go but to Jesus. The twelve disciples were beginning to comprehend that he was the Way, the Truth, and the Life; and if the sinner chooses any other way, he would be lost.

Jesus smiled his approval and answered Peter, saying, "Have not I, the Savior, the Messiah, chosen you twelve in mercy and in love to the apostolic office? Therefore would it not be a greater sin to betray me? One of you has the spirit, the envy, the malice, and the treasonable designs of a devil hostile to my work."

The twelve and I looked from one to the other. Who among us could possibly betray Jesus? Before anyone had a chance to ask questions, Jesus turned and started off down the dusty road that lay before us. He walked with a staff in his right hand and whistled an unfamiliar tune. Looking back over his shoulder, he waved for us to hurry on. He had someone to heal, someone to teach, and others to save.

The Foray at the Feast of Tabernacles

WE STAYED IN the countryside of Galilee for a few days to rest and pray. I had the ultimate pleasure to attend to Jesus's needs, to cook for him, to mend tears and worn areas in his tunic, to wash his feet, and best of all, to be on my knees with him in prayer.

Jesus's mood began to change and take on a more somber character. In the past, he would often go off by himself to pray, but now, he seemed to want prayer time in solitude more than ever. When I was of service to him in some small way, he would always thank me and cast a smile my way, but it wasn't that broad toothy smile that I had instantly been attracted to at the first, or the smile that would cover his face from ear to ear. It seemed now it had become more of an effort to smile. His smile became perhaps a bit forced.

I went to Jesus one night about half an hour after we had finished the evening meal. I sat down next to him on the ground to help keep watch on the heavens for several minutes. Finally, I worked up the courage to ask, "Jesus, what has been troubling you? Why are you so serious and downcast?"

It appeared for a moment that he either had not heard my questions or had chosen to ignore them. Finally, he cocked his head to one side in order to look me in the eye and answered me with questions. "Mary, can you conceive of what it's like to have the weight of the world upon your shoulders? Have you ever considered what it would be like to have the destination of men's souls in the palm of your hand? Has it ever occurred to you how frustrating it is to teach in the synagogues to deaf men or try to enlighten the blind? Can you see in your mind's eye being hounded because you can feed the hungry multitudes with just a few loaves of bread and a few small fishes and be misunderstood because of pride or fear or because you are simply content with the way things are?"

Jesus turned his eyes toward heaven, crossed his legs, and leaned back on both his elbows. He stared for a time at the billions upon billions of stars that shone above us just as intently as they stared at us. After a time, he turned on to his side, propped himself up on one elbow, and said to me, "You know, Mary, I think that I will walk in Galilee only from now on and not among the Jewry in Judea."

"I think that is a very good idea," I agreed earnestly.

"And why is that, Mary?" he asked with a smile.

I answered most seriously, "Because the Jews seek to kill you, don't they?"

"Why, yes, they do," he said pensively. Then he interlaced his fingers behind his head and lay back flat on the ground and returned his stare into the heavens.

I could feel that his heart was heavy. He came to help the people, to give them hope, to preach the Gospel of the kingdom of God to them; but instead of receiving him, they rejected him and had their anger heightened to the level of wanting and plotting to take his life. I wanted so badly to hold him and give him comfort like he did for so many others, but every time I tried to get close to him he treated me indifferently, as if I were his sister. I didn't want to be his sister; I wanted him to love me like a man loves a woman. I figured eventually he would come around. I thought to myself, *I know he loves me. I guess he's just scared. That must be it. I'm scared of how he makes me feel, and I am just as sure he is scared of me. How funny is that?*

I turned to tell him how I felt, but his eyes were closed and his breathing was deep and heavy. I kissed the tips of my fingers and placed them upon his cheek and whispered, "Sleep well tonight, my love. Tomorrow will be another day, and we will see."

We all slept well that night. Our travels were arduous, and the reaction of the Jews sapped our energy. But tomorrow was going to be a better day.

We rose early to go back into Capernaum to Jesus's mother's house for a hearty breakfast that was sure to be waiting for us. John, Phillip, and Nathanael had gone on before to tell Mother Mary that her son and the rest of us would be coming.

By the time we had reached her house, the sun was beginning to break over the horizon. As we entered, we could savor the smell of fresh baked bread and of newly made goat cheese and of eggs frying on earthen plates placed atop an open flame. We were starving. We made our way around the low table that took up the center of the room. Knowing that there would be fourteen of us for breakfast, Mother Mary had already fed Jesus's bothers and his one sister that had not yet married. All leaned to their left around the table, but Jesus remained seated on his heels to offer up thanks for the food.

He looked up toward the ceiling, held his hands high over his head, and said, "Our Father, we give you thanks for this day, thanks for a good night's sleep, and thanks for the way you look out for our every need. We give you thanks for your mercy and for your long-suffering and for your provisions. We ask, O Father, that you bless this food to the nourishment of our bodies that we have strength to serve you in the manner that is consistent with your will. Thank you, Father, for hearing our prayers. Amen."

He then reclined to the left as we all had done and we enjoyed not only the food set before us, but the conversation and fellowship as well.

It was mid-Tisri (mid-October) and it was time for the Jews' Feast of Tabernacles (Booths). During the continuance of this feast, the people dwelt in tents as their fathers had done in the wilderness, and for seven consecutive days, a procession of priests carried water in golden vessels into the temple area. The pouring of water was thought to have some sort of physical as well as spiritual significance, but on the eighth day, the "great day," no water was carried. Instead, the people carried about the branches of palms and willows and branches of other trees that bore thick foliage as well as branches of the olive tree and the myrtle. It was the *greatest* feast and was one of the three feasts that every male among the Jews was obliged to attend.

When we had finished eating, Jesus's half brothers came into the room. Supposing that Jesus came under the same influence as others, that he would seek popularity among men, James said to him, "Jesus, there will be a great multitude assembled in Jerusalem to celebrate the Feast of Tabernacles. You need to depart right away and go into Judea that your disciples may see the works that you do." Then in his unbelieving fashion, he said, "There is no man that does anything in secret while he seeks to be known openly. If you really do these things that everyone says you do, show yourself to the world. Don't hide up here in Galilee."

Turning to face his half-brother, Jesus responded, "The proper time for *me* to go up to the feast has not yet come."

James furrowed his one, continuous eyebrow and quickly shot back, "Are you afraid that if you go with us while multitudes are going up to Jerusalem that you would be perceived to have the appearance of a parade or appearing ostentatious, that the sight of you might excite too much envy and opposition of the rulers?"

Jesus answered without hesitation, "Little brother, it makes no difference to you when you go up. Your going will excite no tumult or opposition. It will not attract attention and will certainly not endanger your life. You profess no principles in opposition to the world, nor do you excite its envy or arouse against you the anger of the civil rulers."

Knowing that none of his brothers yet believed in him, he said curtly, "Since you are of the same spirit and principles with the men of this world, they will not be expected to *hate* you. The main cause of the opposition made against me is because I bear witness against them. Men are depraved, and as a result of that, they hate me. So you all just go on up to the feast for the time of my glorification has not yet come."

His brother turned abruptly to leave the room, waved Jesus off, and remarked blatantly, "Do as you will. You always have!" He stormed past his mother on his way out of the house.

"What was all that about?" she asked.

"Nothing, Mother," Jesus answered, "nothing to worry about anyway. James will write a worthy book of wisdom someday."

Jesus's mother appeared confused. She wrinkled her eyebrows at her son but let it go and said no more.

Jesus rose to his feet, went over to his mother, and took a jug of juice from her. He kissed her on the cheek and whispered in her ear, "Don't worry, Mother, James will believe."

We all left for Jerusalem, but Jesus remained behind until about the middle of the feast, until the mass of the people had gone up, so that his arrival might not draw attention. It was done so that it might not be said that he chose such a time so as to excite a tumult. Though it would have been within the law of Moses for him to go up when all the others left for Jerusalem, and though it would have been a most favorable time to reveal himself, he had decided to forego this revelation rather than to afford an occasion of jealousy and envy within the ranks of the rulers or to have the appearance of exciting an uproar among the people. In spite of his secrecy, the rulers of the Jews sought him at the feast, asking, "Where is he?"

There was considerable dispute among the people concerning Jesus. Some said, "He is a good man," while others said, "No, he's not. He is deluding the people, drawing them away by pretending to be the Messiah."

No one who believed in him and thought he was the Messiah had any confidence to speak openly or boldly about him for fear of what the rulers of the Jews might do. All they dared profess about him was that he was a good man; however, his enemies were not silent. They cursed him, did not believe in him, and gathered together in order to plot his destruction.

Many of the believers praised his morals, his precepts, and his holy life; all the while they were ashamed to speak of his divinity or his atonement, and still more were afraid to acknowledge that they knew that they were going to be dependent on him for their salvation.

At about the midway point of the feast, Jesus entered the temple amidst the great multitudes that were assembled in and around it. He had concluded that it was a favorable time and place to make known his doctrine.

The Jewish leaders marveled at Jesus's teaching. They asked, "How is it that this man knows the science of and has the knowledge of our Scriptures and traditions seeing that he has never attended a school for rabbis? He exhibits in his discourses such profound acquaintance with the Torah that he excites our amazement and admiration."

The Jews taught their law and tradition in celebrated schools. Since they knew nothing of Jesus ever having been instructed in any of those schools, they were mystified by his knowledge.

Knowing their thoughts, Jesus responded to their questions. He rejoined, "What I teach has not been originated by me but comes from the One who has sent me. Though I have not learned in your schools, you are not to infer that the doctrine that I teach is devised or invented by me. I teach nothing that is contrary to the will of God and nothing that he has not appointed for me to teach. I instruct as he has commissioned me.

"Though one may not be able to perfectly keep God's commandments, if he is willing or has a disposition to do his will, has a readiness to yield his intellect, his feelings, and all that he has entirely to him to be governed according to his pleasure, he will have internal evidence of the truth of the doctrine in the very attempt to do the will of God. Man will know whether what I say is divine or whether I speak of myself without being directed by God.

"In an honest desire to obey God, man will be led to discover that his heart is depraved and inclined to doing evil. He will see and understand the truth of the doctrine of depravity and will discover that he is a sinner in need of being born again. He will learn about his own weaknesses and recognize his need of a Savior, his need of atonement, and his need for pardoning mercy. He will know that he is polluted and needs the purifying influence of the Holy Spirit.

"He that speaks by his own authority as mere human teachers do, without being sent by God, seeks after his own reputation and applause. But for the one who seeks the glory of the One who sent him, there is no falsehood or deception in him. Therefore you should be able to see that I am no imposter for I seek not my own glory but the honor of God. Did not Moses give you the law? You freely admit this and pride yourselves for it, and yet none of you keeps the law. Every violation of that law you consider as deserving of death. You have accused me of violating it because I healed a man on the Sabbath, and now you go about seeking to kill me."

Jesus preached to the Jews about their depravity and pointed out that keeping the law of Moses, even if one kept it to the letter, he would not be saved by it. They were in need of a savior, and he was it.

The leaders of the Jews hated Jesus when he did the things that the Messiah was supposed to do when he came, and they despised him for saying that he was the Son of God. They wanted to hear none of the things that Jesus proclaimed. There was no desire to give up their positions in the Roman hierarchy for a man who preached "turn the other cheek" and who would not take up arms to lead a revolt against the occupiers and the oppressors. The things that Jesus had just said were the same things he had said that had incited the people in the synagogue in Capernaum. The people in the crowd were pushing out their jaws as a sign of their anger, and they started to jeer and throw fruit and vegetables at him.

Some of the people who thought Jesus might be suffering from some kind of derangement, and those who were not aware of the designs of the rulers, yelled from the midst of the mob with jeers. "You have a demon in you, *Son of the Most High!* Tell us who goes about with designs to kill you?"

Jesus answered, "You have seen me heal one man on the Sabbath, and you all marveled, especially because I healed him on the Lord's day. I know that this is the grounds for your astonishment, that I should *dare* heal a man on a day that you esteem a violation of the law to work. On this account, Moses gave you circumcision. Not that he himself appointed it as a new institution, but he found it already in existence and being observed by the patriarchs: Abraham, Isaac, and Jacob. He merely incorporated it into his institutions and laws. The Sabbath was also kept before Moses and alike in the one case and the other you ought to keep in mind the design of the appointment. The law requires that a newborn boy should be circumcised on the eighth day after his birth. If that day happens to fall on the Sabbath, you hold that the child is to be circumcised since you think that there is a positive law to that effect. Since this is commanded, you do not consider it a breach of the Sabbath. That the law of Moses should not be broken: a male child *will* be circumcised on the Sabbath. In interpreting the law about the Sabbath you yourselves allow a work of necessity to be done. Why should you be angry with me when I restored the man to health? As you allow circumcision on the Sabbath for the same reason, you ought to also allow a man to be completely restored to health, which is certainly a much more important work. You accuse me of doing things which you yourselves do in other ways."

As always, when Jesus preached in this manner, the crowd became increasingly angry. Like stampeding cattle driven up against the fencing of a corral, these rabid-like men pushed in upon Jesus. They clawed and shoved and screamed obscenities, but they never actually laid a hand upon the Son of God. An invisible wall seemed to separate Jesus from the rabble, and not one person was able to violate that barrier.

Jesus did not shift or change his position but stood his ground. His eyes changed from a soft welcoming demeanor to one of a burning, stern glare. As he glowered at his would-be attackers, Jesus shouted above the clamor, "Judge not as a thing first offers itself to you without reflection or candor. In appearance, to circumcise a child on the Sabbath might be a violation of the law, yet you do it, and it is right. So as it appears, it might be a violation of the law to heal a man on the Sabbath, yet it is right to do works of necessity and mercy. When you judge, judge candidly. Look at the law and inquire about what its spirit really requires."

Then some of the men of Jerusalem yelled above the clamor of the crowd, "Is this not the one whom the members of the Sanhedrin seek to kill? This man speaks boldly, and yet they say nothing to him. Have the rulers been convinced that this man is the Messiah, that he is the one that should come? Does their suffering him to speak without interruption speak to their having evidence of this?"

Focusing on Jesus's claim of being the Messiah, these men had no question in their minds that he had made this perfectly clear, but their response was confused and divided. They had three very good reasons for accepting his claim: the hesitancy of the members of the great council of the nation of Israel who had command of religious affairs to stop him, the miracles that Jesus did, and the excellence of his speaking. However, they found three reasons for rejecting his claim: it was commonly believed that the Messiah would come in a spectacular fashion, they did not know Jesus's real origin, and the Messiah was to sit on the throne of David and, as prophesied, be a Judean from Bethlehem, the city of David. All these people thought Jesus was born in Galilee. The Messiah was to be a defender of the law, yet Jesus seemed indifferent to it by healing on the Sabbath.

Then others in the crowd cried out the reason why they supposed Jesus could not be the Messiah, "How is it we know where this man was born and where he lived all these years? We know that Messiah will be born in Bethlehem, that he will be hidden in some mysterious manner and appear again from some unexpected quarter."

Still standing in their presence in the temple, Jesus spoke as part of his teaching. "You have sufficient evidence of my divine mission, that I am the Messiah. I have not come of myself, but he that sent me. I have given evidence that I came from God, the One whom you do not know. But I know him, for I have come from him. He has sent me and is worthy to be believed."

Because of his reproof and because of his claim to be the Messiah, the rulers and their friends sought to take him, but no man laid a hand on Jesus because his hour had not yet come. They rushed him but were repelled by that invisible barrier that surrounded and protected him.

Many people believed that Jesus was the Messiah and spoke up. "When the Christ comes, will he do more miracles than this man who has given abundant evidence of his power to work miracles?"

The Pharisees and the chief priest who stood at the back of the crowd heard what the people were saying about Jesus. They called for their guards to seize him, if possible remove him from their presence.

Jesus held up his hand in the face of the approaching armed guards sent by his persecutors and future murderers and said sternly, "I am fully aware that you desire to take my life, yet for a little while will I be with you, but then I go to him who sent me. You should be diligent in seeking after me while I am yet to be found. Such troubles and calamities will come upon this nation that you will earnestly desire the coming of the Messiah. You will seek for a deliverer and will look for him that he might bring deliverance, but you will be bitterly disappointed for you will not find him. He will not come to aid you according to your expectations. Where I am you cannot come. This nation will not be delivered."

Then the rulers of the Sanhedrin talked among themselves and questioned, "Where will this man go that we won't be able to find him? Will he leave an ungrateful country and go into the distant nations, to the Greeks and teach them? What manner of saying is this that he said, 'You shall seek me, but not find me, and where I am you cannot come?'"

Jesus did not answer their inquiries but rather chose to turn off their minds from a speculation about the place to which he was going to the great affairs of their own personal salvation.

On the eighth day of the festival, the last "great day" of the feast when the holy convocation and solemn assembly were held, the reading of the law, which they commenced at the beginning of the feast, was concluded. The priest proceeded to fill a golden vial with water from the Fountain of Siloam. Attended with the clangor of trumpets, he bore it with great solemnity through the gate of the temple. The priest next mixed the water with wine and poured the mixture on the sacrifice on the altar. This custom was done in a misinterpretation of the verse from Isaiah: "With joy shall you draw water out of the wells of salvation."

That he might illustrate the nature of his doctrine by this, Jesus stood in the midst of thousands of people and spoke while they were performing this ceremony to stop performing a rite that was not commanded that could not confer eternal life. He cried out, "If any man thirsts, if he feels his need of salvation, let him come unto me and drink. My invitation is full and free to all. It does not depend on this ceremony of drawing water. Come unto me, the Messiah, and you shall find an ever-abundant supply for all the wants of your soul. He that acknowledges me as the Messiah and trusts in me for salvation, just as the substance of what the Scriptures teach, out of his heart will flow rivers of living water, and his piety shall be of such a nature that it will extend its blessings to others. They shall be the instruments by which the Holy Spirit shall be poured down on the world. The Gospel shall be constant and life-giving in its blessings." (Jesus spoke here of the Holy Spirit which they that believe in him should receive. Since he had not yet ascended to heaven to the glory and honor that awaited him there, the Holy Spirit had not been sent down to attend their preaching or to convert sinners.)

Many of the people, when they heard what Jesus had said, declared, "Of a truth, this is the prophet we look for, the one who is to precede the coming of the Messiah." Others made the statement, "This man is the Christ." But others said, "Shall the Christ come out of Galilee? Did not the Scriptures say, 'That the Christ comes of the seed of David, and out of the town of Bethlehem where David was?'"

There was clearly division among the people. Some of the mob wanted to lay hold of Jesus and kill him, but not a single one touched him.

Later that same day, the officers of the chief priests and the Pharisees returned empty-handed to their employers. Those in authority eyed their hired guards so sternly they shrank back in fear. Then Caiaphas, the high priest that year, yelled at the shrinking violets, "Why have you not brought Jesus to us?"

The officer in charge responded fearfully, "Never have I heard anyone speak as this man spoke, Your Eminence. What he said was so awe-inspiring that we dared not take him. There have been very few instances in my life where I have heard such eloquence. His speaking seemed to have so much evidence of truth, so much proof that he was from God, and was so impressive and persuasive that I was convicted of his innocence. I am sorry, but I could not execute my commission."

Three of the Pharisees that were seated nearest Caiaphas sprang to their feet. In anger and frustration, they screamed in unison at the guards, "Are you so foolish as to be deceived as well?"

Like thousands who had not taken the time to examine the claims of Jesus, they determined to believe that he was a deceiver. Hence they did not ask them whether they were convinced or had seen evidence that he was the Messiah but, with mingled contempt, envy, and anger, surmised that they had been taken in. One of the members of the Sanhedrin swiped his hand from one side of the room to the other like an artist broad-strokes his canvas with oils and said with a snarl, "Has there ever been an instance in which the rulers or the Pharisees or anyone else high in authority for that matter embraced this Jesus as the Messiah?"

With an air of contempt, the last to speak said as he stalked the intimidated guards, "This rabble who has not been instructed in the schools of the Pharisees, nor been taught to interpret the Torah as we have, are execrable, are of no account, and are worthy not only of contempt but perdition!"

The rulers supposed that any who believed in the humble and despised Jesus must be ignorant of the true doctrines of the Torah as they held that a very different Messiah from him was foretold. Of course if the people were ignorant, it was the fault of the Pharisees and the rulers, for it was their business to see that they were taught. There can be no so common an attempt to oppose the followers of Jesus as by ridiculing its friends as poor and ignorant, weak and credulous. It could just as well be said that food, raiment, friendship, and shelter be held in contempt because the poor needs the one or possesses the other.

God often places one or more pious men in legislative assemblies to vindicate his honor and his law, and he often gives a man grace on such occasions to boldly defend his cause. At one time, a member of the Sanhedrin, the timid and fearful Nicodemus, the one who had come in secret to Jesus at another feast event to ask questions about being "born again," stood up in front of his reserved seat and said with an air of dignity, "The law requires justice to be done and gives every man the right to claim a fair and impartial trial. Your condemnation of this man, Jesus, is a violation of every rule of right. He has not been arraigned, he has not been heard in self-defense, and not a single witness has been adduced. Every man should be presumed to be innocent until he is proven to be guilty. This is a maxim of law and a most just and proper precept in our judgments."

Other members of the Sanhedrin sprang to their feet and, with condescension in their voices, yelled at Nicodemus, "Are you also of Galilee?"

This, of course, was a slur on Nicodemus. To be called a Galilean was to be called something of the highest reproach. They knew well that he was not a Galilean, but they were asking whether he also had become a follower of the despised Galilean. Ridicule and a gibe are unhappily the only weapons that the proud and haughty often use in their opposition to a religion that is not their own.

"Be diligent, my dear Nicodemus," Caiaphas mocked. "Search and you'll see that out of Galilee arises no prophet."

Caiaphas was saying that there had been no prediction that any prophet should come out of Galilee, especially no prophet that was to attend or precede the Messiah. Therefore, Jesus could not be the Christ. But of course, they were wrong. Jonah came from Gath-hepher in Galilee; Nahum was from El Kosh, later named Capernaum; and Hosea came from a village in Galilee. They did not know that Jesus, even though from Galilee, had been born in Bethlehem just as prophesized.

Other members of the Sanhedrin joined Nicodemus in opposing the Pharisees. After this foray, the Sanhedrin broke up in confusion and disorder, and every man went to his own house. It can be said it is a most melancholy exhibition of the influence of pride, envy, contempt, and anger when brought to bear on an inquiry, especially when there is manifest opposition to candor, argument, and truth. They had wished to destroy Jesus, but God suffered their passion to be excited; a tumult to ensue, the assembly thus to break up in disorder, and his Son Jesus to be safe, safe for his time had not yet come.

Under Attack

When the Feast of Tabernacles came to a close and after his foray with the scribes and the Pharisees, Jesus came to me and said, "Mary, I'm going up to the Mount of Olives and I want you to go with me."

I was so excited to be asked to accompany him alone that I could hardly contain myself. My heart began to flutter like my chest was filled with the beating wings of thousands of butterflies. The skin on my arms and legs chilled, and goose bumps rose up high. I began to rub my arms vigorously when Jesus asked me, "Are you all right, Mary?"

"I just felt a chill, that's all," I responded. "I'll be fine."

I felt like such a fool, but the love I had in my heart for this man could hardly be contained. My breathing became more rapid; I could hardly keep pace with him as he strode across the Kidron Valley to the Mount of Olives.

When we arrived at the mount, Jesus led me to a spot where the ground was well worn underneath three olive trees. He stopped and took off his outer vestment and laid it on the ground. He pointed to the vestment underneath a tree and said sweetly, "Sit here, Mary."

I sat down on his warm covering, pulled my legs to one side up underneath me, and cooed, "Why, thank you."

Jesus sat down at arm's length from me, leaned back against the trunk of an olive tree, and placed both feet flat on the ground in front of him. He interlaced his fingers behind his head and sat motionless, not saying a word.

After an inordinate amount of time, he cleared his throat and said, "You know, Mary, certain ones of those men today wanted to kill me."

"I know," I answered. "I was so frightened for you. Why do you rile them so?"

Jesus just shrugged. For a moment, he looked like a little boy contemplating mischief. He picked up a small branch that had fallen from the tree under which he sat, stripped it of all its outcroppings, and started to scratch in the dirt between his feet.

"You know it's not that I have to intentionally cause consternation in these people," he replied. "They know the Scriptures and yet they refuse to see the truth because of their pride. Since they are children of Abraham, they don't believe they are in need of a savior. They reason because they have the law of Moses, that is all they need. The Scriptures are clear about the coming of the Messiah and yet they have put their own interpretation on them. They believe that the Christ will come as some great military leader and drive out the occupying Romans. Even my 'disciple' Judas is constantly whispering in my ear, 'When are you going to announce yourself and lead us into battle against the infidels?' It is amazing that they refuse to check into my background to see where I was born, to see that I lived in Egypt from age two to age nine, or to recognize the words that I speak to them. I came to give them life and to give them freedom in me, not give them freedom from their occupiers."

He fell silent again. The curls of his long brown hair hung in his eyes. His focus was on the ground where he kept scratching out three *X*s side by side, rubbing them out, and drawing them once more. I watched him for a time not understanding what the *X*s in the dirt were.

Then he drew in a deep breath and said with such melancholy, "These people, Mary, will kill me, but not before I allow it, not before I finish the work my Father has sent me to do."

"Jesus!" I snapped. "Why do you say such things? If you have the power to keep them from killing you, then why do you say those things that anger them so? I just don't understand."

"It is what I came from heaven to do," he reacted. "Yes, I have the power to prevent them from killing me, but I also have the power to lay down my life and the power to take it up again. No one takes my life from me unless I allow it!"

"I just don't understand" I said, shaking my head. "You say that you are the Son of God, yet here you are, a man! I have seen you sweat, I have seen you hungry and thirsty, I have seen you frustrated, and I have seen you wear blisters on the souls of your feet. How is it then that you experience all these things and expect me or anyone else to believe that you are the Son of God? It just doesn't add up!"

Just as the last word left my lips, he responded, "You know by the words that I speak, and you know by the miracles that I do. You know by recalling what the Word of God says in Holy Scripture. It is a mystery to those who have scales over their eyes and those who refuse to believe. You believed the moment the last demon fled from your person, the moment the Spirit changed your heart from a heart of stone to a heart of flesh. And that belief given to you by the Spirit has saved you. You still are like an infant when it comes to spiritual things, Mary, but John will help you when I return to the Father."

"I hate it when you talk like that, Jesus," I scolded. "If you are the Son of God and are supposed to have all this power, then why are you going to allow them to take your life? It just doesn't make any sense!"

"It will at some point," he replied.

We sat there in silence for a long while. I was wondering if he said these things to test my love for him or to shock me. I just didn't know! I knew in my heart of hearts he had become my world. I loved him desperately and knew that there was no way that I wanted to live without him. I knew that he said that I had been given eternal life, whatever that entails. I also knew that I wanted to be with him the rest of my life. I wanted to be his bride. Finally, I managed enough courage to say to him, "I love you, Jesus. I have from the moment I saw you in my right mind. You drove those possessing demons out from me and gave me my freedom, the freedom to experience life, to feel again, and to love again. Do you understand what I am saying to you?"

"Yes, I do, Mary, and I love you too," he said softly. "But my love—"

"Jesus! There you are!" a familiar voice bellowed out from below us. "We've been looking all over for you."

What impeccable timing, I thought. *There is just no way of getting away from Peter.*

He and the other disciples came pouring into the grove where Jesus and I had been sitting and talking. They came and plopped themselves all around and took over the conversation, talking about what they had witnessed the last day of the feast and how scary things had gotten back in the temple. In spite of their concerns, however, they all proclaimed wholeheartedly that they knew that Jesus would be the victor.

After an hour or so of recounting the day, Jesus excused himself to go off alone to pray. It wasn't long after he had left us that one by one, his disciples drifted off to sleep. I wanted to go to Jesus after his followers began their snoring, but I knew he liked his quiet time. So, wrapped in his vest, I curled up and drifted off to dream about him.

Early the next morning, Jesus roused each of us by tapping on our feet with an olive branch. "Come with me," he instructed. "We must go to the temple again."

Oh no, I thought, *not again.*

Wiping sleep from our eyes, we followed Jesus back down the side of the Mount of Olives and crossed the Kidron Valley where we traversed the creek that ran through it. The water was still red with the blood of the thousands of sacrifices from the week of the Feast of Tabernacles. We ascended the hill into Jerusalem, back to the temple, which had been rebuilt by the appointed Roman king, Herod. When we reached the temple, Jesus went inside, sat down in the courtyard, and began to teach the people that came in and encircled him. The disciples and I stood just to the right of where he sat so that we too could receive his teaching.

After about half an hour, the scribes and Pharisees brought before Jesus a woman that had been caught in adultery. They shoved her like so much garbage to the ground in front of him.

One of the Pharisees who seemed to be the leader of the pack said to Jesus, "Teacher, this woman was caught in the act of adultery, in the very act."

It certainly was not normal for them to have brought a person caught in adultery to Jesus. I thought it ironic that they would bring a woman who had been caught in adultery, but not the man. Was he so slick that he was able to evade capture or was it yet another setup by the Pharisees to lay a trap for Jesus to see if he would uphold the law or defend this reprehensible sinner?

Then the one who had taken the lead said to Jesus scoffingly, "Now the law Moses commanded us that such a one as this woman should be stoned to death, but what say you, Jesus?"

Jesus knew that the particular manner of the death was not specified in the law, but the Jews had themselves, in this period of time, determined that it should be by stoning. The punishment for adultery varied. In some cases, it was strangulation. In the time of Ezekiel, it was stoning and being thrust through with a sword. If the adulteress were the daughter of a priest, the punishment called for her to be burned to death.

The Pharisee was not able to disguise his intentions, not even to me. It was obvious he said what he did in order to test Jesus that they might have something concrete of which to accuse him. If he decided the case, they expected to be able to bring an accusation against him. If he decided that the woman ought to die, they might accuse him of claiming power which belonged to Rome, the power of life and death. If he decided otherwise, they could allege that he denied the authority of the law, that it was his intention to abrogate it. They previously had a controversy with him about the authority of the Sabbath, and they perhaps surmised that he would decide the case as he did against them. They doubtless wished to make it appear that he was a glutton, a wine-bibber, a friend of sinners, and disposed to relax all the laws of morality, even in the case of adultery.

There was never a plan so artfully laid, and never was more wisdom and knowledge of human nature displayed than in the manner in which it was met. Jesus stooped down and, with his finger, wrote in the dust that covered the stones of the temple courtyard. In doing this, Jesus showed them clearly that he was not solicitous to pronounce an opinion in this case and that it was not his desire or intention to meddle with the civil affairs of the nation.

When Jesus did not immediately answer, the leader of the Pharisees pressed the question upon him. Persevering in their evil, this horde of Pharisees and scribes were determined to exhort an answer from him. Jesus rose up from his squatted position and stared into the eyes of each of the men standing before him. He crossed his arms and said to them collectively, "He that is without sin, let him be the first one to throw a stone at her." He stooped down once again and resumed writing whatever he was writing in the dust.

In a sentence of death, one of the witnesses would throw the culprit from a scaffold; another would throw the first stone or would roll down a stone to crush the head of the one sentenced to die. This was done in order that the witness might feel his responsibility in giving evidence as he was also to be the executioner. Therefore Jesus put them to the test. Without passing judgment on her case, he directed them to perform the office of executioner if any of them were innocent. Of course Jesus was able to say these things to them knowing full well their own guilt and discerning that no one would dare do it.

From where I stood, I couldn't see what Jesus was writing in the dust, so I asked Peter and John who stood beside me if they could see what he was writing. Neither of them could make it out. Peter, however, towering over us and over those who stood with us, was able to make out that the writing appeared to be a list of names.

Everything stopped moving. There were no birds flying in the sky, no barkers offering their wares, no children tossing pebbles into a circle, and certainly no Pharisee or scribe throwing the first stone. Perhaps they became convicted by their own consciences or possibly saw their own names written in the dust. One by one, they dropped the stones they had brought with them, beginning with the oldest to the youngest. Conceivably, they left in this order because the eldest was convicted of more sins, and would be more anxious to leave Jesus's presence.

All the woman's accusers departed, leaving Jesus and her alone. When Jesus rose to his feet, he saw none but the woman, and he said to her, "Woman, where are those that accuse you? Has no man condemned you?"

None of those that had accused her had proceeded to act expressive of judicial condemnation.

The woman stood, staring at the ground before Jesus. She had long black hair that hung halfway to her waist. Her lips were painted bright red, her ears were pierced and modeled large hoops, her emerald green eyes were encircled with a black dye that came to a point at their outer corners, and her blouse was cut low intentionally to show off her womanly curves. She was embarrassed and responded to Jesus's questions in a voice that was faint and filled with remorse, "No man, my Lord."

Jesus approached the woman and took her chin in his right hand, raised her head, and said to her tenderly, "Neither do I condemn you. I want you to go and sin no more. Do you understand?"

She answered, "Yes, my Lord," and she walked away slowly. Every few steps, she stopped and looked back at this man who had not condemned her or been unkind to her but, in fact, had saved her life.

In his dealings with the woman, Jesus had not been asked for his opinion about her adultery; he was queried to obtain her condemnation. As he had claimed no civil authority, Jesus said that he had not exercised it and therefore should not condemn her to die. Jesus told the woman to go and sin no more. She had sinned, been detected, and brought forward as an accused. Her sin was great, but Jesus did not claim power to condemn her to die. Instead, he spoke words of wisdom; she should go and sin no more.

It appeared that the scratching Jesus had done in the dust in front of the woman's accusers had made them realize that he knew their hearts and their lives. He made them appreciate the fact that men often are very zealous in accusing others of that for which they themselves are guilty. Jesus displayed an astonishing wisdom in making known the devices of his enemies and evading their deep-seated plans to bring him to ruin.

Jesus remained unmoving as he waited for the accused woman to walk away. I ran to him and exclaimed, "That was an incredible display of not only kindness but understanding as well."

Jesus looked at me but said not a word.

Instantly, I knew how ridiculous that must have seemed to him. I tried to explain it, but the more I said, the worse it got.

Finally, Jesus said to me, "Mary, Mary, there is no need for you to explain or try to amend your statement. What you said was perfectly fine. Don't worry yourself so much."

"I…I…I just want…," I stuttered. "I just wanted you to know that I admire you so very much and do not want to sound ignorant before you."

"All is well, Mary," he said empathically. "It's really all right. I have more to do here today and must get to it."

Naturally, I sought permission to accompany him.

He replied, "I'm not going very far. You just stand there, Mary."

I know I must have looked puzzled, but I agreed.

Jesus walked away from me and began to speak to the people who had been watching all that had happened. Then he said something very curious. "I am the Light of the world. He that follows me shall not walk in darkness but shall have the Light of life."

The Pharisees that were in the crowd were quick to discount Jesus's authority and consequently asked him, "Are you a witness for yourself? The law requires two witnesses to prove all cases. If the only evidence you have is your own assertion, you cannot be entitled to be believed. Therefore your testimony is not worthy of belief because it is not substantiated by sufficient evidence."

Even though I stood some fifteen feet from Jesus, I could see his face grow red at the Pharisees' statement.

Unlike most people who would have had to collect their thoughts and calm their inner spirit, without hesitation, Jesus candidly and confidently answered their objections. "You know even though I bear witness of myself, yet my record is true and my case is such that my testimony alone ought to be received, and I also have the evidence given to me by my Father. Of course in everyday life, in courts, and in minor human transactions, it is true that one ought not to give evidence in his own case, yet in this particular instance, such is the nature of the case that my word is worthy to be believed. I know by what authority I act. I know by whom I have been sent, and what commands were given to me. You cannot determine this for you do not know them unless I bear witness of them to you. As I came from heaven, I know my Father's will. As I have seen the eternal world and have known the counsels of my Father, so my testimony is worthy of confidence. Since you have not seen and known these things, you are not qualified to judge. One who is an ambassador from a foreign court knows the will and purposes of the sovereign who sent him and is competent to bear witness of it. All that is required is that I give my credentials that I have been appointed, and this I have done both by the nature of my doctrine and by my miracles. You cannot determine from whence I came and to where I go.

"You judge according to the flesh, according to appearances, according to your own carnal and corrupt mode, not according to the spiritual nature of my doctrine. You have preconceived opinions and prejudices that prevent you from believing that I am the Messiah. However, I judge no man after the manner in which you judge. I came not to condemn the world in a harsh, biased, or unkind manner. However, if I were to express my judgment of men or things, understand that I am not limited or forbidden to do so. My judgment is true and worthy to be regarded. You freely admit that God's judgments would be right, and I tell you that my judgments accord with his. Since I have been commissioned by my Father, my judgments will coincide with all that he has proposed or revealed. This has been shown by the evidence that my Father gave showing that he sent me into the world.

"It is written in your law that the testimony of two men is to be taken as truth. This relates of course to cases involving the life of an individual, but I tell you that if the testimony of two men were sufficient to establish a fact in that kind of case, then my own testimony and that of my Father ought to be esteemed as ample evidence in the case of spiritual doctrine.

"I am one that bears witness of myself. In your courts, a man is not permitted to testify for himself because he has a personal stake in the outcome of the case, and the court would have no proof that the man spoke impartially of the evidence. In my own case, it is otherwise. I have no party end to serve. I am willing to and have denied myself. I make great sacrifices and, by my own life, give all conceivable evidence of sincerity. My own testimony may be admitted in evidence of my motives and designs. It is not right for you to reject the testimony of one who has given so many proofs that he came from God. The Father that sent me bears witness of me, and he did so by his voice from heaven at my baptism. The miracles that I do give proof of who I am, as do the prophecies found in the Torah."

Then with grit in their craw and derision in their speech, and knowing that Jesus meant God when he said, "my Father," the listeners inquired of Jesus, "Where is your Father?"

Giving no heed to their cavil and displaying no irritation at their contempt, Jesus answered them with words that were worthy of the Son of God. He meekly said, "You don't know me, nor do you know my Father. If you had listened to my instructions and had recognized me as the Messiah, you would at the same time have been acquainted with God."

Truly, the Jew's spiritual preparation was inadequate. They could not become his disciples because they were of this world, they did not believe in him, and they did not understand his words. Jesus spoke these things to them near the treasury as he taught in the temple. The time for him to die had not yet arrived, and God restrained the crowd, thereby protecting Jesus's life. God indeed has power over wicked men to control them and to have them accomplish his own agenda.

Then Jesus said to the people who appeared totally dumbfounded, "I am going away. You shall seek the Messiah. You will desire his coming, but the Messiah that you expect will not come. And as you have rejected me and there is no other savior, you shall die in your sins. You will die without pardon, and as you did not seek me where you might have found me, you cannot come where I go."

Then in their malice, the Jews said gleefully, "Since he said, 'Where I go you, cannot come,' does that mean he is going to take his own life?"

They bent over with laugher until their bellies hurt in spite of the fact that they knew self-murder was esteemed as one of the greatest of all crimes. Yet because of their great hatred and contempt for Jesus, they said these unthinkable words. Many of the jocular evil-wishers exclaimed, "He is a deceiver. He has broken the law of Moses. He is mad, and it is probable he will go and kill himself!"

What wonderful patience Jesus displayed in enduring the condemnation of these sinners. He bore their contempt without rendering railing for railing. Ultimately, Jesus cried out to them that would have him destroy himself, "You are of the earth and therefore are influenced by earthly, sensual, and corrupt passions. You are governed by the basest and vilest feelings, such as are opposed to heaven. But I am of above, from heaven. Since my words are heavenly, they should have been interpreted as such. You act and think like all corrupt men of this world. My views are above these earthly and corrupt notions. I have said to you who I am, therefore you will die in your sins for if you believe not that I am the Messiah, you will certainly not escape the damnation that comes with unrepentant sins."

The things that to them seemed so humorous stopped being so. Their laughter dried up like a riverbed in summer, and their demeanor turned from whimsical to serious. Professing still not to understand Jesus's words, they asked him, "Who are you to threaten us in this manner?"

Appreciating that they regarded him as a mere pretender from Galilee who was poor, without friends, and persecuted by those in authority, it was astonishing to witness the patience with which he bore all they threw at him and the coolness with which he answered them.

"What I profess to you is true. I am the Light of the world, I am the Bread that came down from heaven, and I come into the world having been sent by my Father. From this, you might have gathered that I claim to be the Messiah. I have assumed no new character. I have made no change in my professions. I am the same yesterday, today, and forever. As I once professed to be the Light of the world, so in the face of your contempt, persecution, and threat of death, I maintain that profession.

"There are many things which I might say to reprove and expose your pride and hypocrisy. I understand well your character, and I am capable of exposing it. There are many things in you which I could condemn. However, he that sent me is true and is worthy to be believed. I have not come that I might exalt myself, but I have come to execute his commission. He is worthy to be heard and feared. Never think that my judgment is rash or harsh, but remember that it is a command from God."

Despite everything that Jesus had said, they undoubtedly grasped that he spoke to them concerning the Father and that he spoke to them about God, but they were unwilling to acknowledge that he really was sent from and indeed came from God.

Then Jesus spoke some strange, ethereal words that I was unable to comprehend, things that could not be fathomed in the real world. He said, "When you have crucified the Son of man, then shall you know that I am the I Am, and that I do nothing on my own but do only the things that my Father has taught me. These are the things that I speak, and he that sent me is with me in working miracles. Though men have forsaken and rejected me, yet God attends me, for I do always those things that please him."

There was grumbling amongst many of the people in the crowd that surrounded Jesus. They were especially disturbed at him for equating himself with God, for calling himself the Son of the Most High. After Jesus spoke these last words, the crowd started walking away by twos and threes, leaving behind just a handful of people who believed in him. Those who were left asked Jesus to tell them more. It was if someone had turned on a lightbulb, illuminating their consciousness.

Then Jesus said to those Jews that stayed behind, those who believed him to be who he said he was. "If you continue to obey my commandments, to receive my doctrines and live a holy life, that will be proof that your faith is genuine, for the tree is known by its fruit. The newly realized faith that you have has not been tried, and if it does not produce a holy life, it is vain. If you abide in me then you are my disciples indeed. You shall know the truth, and the truth shall make you free, free from the slavery of evil passions, corrupt propensities, and groveling views."

In essence, Jesus was saying to his latest converts that the condition of a sinner is that of a captive or a slave to sin. He is the one who serves and obeys the dictates of an evil heart and the promptings of an evil nature. Jesus was saying to these new believers that the effect of the Gospel is to break the hard bondage to sin and to set them free. He wanted them to understand that religion does not bind them to slavery, nor does it have the effect of oppression. It was true freedom, for the service of God is freedom from degrading vices and carnal propensities, from the slavery of passion and inordinate desires. It is the willful and cheerful surrender of one's self to the One whose yoke is easy and whose burden is light.

Some of the men that had been standing before Jesus, taking in every word that he uttered but who still did not believe in him, answered, "We are the descendants of Abraham, who was not a slave and was never in bondage to any man. We have inherited his freedom as well as his spirit. How can you say, 'You shall be made free'?"

Their declaration was certainly surprising given that their fathers had been slaves in Egypt, their nation had been enslaved in Babylon, had repeatedly been subject to the Assyrians, was enslaved by Herod the Great, and was at this very time under the grievous and insupportable bondage of the Romans.

Men will say anything, however false or ridiculous, to avoid and oppose the truth. At this very moment these people were in bondage to the Romans, but this is the case with sinners. Sin and the bondage of sin produce passion, irritation, and a troubled soul. A man under the influence of passion regards little what he says and is often found to be a liar.

Jesus knew what they were thinking and answered them in such a way as to show them that he was not referring to political bondage but to the slavery of the soul to evil passions and desires. "Truly, truly, I say to you, whosoever commits sin is a slave to sin. The servant does not remain forever with his master. If he is disobedient and wicked, the master sells him or turns him out. He is not the heir and may at any time be expelled from the house of his master. The son abides forever. He is the heir and is privileged with the right of remaining in the family.

"You are in the condition of servanthood. Unless you are made free by the Gospel and become entitled to the privileges of the sons of God, you will be cast off like unfaithful slaves.

"If the Son of God, heir of all things who is forever with the Father and who has therefore the right and power to liberate men from their thralldom, deliver you from the bondage and dominion of sin, you will be truly and really free. You shall be blessed with the most valuable gift possible: freedom, not from the chains and oppressions of masters who dwell upon the earth, but from the bondage of sin.

"I admit that you are the descendants of Abraham. I do not wish to call that into question. What I endeavor to show you is that you can be descendants and still lack his spirit entirely. What is truly interesting is that you seek to kill me because you do not embrace the principles of my religion and the spirit of my doctrine is not in you. It seems, therefore, that there is no room for my doctrine in your minds. You are filled with pride, prejudice, and false notions. You will not receive the truth. Because you do not have my spirit of truth and cannot bear it, you seek to kill me.

"I speak about those things that I have learned from My Father, but you do the things which you have learned with your father."

The blood coursing through the veins of the nonbelievers started to boil. Jesus didn't have to mention the name of Satan for them to know that he referred to the devil as being their father. Shaking their fists in Jesus's face, those whose hearts had not been touched by the Holy Spirit answered him obstinately, crying out, "Abraham is our father! We are his descendants. To charge us with being the offspring of any other is slander and calumny."

Jesus quickly responded to them, "If you were worthy to be called the children of Abraham, you would do the works of Abraham. You are different from Abraham, however, for you possess a murderous and bloody heart. You reject the truth as God has revealed it. Abraham was distinguished for his love of man as well as to God. He liberated the captives, was distinguished for his hospitality to strangers, and received the revelations of God regardless of how mysterious or however trying was their observance. But you show none of those attributes that so distinguished Abraham."

Wanting his listeners to infer whom he meant and wanting them to understand the awful offensive truth of his words, Jesus once again made his charge by touching their minds so that the truth might make the deepest impression. "You do the deeds of your father," he said.

His listeners continued to act as if they did not understand him, and because he said that they were not the children of Abraham, they surmised that Jesus meant that they were a mixed, spurious race that had no privileges in the covenant of the Jews and did not serve the one true God. In rage, they vociferated, "We were not born of fornication! We have one Father, even God, and we have the evidence of our genealogy. We are descendants of those who acknowledged God, and we acknowledge him as well."

Not letting up for a moment and showing a measure of intolerance, Jesus came right back at them, "If God were your Father, you would love me for I proceeded and came from him. All who truly love God but reject his Son show no evidence that they are the friends of God. I tell you the truth. I did not come on my own accord. I came because the Father sent me. If you loved God my Father, you would love him who came from him and bears his image.

"If you were so inclined to understand me, you would not misunderstand my meaning. Is my doctrine so offensive to you that you cannot tolerate it? Is that why you continue to pervert my meaning? Are you therefore resolved in your minds not to understand me? Is it your pride, vanity, and wickedness that keep you from accepting it?

"You certainly are of your father the devil for you do the things he desires. You have his temperament, his disposition, and his spirit. You certainly are influenced by him for you imitate him. There is no doubt in my mind that you should be called his children. It is Satan's nature and his work to deceive. His own propensities result in speaking lies. He exclaims the expressions of his own character. He is the originator of falsehood, and since you refuse to hear the truth that I have spoken to you, you demonstrate that you are children of the father of lies. And even though I tell you the truth, you believe me not.

"From the beginning of the world, he was a murderer. He deceived your first parents, Adam and Eve, and caused them to be subject to death. When he rebelled against his Creator, he departed from the truth. Satan deceived Eve, and in his deception, he cast man down to perdition.

"Which one of you convicts me or can prove that I am guilty of falsehood? A doctrine might be refused if it were possible to prove that the one who delivered it turned out to be an impostor, but as you are unable to prove this of me, you are bound to accept my words.

"He that loves, fears, and honors God adheres to the doctrines and commandments of God just as a child who loves his parents will regard and obey their instructions. But since you do not show a readiness to obey the commandments of God and since you reject his Son, that is proof positive that you are not of him."

The Jews who remained standing before Jesus were now of two kinds: those who believed in him and those who hated everything for which he stood. Those that believed shook their heads incessantly in agreement with the words he spoke, while those who rejected every word he spoke shook their fists in his face and yelled obscenities in his direction.

Then those who were angry enough to kill Jesus on the spot because they considered him with contempt and reproach screamed, "You must be a Samaritan, and you have a devil dwelling within you!"

They brought this charge against Jesus because he had said they were not of God. They considered this the same thing as siding with the Samaritans, for the question was always who between the Samaritans and the Jews worshiped God in truth. As Jesus had affirmed that the Jews were not of God, and as he, contrary to all their views, had preached to the Samaritans, they regarded it as proof that he was disposed to take their part. Having preached to the Samaritans, the Jews that he addressed regarded it as proof that he had a devil dwelling within him.

Jesus quickly retorted, "I am not possessed with demons. I pay homage to my Father, but you do dishonor to me. I teach that my Father is holy and true and that men should love him and obey him. There is proof enough that an evil spirit would not do this. I do not seek my own praise or honor nor do I seek to exalt or vindicate myself. God will take care of my reputation. He seeks my welfare and my honor. I can commit my cause into his hands without attempting to vindicate myself."

Jesus looked upward and lifted his hands toward heaven, as if he were pointing out God. A waft of wind blew his hair away from his face. To those who were angry with him, the gust of wind meant nothing, but to us who believed and loved him, we recognized that the Spirit of God was displaying the Father's approval. Not that Jesus needed any encouragement, but this demonstration of the nearness of his Father, he being in the Son and the Son being in the Father, made Jesus stand even taller. He lowered his eyes and stared at the crowd for a very long time. Then he dropped one hand to his side and with the other he pointed to his would-be assailants and cried out, "Truly, truly I say to you, if a man keeps my word, he shall obtain eternal life. He shall be raised up to that life where there shall be no death."

Many in the crowd became absolutely livid. They left their guarded disposition behind and pushed in upon Jesus. As if there had been a death, the Jews began wailing and gnashing their teeth and pushing and shoving.

John, Peter, and I had been standing by a marble column that supported one of the porticos. When we realized that Jesus was coming under attack, we rushed into the crowd to put ourselves between him and those that would do him harm. Without hesitation, he pushed us to the side that we might avoid being hurt ourselves.

I cried out, "Jesus, get behind us!"

But he ignored my pleading. Instead, he exclaimed, "Mary, I've told you before to not interfere. I am here to do the will of the Father who sent me. Now stay back or leave immediately."

What arrogance! I thought. *I'm here to lend a hand, to give some protection, and he tells me to get out of the way! What is wrong with this man? Does he not realize that his disciples and I would give our lives for him?*

Before I could utter a single word in my defense, Jesus pushed the three of us aside and stepped in front of us to confront the Jews head-on.

A burly Jewish man about forty years of age and a head taller than Jesus elbowed his way to the front of the crowd. His eyes were glazed over with rage. He came just within inches of my Savior's face and shook his massive index finger at him. He growled with a foul hot breath, "Now we know that you are possessed by a demon! You have affirmed a thing that is contrary to all human experience, Jesus. We know it to be impossible!"

The crowd cheered as if the giant of a man had won a debating match. They chanted repeatedly, "The man of Galilee is a liar. He knows not what he says. The man of Galilee is a liar. He knows not what he says."

Then the big man bellowed, "Abraham and the prophets are dead and you have the audacity to say, 'If a man keeps my sayings, he shall never taste death!' Are you greater than our father Abraham who is dead? Are you greater than the prophets who are dead? Although all our great prophets have passed on, yet you, a Nazarene, a Samaritan, and a devil, pretend that you can keep your followers from experiencing death! The real question is, who's going to keep you from experiencing death, Jesus of Nazareth?"

As the bigger-than-life man spoke, he kept shaking his finger in Jesus's face. When he had asked just who he was anyway, Jesus caught the man by that wagging finger and, with a modest amount of pressure, froze the man in his tracks. Then Jesus said in a voice that was calm and collected, "If I commend or praise myself, if I had no other honor and sought no other honor than that which proceeds from a desire to glorify myself, the commendation and praise of myself would be of no value, would it? However, it is the One you say is your God who honors me. Yet I can tell you, you have not known him. But I know him. If I were to say that I did not know him, then I would make myself a liar as you have made yourselves liars. The fact is I do know him and I keep his word.

"Since you consider the testimony of Abraham to be supreme and you feel a signal honor to be his descendants, I tell you that he *rejoiced* in being shown the advent and the manner of life of the Messiah. As it was in the days of Noah, so shall it be in the days of the Son of man. Abraham was not permitted to live in the times of the Messiah, yet he was permitted to have a prophetic view of him and also of the design of his coming for God revealed his advent clearly to him. After Abraham was told to sacrifice his son Isaac and then a substitute was provided, he was impressively told that a parent would not be required to offer in sacrifice his sons for the sins of his soul, but God would provide a victim, and in due time, an offering would be made for the world. Abraham was not only permitted to see that day, he was glad in view of the promise, that he was permitted so distinctly to see it represented."

The believers in the crowd wore smiles on their faces, and their teeth shone in the light of the sun like the teeth of a braying donkey. They had grasped what Jesus was saying to those who could not or would not believe. Those who did not believe wore a scowl on their faces, a wrinkled-up old mask that would scare children who saw them. They growled and gnashed their teeth and stuck out their lips in disapproval! Then the unbelieving Jews said to Jesus, "You are not yet fifty years old, have you seen Abraham?"

They really were trying to pervert Jesus's words, for Jesus had not said that he had seen Abraham, but that Abraham was glad to have been shown *his* day. The design of Jesus was to show them that he was greater than Abraham. To do this, he said that Abraham, as great as he was, earnestly desired to see *his* time, acknowledging his own inferiority to the Messiah. But in order to get a laugh and try to show how absurd the words of Jesus were, the unbelieving Jews affirmed that it was impossible that he and Abraham could have ever seen each other having lived centuries apart.

Jesus answered them, saying, "Verily, verily, I tell you the truth, before Abraham ever lived, I am that I Am."

Now the heated debate intensified! The objection of the Jews was that Jesus was not yet fifty years old and, in his wildest imagination, could not have seen Abraham; but going way beyond that, Jesus had just told them that he existed before Abraham. By using the term they were all familiar with from the five books of Moses, Jesus affirmed his existence as God.

Screaming and yelling emanated from all directions. The unbelievers accused Jesus of blasphemy. They didn't wait to take him and hold him for trial for the crime of blasphemy; rather, because Herod the Great had not yet completed repairs to the temple and stones lay scattered everywhere upon its floor, they picked them up to throw at Jesus. Pushing and shoving to get to him, the unbelievers had become so enraged they never noticed Jesus intermingle with them. In a moment, he simply slipped through the enraged mob to the edge of the stairs where Peter, John, and I had been waiting after we were told to move away. We whisked him away to safety. In retrospect, I know that it was not we who took Jesus to safety, but he who delivered us.

I was the first to voice an opinion as we ran through the narrow alleyways of lower Jerusalem. Shrieking between gasps of breath, I said, "Jesus, those people were on the verge of killing you right there in the temple. You must be more cognizant of your surroundings. You must stop baiting these people!"

I couldn't believe my ears when I heard Jesus, running stride for stride with me, burst out laughing. I stopped in my tracks so suddenly that Jesus, Peter, and John ran smack into my back. We all four went crashing to the ground. I collected myself quickly and said with venom on my tongue, "So you think that this is all a joke? The fact that that mob was preparing to stone you to death, doesn't bother you? I—"

Jesus interrupted me before I could continue berating him for treating the situation so casually. In that lyrical mesmerizing voice of his, he said to me, "Mary, Mary, you are troubled way too much. I have told you and all who follow me my time is not yet come. Those disbelieving, misunderstanding men cannot harm me. There is nothing they can do to me until all things have been fulfilled, until my Father relents and gives them their lead. Did you see Peter or John try to stop me? No! They understand!"

Jesus turned and looked at both of his dear friends. "It took awhile," he said, "but they finally understand that no man can touch me without my permission. I came to do the will of my Father, and until all things come to pass as he wills, I cannot be taken, harmed, or killed. When all things have been accomplished, then I lay down my life of my own accord."

"That may be true," I protested, "but suppose something goes wrong and everything becomes fulfilled before you realize that has happened? What if your Father changes his mind? I am so afraid for you, Jesus! I can hardly stand it!"

Jesus put his muscular arms around me and held me close and tight. He whispered in my ear, "Mary, I and the Father are one. No one can touch me unless I know beforehand that he is going to do it, and unless I grant it be done. Do not fear, Mary, for it is I Am. All things are under my control. All things are going according to the plan that my Father established before the foundation of the world."

I pulled free and snapped curtly, "Well, I don't understand it, and I certainly don't like it."

"I know," Jesus said, "you truly are special, Mary. For all your caring and for all your love, you will be first among women. You will have a privilege no one else will have."

"What is that, Jesus?" I implored rudely. "What is my privilege? What will make me first among women, Jesus, to watch you be torn limb from limb by an angry mob? Tell me!"

"Not now, Mary," Jesus replied. "You will know in due time, and you will rejoice for it. For now, just know that you are favored."

I stomped off, leaving the three know-it-alls behind. I thought to myself, *I am favored, all right! I am favored to love a man who is so blinded by his own ambition, so much on a quest to self-destruction, so obligated to some "Heavenly Father" that he cannot see that it is only a matter of hours before those in authority here in Jerusalem will tear him limb from limb. What glory will that bring? How will that bring salvation to those few who believe what he is telling them? Does he really believe what he is saying to the multitudes? Sometimes I think I was better off being out of my mind! At least back in Magdala, I didn't have mind enough to know that I was bad off. At least back there, my heart didn't ache so much that I felt nauseous and felt like I wanted to throw up all the time.*

I stopped dead in my tracks and turned so that I could clearly see Jesus's face. I studied him for a moment and wanted to scream at him, "You are crazier than I ever was in Magdala! Back there I was possessed, out of my mind, and didn't know any better, but you, you say that you are omniscient. You and that Father of yours know all things, but you don't seem to get the fact that I am head over heels in love with you, and that doesn't seem to make a bit of difference."

I held my tongue and stomped off in total distress.

Raising Lazarus Raises a Ruckus

IN THE VILLAGE of Bethany, John the Baptist had been baptizing people for the remission of sins, pointing out that Jesus was the Lamb of God who takes away the sins of the world. In that same village was a man called Lazarus. He and his two sisters, Mary and Martha, had befriended Jesus. While visiting with his dear friends, Jesus was confronted and tested by a young lawyer who asked him, "Teacher, what shall I do to inherit eternal life?"

Knowing that the young lawyer was testing him, Jesus responded with a question, "What is written in the law? How do you read it?"

The young lawyer was very smug and answered Jesus with an answer that most anyone would have been happy to give. "You shall love the *Lord* your God with all your heart and with all your soul and with all your strength and with your entire mind." Then trailing off, he said just above a whisper, "And love your neighbor as yourself."

Jesus replied to the young lawyer gleefully, "Ah! You have answered rightly. Do what you have said and you shall live."

But the young lawyer wanted to justify himself. Without realizing that he was opening a dangerous discourse, he asked Jesus arrogantly, "Who is my neighbor?"

Jesus had already turned to walk away with his disciples; however, when the young lawyer asked this last question, Jesus whirled around like a man standing on a turntable and said to the young man, "Well, let me tell you just who your neighbor is."

Jesus invited the young man to sit down across from him and began to tell him a story, a parable. "There was a certain man who went down from Jerusalem to Jericho, and as he went along, he was attacked by thieves. The thieves robbed the man of his clothing, beat him severely, and left him on the side of the road to die.

"By chance, there came down that same road a certain holy man, a priest. When he saw that the man lying beside the road had been severely beaten, he crossed to the other side of the road and passed the man by. Likewise, a Levite, when he had come upon the scene and saw the man who had been severely beaten lying beside the road, he crossed to the other side and passed the man by. Neither of the temple people offered any aid to the potentially dying man. They were either in too much of a hurry, didn't want to get involved, were afraid, or they just didn't care.

"A little while later, a certain Samaritan, as he journeyed along, came to the place where the beaten man was lying. Unlike the priest and the Levite, he took compassion on the injured man. He crossed the road to where the man lay, rolled him over, covered his wounds with bandages, poured oil on the bandages, gave wine to the man to drink, and placed him on his own beast of burden. He took the victim to an inn where he continued to take care of his injuries until the next day. Before time to depart the inn, the Samaritan took two denarii from his pocket and gave them to the innkeeper. He instructed the innkeeper to take care of the injured man, keep count of any additional expenses for his care, and when he came back this way, he would settle the account."

Then Jesus asked the young lawyer, "Tell me, which of these three men was a neighbor to the injured man who had fallen prey to thieves?"

Not able to bring himself to say the word *Samaritan*, the young lawyer answered, "The one who showed mercy on the injured man."

Illustrating that racial considerations are utterly transcended by God's command to love him and thus to love others as he does without prejudice or partiality, Jesus raised one eyebrow and said sternly to the young lawyer, "Go your way and do the same as the good Samaritan."

The young lawyer got to his feet and walked away with his head hung low. He knew what Jesus had said was the right thing; he just could not think of himself doing the right thing for a Samaritan.

After Jesus had the conversation with the young lawyer, he and his disciples went to Martha's house where she welcomed them and invited them to stay while they were in Bethany. They settled in and sat around, talking, whereupon Jesus began to teach them about the kingdom of heaven. Martha's sister, Mary, came into the room and walked over to where Jesus sat. She broke open a vial and anointed him with a fragrant oil. Using her long flowing hair, she wiped his feet. She sat down at Jesus's feet and listened intently to every word he uttered.

I was livid! It was my place at Jesus's feet, not some other woman's. I don't care if they were friends before. How dare she anoint my man with some "cheap" perfume. Did she really think that that would impress him?

My mind said, *Jesus is mine. He came to my rescue, not yours. Did he do that for you, missy? How dare you think that you can have the best seat in the house! I love this man. He saved me!*

How I hated this woman that bore my name! I sat down near the back of the room, away from my man. I was not happy! How could this Mary assume that she should have the place of honor? I placed my arms around my knees and pulled them tight up against me and rested my chin on top. *I am not going to say a word*, I thought. *Jesus will see me and know that he is in love with me, not some Jezebel that shares my name. You think you're so desirable! When we leave this place, Jesus will once again be mine. You'll be just a memory. I am the one who can travel with him and help in his support, not you. Enjoy your little triumph. It won't last long!*

Martha came into the room and spotted her sister sitting at Jesus's feet. She motioned to Jesus to come to her. When he stood beside her out of earshot of the others, she said to him, "Lord, doesn't it concern you that while I am slaving away in the kitchen preparing the meal and coming in and out serving you and your group drinks and snacks, my sister has left all this for me to do? Could you please just tell her to get up and help me?"

Jesus smiled at her tenderly and said her name twice to show the intimate closeness that they shared. "Martha, Martha, you are unduly concerned about this world. You show an unbelieving attitude that hinders proper attention to the things of God. You are too worried and troubled about mundane matters. The primary thing that is needed is spiritual nourishment, and Mary has chosen that good part. She craves to be fed spiritually, and I certainly will not take that away from her. Maybe you too should leave the housework for a time and concentrate on a more urgent matter."

Knowing that her complaining was indeed trivial, Martha lowered her eyes away from the eyes of Jesus. For a time, she too came and sat at the Master's feet and received food for the soul.

The next day, Jesus, his disciples, and I hugged and kissed our hosts in gratitude for a wonderful stay and said our good-byes. Of course I didn't hug Mary. That was something I didn't feel like doing. We were off again to spread the good news of the Gospel.

Some time had passed since Jesus had seen or heard from his friends, Mary, Martha, and their bother Lazarus. In that time, Lazarus had fallen gravely ill and was near death when Mary and Martha learned that Jesus was preaching in a village beyond the Jordan River where John baptized. Believing that Jesus had the power of healing and assuming he would be desirous of seeing Lazarus at least one more time, Martha asked one of her neighbors if he would go to the village where Jesus was preaching and ask him to come quickly and heal Lazarus.

The members of this family were among the few special and intimate friends of Jesus. He had spent a considerable amount of time with them, showing to them marks of close friendship, and in return, they showered upon him many proofs of affection.

Jesus saw Martha's neighbor approaching and knew exactly why he had come to seek him out. After the man had delivered his message, Jesus said, "This sickness is not fatal. It is not designed for his death but to provide an opportunity for a display of the glory of God and to furnish a standing proof of the truth of religion. It is intended to exhibit the power of the Son of God and to be a proof at once of the truth of my mission, of my friendship for this family, of my tender, peculiar love as a man, of my power and glory as the Christ, and of that great doctrine that the dead will raise."

How peculiar was that statement, I thought. *Why did Jesus say that Lazarus's illness would not end in death? The words to follow showed that he would expire and somehow Jesus would be glorified.*

Jesus told the messenger, "Go and tell Mary and Martha that I'll come in due time."

The messenger left to relay the words of Jesus to Lazarus's sisters. Despite our urgings, Jesus purposely stayed two more days there in Bethabara, some thirty miles from Bethany. Somehow,

I sensed that Jesus knew that Lazarus had died within minutes after the messenger had left Martha's home. Even though Jesus knew that, he did not hasten to Judea. It was hard to reconcile his delay with the friendship that he had with Lazarus and his two sisters.

After a couple of days preaching and teaching, Jesus said to his disciples, "Let us go into Judea now."

His disciples quickly reminded him that for four months, the unbelieving Jews there had sought to kill him and therefore questioned this return to that land.

Jesus gave them an answer they would have difficulty in understanding. "Are there not twelve hours in the day? There is an allotted time for me to live and do my Father's will. If any man walks in the day, he stumbles not. He can see because of the sun, the light of this world. The will of God is that I should do well. Therefore the Father will take care of me when I do the works of beneficence and mercy, which he has commissioned me to do, and which are expressions of his goodness and power. But if a man walks in the darkness, he stumbles because he is unable to see danger or obstacles, because there is no light by which he can see. Does not a traveler journey on until night? Is it not proper for me to travel the twelfth hour as any other? So it is proper for me to labor until the close. The night of death is approaching, and no work can then be done. I have nothing to fear. God will defend me in this until the appointed time. We should be diligent to the end of life, fearless of enemies when we know that God requires us to labor, and confidently commit ourselves to him who is able to shield us. And in whose hand, if we have a conscience void of offense, we will be safe. Besides," Jesus mused, "our friend Lazarus just sleeps. But I will go that I may awaken him."

Mystified, the disciples looked at one to another and said to Jesus, "Well then, Lord, if he just sleeps, he will be all right. There's no need for us to return to Judea. After all, sleeping is a favorable symptom in sickness. It is a sign of recovery, is it not? The violence of the disease surely has abated."

I don't believe the disciples and Jesus were on the same page. Jesus spoke of Lazarus's death whereas they thought he had spoken of taking a rest from the illness by sleeping.

Jesus faced his followers and spoke plainly. "Lazarus is dead, and I am glad for your sakes that I was not there to heal him. If I had been there during his sickness, the entreaties of his sisters and his friends would have prevailed upon me to restore him to health. I could not have refused them without appearing to be unkind. Though a restoration to health would have been a miracle and sufficient to convince you, yet the miracle of raising him after after four days being dead will be far more impressive. On that account, I rejoice that an opportunity is thus given so strikingly to confirm your faith, to furnish you evidence on which you might be established in the belief that I am the Messiah."

One of the twelve disciples known as Didymus (which means the twin), Jesus called him Thomas, exhorted his fellow disciples to go and die with Lazarus. Didymus said, "What hope have we if Jesus returns to Judea? Recently they have attempted to stone him, and now I have no doubts that they will put him to death. And we, like Lazarus, will be dead as well. Jesus is about to place himself into danger. The Jewish leaders have sought his life, and they will again. They will put him to death if they get the chance. Let us not forsake our Lord but stand firm and die with him."

There was no more conversation; Jesus had set his sights on Bethany. It took a day of hard walking to reach the township of Bethany. Jesus had already informed his disciples that Lazarus was dead, and upon their arrival. they learned that Lazarus had indeed died and had been in the grave for four days. Being that Bethany was only two miles from Jerusalem, many of the Jewish leaders who were distant relatives had come to comfort Mary and Martha concerning the death of their brother.

Being entrusted with the management of the affairs of the family, as soon as she had heard that Jesus was coming into Bethany, Martha went out to meet him. Stricken with grief, her sister Mary remained alone in the house.

When Martha came face-to-face with Jesus on the road leading into Bethany, she stopped him and railed, "Lord, if you had been here, I feel certain that my brother would be alive today. I know that even now, whatever you deem necessary for our consolation, you will ask and it will be granted to you."

With empathy, Jesus said, "Martha, your brother shall rise again."

"Yes, I know, Jesus," she replied with indignation, "I know and am fully convinced that Lazarus will rise again in the resurrection at the Day of Judgment."

Trying to placate his friend, Jesus said, "Martha, Martha, don't you know that I am the author of the resurrection? It so depends on my power and will that it may be said that I *am* the resurrection itself." Jesus pointed to himself and said, "The whole doctrine of the resurrection comes from me, and the whole power to affect it is mine. As the resurrection of all depends on me, I tell you that it is essential that it should be deferred to the last day. I have the power to do it now as well as at the last day. He that believes in me, though he may be dead, shall yet live. You understand that faith does not save us from temporal death. But even though the believer, as others, will die a temporal death, he will hereafter have life, life eternal. Even if he dies, he will be restored to life in the resurrection."

Jesus had just spoken of the prospects of the pious dead. He said that the same prospects are before the living, which was like faith. Though they are dead, yet they shall live. The living shall have the same kind of life. They shall never experience eternal death.

It seemed appropriate to test Martha's faith, so Jesus asked her, "Do you believe what I have said?"

Death of a loved one is the perfect time to test one's faith. If we still have confidence in God, if we look to him for comfort in such seasons, it is certain evidence that we are his friends. The person who still loves God when he has taken away their comfort has the best evidence possible of true attachment to him.

Martha answered Jesus with a noble confession, "Yes, Lord, I believe that you are the Christ, the Son of God, who was to come into the world. I have full confidence in you as the Messiah. I believe that all that you have said is truth."

Jesus told her to go home and ask her sister Mary to come to him. Saying nothing more, she left immediately.

As soon as Martha came to her sister, weeping in private, she told her that the Teacher had come and had asked for her. Without a single word, Mary got to her feet and raced to meet Jesus.

Because Mary left so abruptly, the mourners who were there in the house to comfort the sisters assumed she had left so hastily because she had need of going to the tomb to weep, so they followed her. Within half an hour, Mary came to the spot where Martha had met with Jesus, to where her Lord and Master stood waiting. When Mary laid eyes upon Jesus, she fell down at his feet and said, "Lord, if you had only been here, my brother would not have died."

When Jesus saw her weeping, as well as the mourners who had followed her, he was grieved in his own spirit. He perceived the sorrow of the others and was moved with sympathy and love as well.

Speaking as a friend and as a man, Jesus asked Mary, "Where have you laid him?"

Mary and the mourners answered, "Lord, come and see."

Knowing that death had come because of the curse put on man at the disobedience of Adam, Jesus wept for his friends. He felt tenderness toward them and revealed his nature as a man.

I've seen Jesus weep, I've seen him sweat, I've seen him stump his toe and experience pain, I've seen him with blisters on his feet, and I've seen him hungry, thirsty, and tired. From all that I have observed in the relationships that Jesus has with his friends and with those that follow him, I can say with surety piety binds stronger the ties of friendship, makes more tender the emotions of love, and seals and sets apart the affections of friends. I have found it to be right, natural, and indispensable for one person who believes in Christ to sympathize with others in their trials and tribulations. With him at our side, we experience a tempering and a chastening of our grief; we are taught to mourn with submission to God, to weep without murmuring, and to seek to banish tears, not by hardening the heart or forgetting the friend, but by allowing the soul, made tender by grief, to receive his sweet influence and to find calmness and peace in the God of consolation.

I heard many of the Jewish leaders that had come out to see Jesus say, "Behold how he loved this man, Lazarus. Could not this man who healed the sick, opened the eyes of the blind, and caused the lame to walk have prevented even this man from dying?"

We walked together to the tomb of Lazarus. You could just see Jesus groan within himself as the others present wept openly. Mary, her sister Martha, and their attendants cried tears of sorrow at the loss of their brother while the mourners cried no tears but put ashes on their heads and lamented loudly. All who came from Bethany were in black; Jesus's band was in an array of colors.

When we arrived at the tomb, we saw a cave with a stone rolled in front to seal its opening. Without hesitation, Jesus commanded two men standing beside the entrance, "You men there at the tomb, roll away the stone."

Martha stopped weeping, took hold of Jesus's arm, and said to Jesus, "But, Lord, Lazarus has been dead now for four days. Surely he will have started to stink. Please do not uncover the tomb."

Jesus pulled free of Martha's grasp, put his hands on Martha's shoulders, looked straight into her eyes, and whispered softly, "Did I not say to you that if you believe, you would see the glory of God?"

"Yes," she answered, "but—"

Jesus did not give her a chance to speak further. He once again commanded, "Take away the stone!"

The two men did as they were instructed and rolled the stone away from the entrance to the cave. A smell of rotting flesh filled the air so that those near its entrance placed their hands over their noses and mouths to stifle the gut-wrenching stench.

Lifting his eyes up toward heaven and extending his open hands above his head, Jesus prayed aloud, "Father, I thank you that you have heard my prayer and committed to me power to raise up Lazarus. As for me, I have had no doubts concerning myself that I should always be heard, but the particular basis of gratitude is the benefit that will result to those who are witnesses that they might believe that you have sent me."

When Jesus had finished praying to the Father, so that there might not be any suspicion of charm or incantation, he cried out in a loud, distinct, clear voice, "Lazarus, come forth!"

There was a rumble from deep down within the earth as if there was an earthquake starting to develop. Our footing became unsure, and we swayed back and forth like the giant cedars of Lebanon in the wind. A gush of putrid air came bellowing forth from deep within the dark cavern that caused everyone close to the entrance to retreat. There appeared in the entrance to the cave a "thing," a corpse that was wrapped from head to foot in grave clothes and was topped off with a burial napkin.

From where he stood, we could hear Jesus instruct those that were closest, "Unbind him so that he may walk freely."

The ancient heathen might have declared it to be beyond the ability of God to have the power to raise the dead, but Jesus not only displayed the power to give life to the deceased body, the power to enter the world of the spirits, the authority to recall the departed soul but also the omnipotence to reunite it with the body. He that could do such a thing must be omniscient as well as omnipotent, and if Jesus did this by his own power, it was a proof that he was divine.

The odor was so bad for those that loosened Lazarus that one of them swooned and nearly fainted. Within minutes after the grave clothes that had bound Lazarus had been unraveled, the stench dissipated, the necrotic soaked rags dried up, and Lazarus began to wriggle free of those garments holding him captive. The only thing left on his person was the burial napkin that covered his face. The once-hideous figure that had come forth from the tomb shed its grave clothes, and the necrotic flesh that covered its body now had new blood coursing through its veins. He reached up and pulled the burial napkin off. There for the entire world to see stood Lazarus, six feet of resurrected body.

Everyone, including Mary and Martha, gasped to see a dead man having come back to life. At first they were afraid of him, but once Lazarus had pulled the burial napkin off his face, those who knew him recognized him. Mary and Martha ran to their brother and hugged him with abounding unspeakable joy.

Many of the Jews who had come to the tomb with Mary, who had witnessed a dead man resurrected, believed in Jesus. However, many of those Jews who had come to spy on him, to report back to the leaders on what Jesus was up to, hurried back to the Pharisees and told them all the things they had seen him do.

It was hard to believe what I had just witnessed; however, there was no denying what I had just seen with my own two eyes. With just his word, Jesus called a man who had been dead for four days to come forth from the grave, and he came. He was already ripe. He had been buried in clothes with embalming oils and spices deep within a cave, and yet, there he stood before us. His flesh looked ashen and puffy from putrefying from the inside, but as soon as he started to walk and talk, the color came back into his cheeks and the odor dispersed. The smell of the burial wraps soon vanished, and with each step he took, the stiffness with which his legs moved melted away.

Overjoyed to have him back among the living, Martha and Mary hugged and kissed their brother over and over again. In spite of my animosity toward Mary, I went to her and offered my congratulations to a reunited family blessed with renewed opportunity to talk with and love one another again. I felt sure they would not be taking one another for granted any time soon.

The tomb that had once been a place of mourning now was a place of laughter and celebration. Once the jubilation began to subside, Martha and Mary, one on either side of Lazarus with their arms interlaced with his, walked back toward Bethany. They yelled back for Jesus and his disciples (and for me of course) to come to their house for a celebration feast. Jesus readily accepted the invitation for us, and soon, the burial site was deserted.

That night, the food and wine were plentiful. There must have been a hundred individuals that came to the house of Mary, Martha, and Lazarus to celebrate the resurrection of life. There was music made with the timbres, the drum, the lyre, and the flute. Wine, diluted with water, flowed as if we were celebrating a wedding, complete with toasting, dancing, laughter, and praising God for his grace and his mercy. There was hugging, kissing, and thanksgiving offered to Jesus for using the power that he shared with his Father.

Wasted Oil

BLACKNESS COVERED JERUSALEM like a blanket; not one moonbeam could be found. A council of the chief priests and the Pharisees gathered under this cloak of darkness, this night concealed from the eyes of onlookers. They were worried, afraid, and angry that someone like Jesus should come along and upset their apple cart, should throw salt into their vat of brew. The Pharisees had wanted to kill Jesus on several occasions by the orthodox Jewish method of stoning; however, the Sadducees insisted they could accomplish the dastardly deed through their political union with the Roman occupiers.

The Sadducees were particularly agitated by Lazarus's resurrection since they themselves did not believe in a resurrection. However, their main concern with Jesus was that he might cause a messianic uprising. Unlike the Pharisees, the Sadducees' interests were political, not theological. Blasphemy or healing on the Sabbath did not particularly disturb them.

A meeting of the Sanhedrin, the general council of the nation of Israel, was convened. Reserving the right of regulating all the affairs of religion, the members of the Sadducees asked, "What measures are we taking to arrest the progress of Jesus's sentiments? We see that this man does many miracles. If we admit that he performs miracles, the common people will want us to receive him as the Messiah. We know that there have been many imposters and we know about the miracles and wonders that were performed by the magicians in Egypt. Since we see the tendency of the doctrines of this man to draw off the people from the worship of God in the Temple, from keeping his law, we do not suppose ourselves bound to follow him even if he did work miracles. If we leave him alone to do as he pleases, the whole nation might believe in him and the Romans, to whom we owe our privileges, will come and take away both our place and the nation."

Whatever privileges they held were at the will of the Roman emperor. They feigned to believe that Jesus intended to set up a temporal kingdom. As he claimed to be the Messiah, they surmised that he designed to be its temporal prince. They professed to believe that this claim was in fact hostile to the Roman emperor. They were afraid that the nation would become embroiled in war if he were not stopped.

Then one of the Sadducees by the name of Caiaphas, the high priest at the time, bellowed in a gravelly baritone voice to the Pharisees that came to see him, "You know nothing respecting the subject under consideration! You are fools to hesitate about so plain a case."

Caiaphas was dressed in a fine off-white linen toga with a purple sash around his waist. A prayer shawl with all its fringes dyed sky blue hung around his neck; a purple headdress with a band of pheasant feathers adorned his head. He paraded around the floor of the Sanhedrin like a peacock displaying his plumage. He felt that there was no one as magnificent as he, and to kiss his ring when you came into his presence was certainly expected.

Then the great one, sashaying around with his fingers interlaced behind his back, said in a condescending manner to those men that cowered before him, "Do you not think it expedient and profitable for us that one man should die? This man Jesus is promoting sedition. He is exposing the nation to vengeance at the hands of the Romans. If we put him to death, the people will be safe."

He sauntered over to his seat in the center of the forum, did an about-face before it, and plopped his rotund body down on its stack of cushions like a frog flopping onto a lily pad. He looked so smug and confident for he had just delivered a speech promoting Jesus's death in order that they could be made safe. He certainly was not intending to speak of Jesus's dying as an atonement or a sacrifice. But what he said, even though by accident, expressed the real truth, the truth that Jesus's death was expedient and infinitely desirable. Jesus should die for the people and for all others, to save them from perishing.

Caiaphas spoke not on his own authority, but being high priest, he prophesied that Jesus should die for the nation, and not for it only, but he should also gather together in one the children of God that were scattered abroad. He spoke not only about those who were already Christians but about all those who God should bring to himself, all who would be in the mercy of God, called, chosen, and sanctified among all the nations. This was not the intent of Caiaphas; he was plotting a murder and a crime. In spite of Caiaphas's wickedness, God so ordered it that he deliver a most precious truth regarding the atonement without even knowing it.

It should never be supposed that Caiaphas was ever a true prophet or that he was ever conscious of the meaning affixed to his words. Regardless, he expressed the truth about the atonement of Jesus. It is a remarkable happenstance that the high priest of the nation should unwittingly utter a sentiment that turned out to be the truth about the death of Jesus.

The judgment of the high priest silenced all opposition and those who were shaking in their sandals before him. He began to devise measures to put Jesus to death in a way that would not excite tumult among the people.

Because of the briskness of the night air, we sat around an open fire in the courtyard of the house that belonged to Lazarus and his sisters. Jesus had been teaching us about the kingdom of God, about the meek inheriting the earth, about counting the cost of following him, and many other things that unfortunately I do not remember. Then something happened that to this day, I just can't explain. Right in the middle of speaking, Jesus stopped so abruptly that if we had been moving, we would all have collided. He got to his feet and said, "I can no longer walk openly among the Jews. From now on, I must walk in the country near the wilderness. In the morning, we'll go to a city called Ephraim. They are now plotting how to kill me, but my time is not yet."

He then sat back down and became very quiet, almost moody to my way of thinking. I moved closer to him and tried to sooth his spirit. I loved this man so, and yet there remained a chasm between us. I openly offered my love, and he seemed to receive it, but outwardly he withdrew. It was as if he could feel the love that I had for him, but because of who he said he was, Jesus never let me into his private world I so desperately wanted to enter.

"Jesus," I said softly, "it is six days before the Passover. Can't you just rest tonight? Do you have to always be so serious? You are surrounded by people who admire and love you. Relax and find some peace for your troubled soul tonight. Would you do that for me?"

Jesus said nothing. He got up from the fireside, and he and his disciples walked inside. It was as if he had never even heard me.

He looked so troubled that it broke my heart, but I knew that I had done what I could. What I didn't understand was if he's truly God, what's the problem? When the Jews try to do something, why wouldn't he just put his hand up and speak a word. Would they not be instantly stopped, and if he so desired, wouldn't they instantly be obliterated?

We all took our places around the table that graced the center of the dining area. Jesus and Lazarus were the guests of honor. To the right of Jesus reclined Lazarus, and to the left, I took my seat before John or Peter had a chance to grab their usual spots. Before I had a chance to say more to Jesus, Martha announced that supper was ready to be served. She saw her beloved resurrected brother sitting by Jesus on the one side and me on the other and her sister near Jesus's feet, where she always sat when he was in the house. The expression on her face said, *Not again. Why can't she ever help me serve?*

Before she had a chance to cause a scene, I jumped to my feet and said, "Martha! Let me help you serve diner. It would be such an honor."

She looked a little disgusted at her sister but certainly was thankful that she had someone to lend a hand.

"Why, thank you, Mary of Magdala." Giving her sister a sharp glance, she added, "It certainly will be wonderful to finally have someone to give me some help."

I followed Martha into another room, where the food had been prepared, to help her as I had promised. On our way back into the room where Jesus, Lazarus, and the disciples were reposed about the table, we stopped in our tracks and watched as Martha's sister, Mary, took a pound of a very costly fragrance called spikenard and anointed the head and feet of Jesus, all the while tears streaming down her cheeks. After having poured the ointment over Jesus's head, she poured the remainder over his feet. She commenced to wipe the excess off with her long velvet hair.

The room became filled with the fragrance of the oil, the oil of burial. All the while there seemed to be an unspoken connection between Mary and Jesus about which I was none too happy. There was not a word spoken between them, and yet her act was received by Jesus as if he were in a hypnotic trance.

There were some present, celebrating the resurrection of Lazarus and the presence of Jesus who became indignant at what Mary had just done. The happiness of the occasion was broken when Judas Iscariot, Simon's son, criticized her harshly. "Why was this fragrance not sold for three hundred denarii and given to the poor? Don't you realize that you just wasted a year's salary worth of ointment?"

I don't know what the others might have thought, but as for me, I thought, *You evil person! You don't care about the poor! You have been given the task by Jesus and the other disciples of keeping the bag that contains the money collected for the poor, and yet, because you are naturally avaricious, everyone knows that you take from it for your own purposes. You are a thief, for crying out loud! Do you complain because you're afraid someone might take some of "your" precious money?*

Jesus rose to his feet and rebuked not only Judas but the others that had ill feelings in their hearts for Mary's unselfish act.

"Let her alone," he exhorted boldly. "Why do you trouble her? She has done a beautiful thing for me! You will have the poor with you always and whenever you desire. You may do them good, but you will not always have me here with you!"

Foreseeing a criminal's death (for only in the case of a criminal's burial is the body not anointed before being laid to rest), Jesus said, "Mary has done what she could. She has come beforehand to anoint my body for burial. Verily I say to you, wherever my Gospel shall be preached throughout the whole world, what Mary has done here tonight shall be kindly spoken of as a memorial to her."

Many of those who had murmured against Mary now hung their heads in shame at what they had thought and said. Judas, however, felt indignation at being rebuked by Jesus. He grabbed his cloak and bolted though the door, leaving without having finished his meal.

Always the first to speak, whether right or wrong, Peter got to his feet and said, "I'll go after him!"

Jesus grabbed him by the arm as he started past and said, "Let him go, Peter! He'll cool off and return to us tomorrow! I have need of him!"

"You know," Peter said, "Judas has always been a hothead. Perhaps we would be better off without him. Maybe it's time he moved on to keep company with those zealots he meets with in secret."

Jesus looked at Peter as if he were surprised by what he had just said. "You know about his affiliations, Peter?" Jesus asked.

"We all know, Lord," Peter answered. "We just don't understand why he continues to be part of our group. He's always at odds with you, demanding that you come forward and take the crown that's rightfully yours. I guess our question to you is why do you put up with him?"

I couldn't contain myself any longer. I stepped into the conversation and added, "He's right, Jesus. Judas is always complaining about you for not taking your rightful place and questioning whether you are who you claim to be. I don't know about your disciples, but I know for a fact that he uses money for himself from the coffers designated for the poor."

"I am aware of that, Mary," Jesus responded, "but I have need of Judas. He will serve the purpose for which he was born. I can assure you of that!"

"But, Jesus," I protested.

"Mary of Magdala," Jesus said firmly, "you do try my patience sometimes. Hear what I am saying: Judas serves a purpose. That's why I called him to serve me. He was born to fulfill prophecy. He will return before the cock crows in the morning, ready to go with us into Jerusalem later this week."

Jesus waved Peter and me off as he returned to his seat beside Lazarus and said to us, "That's the end of it. No more is to be said."

Peter and I looked at each other and simply shrugged it off. When Jesus had made up his mind about something, there was no changing it, so we reclaimed our seats to resume the celebration of the resurrection of Lazarus and to enjoy being in the presence of our Lord who had raised him to life. Because of the resurrection to life of Lazarus, many of the Jews believed that Jesus was indeed the Messiah.

The food was most satisfying, the fellowship was superb, and being in the presence of God's Son was just about more than any of us could ever have hoped for. And me, I was sitting near the man I loved. It was overwhelming to say the least. If only Jesus would see me the same way I saw him. Surely he knows how much I love him.

I Leave My Love

SIX DAYS HAD passed since the celebration at the house of Mary, Martha, and Lazarus. We remained in the town of Bethany with Jesus ministering to the sick, the lame, and the blind. He not only healed people that were brought before him, but he also preached the Gospel, the good news of the kingdom of God.

I felt that we had had a chance to get to know one another a little better. Circumstances allowed me to be with him more than usual. I was allowed to remain in his presence when he prayed to his Father, and he freely answered my questions concerning things that he mentioned in his prayers. The last two nights that we were in Bethany, Jesus walked with me to and from the grove of olives that covered the hillside nearby where he either met with his followers or offered up prayers for them and for the nation of Israel. On one occasion, I overheard him lamenting over Jerusalem saying, "Oh, Jerusalem, oh, Jerusalem, you that kill your prophets and stone those that are sent to you. How often would I have gathered your children together, even as a hen gathers her young under her wings, but you would not believe."

Darkness covered the land, and Jesus walked with me back to the house of Mary, Martha, and Lazarus. I wanted to grab him and hold him so tightly that the breath would have been squeezed right out of him, but I resisted the temptation. I must admit, however, I did secretly pray to God that he would free his Son from the burden that was on his heart and just let him love me the same way I loved him.

Jesus bid me good night and walked away to join his disciples where they would sleep in the open within the walls of the courtyard while I, on the other hand, was granted the luxury of having a mat to sleep on within four walls under a roof.

I thought to myself as I lay upon my bed, *Good night, sweet one. I love you so very much. I just don't understand why everyone with whom you come into contact doesn't feel the same way I do.*

As I drifted off to sleep, I imagined how it would be if Jesus were holding me tightly in his arms. I know I must have slept the entire night with a smile upon my face.

The next day, while we ate the morning meal Martha had prepared for us, Jesus called two of his disciples and said to them, "Go into the village and as soon as you enter, you'll find a donkey along with her colt tied to a post outside a small bungalow. I want you to untie them and bring them here to me. If anyone says anything to you about taking the animals, I want you to say to them, 'The Lord has need of them.' When he hears you say this, straightway he will send them with you along with his blessing."

The two disciples looked at Jesus, somewhat puzzled, so he reminded them, "It was written in Isaiah and Zechariah, 'Tell the daughter of Zion, "Behold, your king comes unto you, meek and lowly, sitting upon a colt, the foal of a donkey."' So I say to you, go, do as I command!"

I don't think they fully understood what Jesus was saying. I know I certainly didn't, but they went and did as he had commanded them.

After almost an hour, the two disciples returned with the donkey and her colt in tow. When they stood in the presence of Jesus, they removed their cloaks and placed them on the back of the colt. With joined hands, they hoisted Jesus onto the back of the donkey colt that had never previously been broken or ridden. For a moment, everyone stood motionless. No one knew whether the unbroken colt would start bucking and throw our Lord to the ground. However, the colt stood there without moving. It acted as if giving someone a ride was commonplace.

Jesus nudged the animal onward with the heel of his sandal, and we all headed to the feast of the Passover in Jerusalem, which was only a mile away. After we had descended the Mount of Olives and before Jesus entered through the gate of the wall surrounding the city, a whole multitude of his disciples began to rejoice and, with loud voices, praised God for all the mighty works they had seen. A greater number of people spread their garments in the path of the colt, and others cut down branches from the palm trees and spread them on the road. The great crowd that went before Jesus and those that followed cried out in loud voices, "Hosanna to the son of David! Blessed is the king of Israel that comes in the name of the *Lord*, peace in heaven, and glory in the highest."

I don't know about the rest of Jesus's family or disciples, but my ears perked up at what the crowd was crying out. They were singing "hosanna," which means "please save." They were rejoicing and shouting, "Blessings on the son of David."

I had been listening to Jesus as he shared with his disciples, but this was incredible. It was as if these people knew that Jesus was from the line of David and that he was the one to come.

As he rode farther into Jerusalem, the entire city was moved, and some said, "Who is this?" while others of the multitude answered, "This is Jesus, the prophet of Nazareth of Galilee."

The people that had been with Jesus when he raised Lazarus from the dead bore witness to this miracle to the throngs of people that lined the streets, that hung over second- and third-story balconies, that jumped and danced before the parade that had formed as Jesus came riding into the Holy City on the colt of a donkey. Others who had heard of the miracle of Jesus raising Lazarus from the dead came out also to meet him. With glee, they sang, danced, and shouted the praises to God and his Son. But the Pharisees, jealous as they were, complained among themselves, "See how he accomplishes nothing? Behold, the world has gone wild for him!"

In the midst of the joyous multitude, some of the Pharisees feared that the crowd's acclamation might bring Roman troops into action. Not wanting to see Jesus proclaimed king, they cried out to him as he rode by in front of the wall on which they stood, "Teacher, rebuke your disciples!"

As he rode past, Jesus shouted back to them, "I tell you that if these people should keep silent, the very stones from which this city has been built would immediately cry out!"

As Jesus came closer and he was able to behold the magnificence of the city, tears filled his eyes, and he proclaimed, "If you had only known, even you, at least in this day, there is still time to repent. But I know that comparatively few will make use of it. Salvation has been here offered, but the city that for so long has rejected God's messengers is no longer capable of discerning its redemptive last chance. Now these things are hidden from your eyes, for the days shall come upon you that your enemies will build an embankment against you, surround you, and close you in on every side. You shall be leveled to the ground, your children shall be killed, and there will not be left one stone upon another because you knew not the time of your visitation."

I watched Jesus pour out his heart for these people. To think that it wasn't that long ago that I too had eyes that did not see and ears that did not hear. My eyes welled up at seeing the passion that this man had for a nation, a people that had rejected all the prophets that God had ever sent their way, including his cousin, John the Baptist, whom King Herod had beheaded. Now even as the multitudes inundated him, singing and dancing and praising God for sending the Messiah to take the throne of David, Jesus knew that it was only a matter of hours before they would reject him for claiming to be the Son of the living God. Not only would they reject him, they would cry out for his death.

Oh, how I wanted to take Jesus in my arms and smother him with affection, wipe the tears from his eyes, mop the sweat from his brow, and keep him from the harm that seemed inevitable. He had brought what was coming on himself with his claims of being God, for his miracle working, for his indictment of the Pharisees and the Sadducees, for his preaching about loving and praying for your enemies instead of cursing and killing them, and for his failure to take the throne as king of Israel.

"Oh, dear Father," I prayed. "Take this burden from my love. Please do not let these awful people hurt him. He claims to be your Son. I don't understand how that's possible. Nevertheless, who am I? I love him so, and if you love him as I do, then please, Father God, tell Jesus to step back and come away with me before it's too late. Please, Father, please."

Suddenly, I was startled back to reality when either Andrew or Philip touched me on the shoulder and Philip said, "Mary, we need to tell Jesus something."

Without thinking, I asked, "What?"

"Well, if you must know," Philip said somewhat harshly, "these men here with us are Hellenists who have come up to worship at the feast and they would see Jesus."

"Well, you can certainly see him over there dismounting the donkey colt," I answered.

"I know, Mary," Andrew interjected. "The problem is that we can't get near him. We thought that you might be able to get the message to him."

I agreed and began to work my way toward Jesus.

When I had finally wiggled and squirmed through the crowd to Jesus's side, I delivered the message from Phillip and Andrew.

Jesus acknowledged those two disciples and said, "I'll go to them."

We squirmed our way through the crowd to where Philip and Andrew and the Greek men stood, and Jesus said to the men that had come to see him, "Shalom."

They responded, "Shalom," in kind.

Jesus said to them, "The hour is come that the Son of man should be glorified, but not in the manner in which you think. As a man, I have been humble, poor, and despised. But the time has come when, as a man, I am to receive the appropriate honor of the Messiah, the honor that is due me in the proper manner—that is, by the testimony that God will give to me at my death, by my resurrection, and by my ascension to glory."

These people had seen his triumph; they supposed that he was about to establish his kingdom. However, they had no idea what in the world he meant by this profession. They could not see how all this could be. It appeared to dash their hopes.

Using a perfect comparison, Jesus took the occasion to illustrate what he meant, "All the beauty and richness of the harvest resulted from the fact that the grain had died. If it had not died, it would never have germinated or produced the glory of the yellow harvest."

So it was with him. By this illustration, Jesus still kept before them the truth that he was to be glorified, but he delicately and beautifully introduced the idea that he must and was going to die.

Then he said in the most humble, heartfelt words that I had ever heard, "Verily, verily I say to you, except a grain of wheat be buried in the earth and die, it remains alone without producing the rich and beautiful harvest. But if it dies, it will bring forth much fruit."

My love for him overwhelmed my heart. Tears streamed down my face as I remembered the things that he had specifically said and all those things that he had referenced in the many hours spent in conversation and in discipleship, the many times that it was even possible for me to listen to him when my heart was racing wildly and my dreams soared unbridled. But this I remember him saying, "I have been made a little lower than the angels for the suffering of death to be crowned with glory and honor. I have humbled myself and will be obedient unto death, even death of the cross, wherefore God will highly exalt me." And finally when he had said, "Who, for the joy that was set before me, I will endure the cross, even though I will despise the shame, but I will sit down at the right hand of the throne of God," I remember having wept openly.

Jesus continued by repeating one of his favorite principles, an axiom which he applied not only to his followers but to himself as well. "He that loves his life shall lose it, and he that hates his life in this world shall keep it unto life eternal. If any man will be my disciple, let him imitate me, do what I do, bear what I bear, love what I love, and where I am, there shall also my servant be. If any man serves me, my Father will honor him. You have seen me triumph, you have seen me enter Jerusalem, and you have supposed that my kingdom was to be set up without opposition or calamity. But it will not be. I am to die, and if you will serve me, you must follow me even in times of calamity, be willing to endure trials, and to bear shame looking for your reward in the future."

Jesus lowered his head and grimaced as if he were in pain and moaned, "Now is my soul troubled."

I noticed that when he mentioned his death, it brought to him its approaching horrors, its pain, its darkness, and its unparalleled woes. He was filled with acute sensibility, and his human nature shrank from the scenes through which he was to pass.

He hesitated for a moment, and you could see the intense anxiety and perplexity that resonated within him. Then he said, "What shall I say? Father, if you will, save me from this hour. But you see, I came specifically for this hour."

Jesus wrestled with himself as if there were a subject of some great debate: whether he could bear those sufferings, or whether the work of man's redemption should be abandoned and he should call upon his Father to save him.

One would have to say, "Thank God that he is willing to endure these sorrows and does not forsake man when he is so near being redeemed."

On the decision of that particular moment the rigid and unwavering purpose of the Son of God determined man's salvation. If Jesus had forsaken his purpose, then all would have been lost.

Then he looked up as if looking directly into the face of God and said just above a whisper, "Father, I am willing to bear any trials. I will not shrink from any sufferings. Let your name be honored and glorified. Let your character, wisdom, goodness, and plans of mercy be manifested and promoted, regardless of whatever suffering it may cost me."

We were startled and confounded to hear an unexpected voice that sounded like thunder come to us from high above, saying, "I have glorified it. I have honored my name by the pure instructions that I have given to man through you by the power displayed in your miracles, by proclaiming my mercy through you, by appointing you to be the Messiah. I will glorify it again by your death, your resurrection, your ascension, and by extending the blessings of the Gospel among all nations."

When some standing there proclaimed that the sound they heard was the voices of angels because they believed that God no longer spoke to men except by the ministry of angels, Jesus answered and said to them, "The voice you just heard did not come to strengthen or confirm me, but came to give you a striking and indubitable proof that I am the Messiah, that you may remember it when I have departed and be, yourselves, comforted, supported, and saved. There was never any question that God would approve me and glorify his name. Now is approaching the decisive scene, the eventual period, the crisis when it shall be determined who shall rule this world. There has been a long conflict between the powers of light and the powers of darkness, between God and the devil. Satan has so effectually ruled that he is the prince of this world, but my approaching death and resurrection will destroy his kingdom, will break down his power, and will be the means of setting up the kingdom of God over man."

Jesus's death was to be the most grand and effectual of all means that could be used to establish the authority of the law and the government of God. He was saying that this would show the regard which God had for his law by showing his hatred of sin and presenting the strongest motives to induce man to leave the service of Satan, by securing the influences of the Holy Spirit, and by putting forth his own direct power in the cause of virtue and of God. The death of Jesus would be the determining cause, the grand crisis, the concentration of all that God had ever done or ever would do to break down the kingdom of Satan, and set up His power over man.

Then Jesus said, "Now the prince of this world, the prince of the power of the air, the spirit that works in the children of disobedience, shall be destroyed, and his empire shall come to an end. And when I am lifted up from the earth, I will draw all men unto myself."

His disciples understood what he had just said was signifying by what means he should die.

People in the crowd who had been listening to his words said to him, "We have been taught by those who have interpreted the law that the Messiah will live forever and will reign as a prince forever over his people. We know that it says in the Psalms of King David: 'You are a priest forever.'

"How is it then that you say that you, the Son of man, must be lifted up? Besides what is written in the Psalms, we also understand that the Son of man is the Messiah spoken of by Daniel, who also said that he is to reign forever. So answer us, who is this Son of man of whom you speak? You certainly cannot be saying that *he* must be lifted up or must die. What other Son of man is referred to but the Messiah?"

He answered them, saying, "Yet a little while is the light with you. Whatever you must do, do it while you still have the light. Make excellent use of your privileges before they are removed that you may learn the way to life lest God should take away all his mercies, remove all light and instruction from you, and leave you in ignorance, blindness, and woe."

Never arousing the prejudices of men unnecessarily and never shrinking from declaring to them the truth in some way, however unpalatable it might be, Jesus admonished them, "While you have light, believe in the light that you may become children of the light."

Jesus was clearly telling them that he was the Messiah, the light of the world, and they needed to believe that so that they might be his friends and followers. Immediately after speaking, Jesus departed to Bethany where he passed the night quietly.

Even though Jesus had done so many miracles in the sight of the Jewish nation, healed the sick, opened the eyes of the blind, made the lame to walk, and raised the dead, the Jews did not believe as a nation, but they rejected him.

The Pharisees' rejection of Christ paralleled the Jews' rejection of Isaiah during his time. His message was despised by the nation, and he himself was put to death. Now it was happening all over again by the same cause, by the same nation, and by that same Gospel message rejected by the Jews. No doubt the Holy Sprit intended to mark both events simultaneously, for the language of the prophet Isaiah expressed both events, *"Lord, who has believed our report? To whom has the arm of the Lord been revealed? You have proclaimed truth to them, truth that resulted in blinding their eyes and resulted in hardening their hearts, that they should not see with their eyes or understand with their hearts and be converted, and I should heal them. Oh, Lord, you knew that this would be the result, as it was the effect of the message, your commandment to me to go and proclaim, as if you had commanded me to blind their eyes and harden their hearts. As the omniscient God of creation, you knew what was in their hearts and minds before I even went."*

The effect of truth on such hearts and minds is to irritate, enrage, and harden, unless counteracted by the grace of God. In proclaiming the truth, there was nothing wrong on the part of God or of Isaiah, nor is there any indication that God was unwilling that the Jews should not see or hear. It certainly does not mean that it was the design of God that they should not be converted, but that it was the effect of their rejecting the message.

These things were spoken by Isaiah when he saw the glory, the manifestation, the *Shechinah*, the visible cloud that represented God. Isaiah saw the Lord sitting on a throne, high and lifted up, surrounded by the seraphim. And since the Torah says that "no man shall see God and live," and Isaiah affirmed that he had seen Jehovah God, the Jews, for that and others reasons, put him to death by sawing him in half with a wooden saw.

Nevertheless, among the members of the Sanhedrin, the ruling council of Israel, many, like Nicodemus, Joseph of Arimathea (the great uncle of Jesus), and others like them, believed in Jesus when they heard him; but because of the Pharisees (the majority of the council), they did not publicly acknowledge him lest they should be excommunicated from the synagogue. They loved the approbation given to them by men more than they liked to praise God. They did not possess a living, active faith, but they were convinced in their understanding that Jesus was the Messiah. They possessed that kind of faith, which is so common—a speculative acknowledgment that religion is true—but no acknowledgement that leads one to self-denial, an acknowledgement that will prevent one from recoiling from the active duties of piety and a knowledge that fears man more than it fears God.

Knowing their hearts and seeing their unbelief, Jesus cried out, "He that believes in me believes not in *me* alone, but in him who sent me. The union between the Father and me is such that there cannot be faith in me unless there is also faith in God. He that sees me sees him who sent me. I have come as a light into the world, that whosoever believes in me should not abide in the darkness, the gross and dangerous errors of sin. And if anyone hears my words and believes not, I have not come at the present time to condemn him, for I came not to judge the world but to save the world. He that refuses to receive me and receives not my words needs not my voice to condemn him. He will carry his own condemnation with him even if I were not to speak a word. His own conscience will condemn him, for a guilty conscience needs no accuser. My words of mercy that the sinner hears and rejects will ultimately be remembered by him. This will make him miserable, and there will be no possibility for happiness. The conscience of the sinner will concur with my sentence in the great day, and he will go into eternity self-condemned. The word that I have spoken, the doctrines of this great Gospel, and the messages of mercy will be that which you will be judged in the last day. Every man will be judged by that message, and the sinner will be punished according to the frequency and the clearness with which the rejected message has been presented to his mind.

"I have not spoken by my own authority," Jesus said, "but by the Father who sent me. He gave me a commandment for what I should speak. I know that his commandment is the source of everlasting life, and whoever obeys that commandment of God shall obtain that everlasting life. This is his commandment: that you believe in the name of his only begotten Son. Whatsoever I speak, the Father spoke unto me, and therefore I speak."

Jesus proclaimed the Word of God in the face of all opposition, contempt, and persecution. He had a deep and abiding conviction that he should deliver a message that was connected with the eternal welfare of his hearers.

When Jesus finished delivering this discourse to the great throng of people and unlike the many times when I had tried to drag him away from confrontation, this time he came away with me without protest.

I tried to engage him in conversation by saying, "You know, Jesus, you certainly know how to stir people up! As always, I could see the look in their eyes. They wanted to take you apart limb by limb."

Barely audible, he responded, "I know." He took a deep breath in through his nostrils and let the air out slowly through his mouth. He added, "These people are lost and dead. They will not hear. It breaks my heart, Mary. It just breaks my heart. Even though there is a redeemed people set aside for me by the Father as a love gift, a gift that he predetermined before the foundations of the world were set, all people still have a knowledge of God implanted in their hearts. They have no excuse, but men love darkness more than they love the light. Ever since Adam took from his wife and ate the forbidden fruit, darkness has ruled people's lives."

Tears welled up in his eyes, and he repeated something that I had heard him say before. "How often would I have gathered them together, even as a hen gathers her chickens under her wings, and they would not?"

He turned to me and said sadly, "You know, Mary, this is the close of my public preaching. From now on, I will employ myself in the private instruction of my disciples, preparing them for my approaching death."

Like some knee-jerk reaction, I struck Jesus on the arm and screamed at him, "You know I hate it when you say those kinds of things! I have begged you over and over to stop agitating these people. You are truly setting yourself up to be killed, and I hate it! I hate it! I hate it!"

Rubbing his arm where I had struck him, Jesus responded, "I know what you have said over and over and over again, Mary, but I have also told you over and over and over again that that is why I came: to do the will of the Father."

"Well!" I snapped, "I can't believe any father would send his son to die for people who don't believe in him or want him. You don't have to do this, Jesus," I argued. "You don't have to do this! I love you, Jesus. Are you just going to ignore that?"

Jesus placed his hand on my shoulder, but I pulled away. I folded my arms and with my back to him, I stomped my foot and stared down at the ground.

"You know, Mary, that I love you as well, but it's different," he replied. "It's different for me. I came to fulfill all righteousness, to fulfill the law."

He placed his hands on both of my shoulders, never tried to turn me around to face him, but continued to speak from behind me.

With compassion, he said, "I know that you don't understand these things, Mary, but I must be about my Father's business. His will for me is to—"

"His will?" I screamed. "His will? What about my will? What about my feelings? You saved me from those demons that had possessed me."

"I came to save you for eternity," Jesus interrupted. "That's far and above what I did for you back in Magdala."

"Why do you say such things to me, Jesus?" I asked. I turned around to look him eye to eye and continued, "Save me for eternity? What about now? What about the way I feel about you now? You know, Jesus, you are right. I don't understand when you talk about your Father wanting you to die, or talk about your need to teach your disciples, or make it so plain that you would rather be with a bunch of poor fishermen and tax collectors and all those other men who claim they love you so much. They don't love you half as much as I love you and yet they always come first! Well, you can just have them! As of now, I stop loving you, Jesus." Then I said the worst thing that I could possibly have said: "I hate you!"

I pulled away from the man I loved more than life itself, and with tears streaming down my face, I ran down the cobblestone street to get away from him. I didn't really know what I was going to do, but the pain that was continually being inflicted into my heart by his rejection was just more than I could bear at this moment. I wasn't sure just how I was going to manage, but I was going to stay away from this man. I had to. Otherwise, I wasn't sure if my heart could withstand the pain. *Oh, Jesus*, I thought as I ran away, *and you think that these people are so blind. What about you?*

Jesus Eats His Last Meal and Holds His Last Class

KNOWING IN HIS heart and in his mind that the hour appointed in the purpose of God that he should depart out of this world back to him, and having given to his disciples decisive and constant proofs of his love, Jesus concluded that he had not wavered in his love for them, even to the end. He had done all this by calling his disciples to follow him, by patiently teaching them, by bearing with their errors and weaknesses, and by making them the heralds of his truth and the heirs of eternal life.

It can be said that Jesus is the same yesterday, today, and forever. He never changes. He always loves the same characteristics, and he does not withdraw his love from the soul. If anyone whom he has called walks in darkness and wanders away from him, the fault lies with them, not in him. His is the character of a friend that never leaves or forsakes his own, a friend that stays closer than a brother.

Jesus had called his chosen disciples to meet with him in an upper room that they might celebrate their last Passover together. A couple of his chosen ones had gone before and paid an innkeeper to reserve a room on the second floor of his establishment and to prepare the Paschal Lamb for the Passover feast.

Jesus and his twelve disciples reclined around a low table in the center of the room that had been prepared for the Passover meal. They had observed all things that the feast meal had called for, and now they relaxed, told stories of all the miracle healings that they had seen Jesus perform, especially raising Lazarus from the dead. That one story was talked about more than any other, and they rejoiced to be in the presence of the One who had the power to give life back to someone who had died and had started experiencing physical deterioration.

While they were still at supper, the prince of evil spirits cast into the heart of Simon's son, Judas Iscariot, the willingness and the inclination to betray his friend, his mentor, his Master. It is not known precisely how this was done, but we know it was done by his avarice. Satan can tempt no one unless there is some inclination of the mind, some natural or depraved propensity of which he can make use. Satan presents objects in alluring forms fitted to that propensity, and under the influence of a strong or a corrupt inclination, the soul yields to sin. In Judas's case, it was two things: his disappointment at Jesus not coming as a warrior to take Israel back from Rome and the love of money. It was necessary to present to him only the possibility of obtaining money, and it found him ready for any crime.

Jesus had full knowledge of his dignity and full knowledge that the Father had given all things into his hands. While the disciples were still eating, Jesus rose from his reclined position and walked over to the door where their sandals had been removed. He took off his mantle, a garment without any seam, and laid it beside their footwear. In the manner of a servant, he took a towel and wrapped it around his waist. He then took an earthen basin and placed it at the feet of the disciple reclined at the end of the table. The disciple instantly rolled over so that he was seated with his feet sticking straight out away from the table.

Jesus went down on his knees and began to splash water over the disciple's feet and to massage them with his hands. After the dust of the road had been washed off, Jesus took the end of the towel that was girded around his waist and dried the disciple's feet.

When Jesus came to his disciple Peter the Rock and knelt before his feet to wash them in like manner, Peter pulled his feet back underneath him in what he thought was an expression of his humility. In his mistaken reverence for his Lord, he said, "Do you, the Son of God, the Messiah, perform the humble office of a servant toward me, a sinner?"

Jesus answered Peter, "What I do you don't understand now, but you certainly will hereafter."

Peter saw the actions of his Master, yet he did not quite understand the design of it. What Jesus did was symbolic, inculcating a lesson of humility, and was intended to teach them in such a manner that it would be impossible for them to ever forget. Had Jesus simply commanded them to be humble, it would not have had the impressiveness and long-lasting power that it now had as they watched him actually perform the office of a servant. Each and every day, they would realize more and more the necessity of humility and of kindness to each other and would see that they were the servants of Jesus and of the church. They would learn that they ought not to aspire to honors and offices but be willing to perform the humblest service to benefit the church.

God often does things that we do not now fully understand, but we will in the hereafter. He often sends afflictions upon us, he disappoints our small minds, and he frustrates our selfish designs. We may not appreciate adversities now, but we shall learn that what happens is for our own good, designed to teach us some important lesson of humility and piety. In heaven, God will remove all doubts, eradicate all difficulties, and reveal to us his plan and the implementation of his mysterious dealings in his leading us in the way to our future rest.

After Jesus had knelt at the feet of his big outspoken disciple, Peter said to him, "You shall never wash *my* feet!"

Jesus had just declared that it had a meaning and that he ought to submit to it, but Peter being Peter did not recognize that he, like every follower of Christ, should yield to all the plain and positive requirements of God, even if it was unclear how obedience would promote his glory.

Jesus immediately answered his slow-to-evaluate, quick-to-answer disciple and said, "If you don't allow me to wash you, you obviously have no part with me."

If Peter showed no confidence in Jesus as to believe that an act which he performed was proper, though he could not see its propriety, if he was not willing to submit his will to that of Christ and obey him implicitly, he had no evidence of piety in him. What Jesus was really saying to Peter was, unless by his doctrine and spirit he purified Peter and removed his pride, his want of constant watchfulness, his anger, his timidity and fear, he could have no part in him. He would show no evidence of possessing the spirit of Christ or be interested in his work. Peter could have no participation in Jesus's glory.

With characteristic readiness and ardor and realizing that everything, including his whole salvation and the entire question of his attachment to his Master, depended on this, Peter pushed his feet out toward Jesus and said, "Lord, wash not my feet only, but also my hands and my head."

In Peter's mind, it was mandatory that he not be seen as being unwilling or not desiring to have his feet washed and be part of his Lord. He wanted it known that he was not only willing but anxious that it should be done, not only anxious that his feet should be cleansed, but his hands and his head—that is, that he should be cleansed entirely and thoroughly. It became evident to him the spiritual meaning of the Savior, and he expressed his ardent wish that his whole soul might be made pure by Christ's work. He had no reserve and wished to be cleansed from all sin, that every thought should be brought into captivity to the obedience of Christ, and that his whole body, soul, and spirit should be sanctified wholly and be presented blameless to the Lord Jesus Christ.

It was as if there were an immediate revelation that his intellect, his affection, his will, his memory, and his judgment should all be surrendered to the influence of the Gospel and the mastery of the body and the mind be consecrated unto God.

Even though Jesus was long-suffering and patient, he must have felt that his big clumsy disciple, the leader of the pack, would never fully understand all that he had taught him. With a supreme kindness, he said to Simon Peter, "He that is saved with the washing of regeneration need not be bathed again except for the feet, for there are sins after salvation that soil the feet that hinder one's fellowship with God." Recalling the one among them that would betray him to the authorities, Jesus added, "But you are not all clean."

The disciples looked one to another but said nothing. Silence fell on the upper room like the humid air of the Mediterranean Sea in summer. They watched with much interest as Jesus knelt before each one in turn, poured water over each one's feet, rubbed them with his hands, and dried them with the towel that he had girded around his waist.

When Jesus had finished washing his disciples' feet, he asked them, "Do you know the meaning of what I have done unto you? You call me Teacher and Lord. You say well, for so *I Am*. If I, your Lord and Teacher wash your feet, you also ought to wash one another's feet. I have given you an example that you should do as I have done to you."

It was the manifest desire of Jesus to instill a lesson of humility, to instruct them by his example that they should condescend to the most humble offices for the benefit of other people. They should avoid being proud and vain and be willing to take up a low place, to see themselves as servants of each other, and be willing to befriend each other in every way possible. Knowing that these men would be the founders of a new religion, the founders of the church and therefore greatly honored, Jesus seized the moment to warn them against the dangers of ambition and arrogance. By setting the example, they would not forget he taught them the duty of humility and servitude.

Jesus continued to teach his men and said to them, "I tell you a universal truth that you are to remember always. Verily, verily I say to you that the servant is not greater than his master, but neither he that is sent greater than the one who sent him. If you understand these things, you will be doing my Father's will if you do them. I expect you to manifest the same spirit that I do, and you can expect the same treatment from the world.

"In addressing you as clean, I do not mean to say that you all possess this character. I know whom I have chosen. I have not chosen you all. Even though I came to you individually and asked you to follow me, I know your hearts and I know that not all of you are pure in heart. Even though I have chosen you all to be apostles and have treated you all as such, you all are not pure in heart and life. Eleven of you shall be saved. You all have been submitted to the same teaching, the same familiarity, and the same office. So that the Scripture may be fulfilled, so that an exhibition of ingratitude and baseness is exhibited like in the case of David, he that eats bread with me lifts up his heel against me."

As if running a race when one might attempt to trip the other up and make him fall, so it was with Judas—the one who was ungrateful for the Master's kindness, and the one who had been admitted to the intimacies of friendship—and yet he was ungrateful and malicious in the way he thought he had been treated. It wasn't the common people, the open enemies, the Jewish nation that had disconnected itself from the Christ, but the one who had received all the usual proofs of kindness.

Jesus pronounced further, "I tell you certain things before they happen so when they come to pass, you may believe that I am He. You will see that I have knowledge of the heart and the power of foretelling events and must therefore have been sent from God. I know that you have faith now, but your faith will be strengthened by what I say to you. I want you to know that he that receives whoever I send receives me, and he that receives me receives him that sent me. You who receive me receive my Father who is in heaven. Everything pertaining to religion is connected together. Therefore a man cannot dishonor one of the institutions of religion without doing injury to all."

When Jesus had concluded his discourse to his disciples, he became troubled in his spirit because Judas, a professed friend, was about to betray him. He not only envisioned his fast-approaching death on the cross but was deeply distressed at the ingratitude and wickedness of one with whom he had shared everything. Despite the fact that Jesus was fully God, he was also fully man and therefore felt the sorrow and the pain that every other man feels. His human nature recoiled at the thought of suffering, no different and no less than any other human being.

With a truly sorrowful look on his face and his brow deeply furrowed by the stress, Jesus testified, "Verily, verily I bear witness to the truth that one of you shall betray me this very night."

The disciples looked from one to another with that kind of perplexity that burdens one's very soul when he knows not what to say or do. There was one who occupied a position next to Jesus at the table, so close, that if he were to lean back, his head he would press against the chest of Jesus when he spoke with him. This man was John, the youngest of the disciples. He was admitted into a peculiar friendship to the Master because the natural disposition of the Lord was more nearly like the amiableness and mildness of this young follower than any of the other disciples. Jesus expressed a tender love for this particular disciple more than the rest because he possessed a meek and quiet spirit, which Jesus valued at great price.

From his position, a mere three persons away from Jesus, Peter mouthed to John to ask their Lord and Master of whom it was he spoke that would betray him.

Reclining back on Jesus's chest, John whispered to him, "Of whom do you speak, Lord?"

He looked down at John with a most amazing tender look. A look more fragile, more compassionate, more pathetic than possibly anyone had ever seen on the Savior's face, a look that said, *John, I am in pain here. I know that my Father created Judas to do what he must do, but for the life of me, it's hard to fathom how he could turn on me, how he traveled with us these months and yet did not grasp what I was preaching, what I offered not only to him but to the nation that my Father chose out of all the nations that could have been chosen.*

Jesus breathed out a sign that could be heard clear across the room, a sigh that brought everyone's attention to him and John. A tear ran down his cheek as he whispered, "John, it is he to whom I will hand a piece of bread that I have just dipped into the Passover sauce."

After Jesus had broken off a piece of unleavened bread and had dipped it into the sauce, he handed it to Judas Iscariot, son of Simon, who, not having heard Jesus breathe who it would be to John, took the morsel and consumed it with pleasure. After he had eaten the sop, Satan entered into Judas, making him aware that Jesus now knew his design and no longer could he conceal his plan.

Jesus did not command Judas to betray him but left him to his own purpose by saying, "What you must do, do quickly!"

Jesus had presented Judas with enough information and enough witness to miracles that he could have chosen to lead a holy life. It was time for a decision. If he could pursue his wicked plan, could go forward with it when he was conscious that the Savior knew his design, he was to do it at once. If he could betray Jesus knowing that God sees all and that he had been given the privilege of being taught by God himself, there was no doubt that his heart was fully set on doing evil and, outside the work of the Holy Spirit, that there was nothing that would restrain him.

Jesus had indicated to John only who it was that should betray him. Some of Jesus's disciples thought that because Judas carried the money bag in which they had placed their money in common, Jesus had sent him off to purchase the things needed for the seven days of the feast of the Passover or that he should give alms to the poor for him and his followers.

When Jesus said to him, "Go and do what you have to do, and do it quickly," Judas's look at Jesus was deadly. Up until this time, Judas had wanted Jesus to behave like the Messiah for whom the majority of Israel was looking, the One who would set up his throne, declare himself to be the true king of Israel, and gather an army to drive out the Romans; but Jesus had become a great disappointment to Judas and all the other Zealots like him. Jesus had preached brotherly love, a turn-the-other-cheek Gospel, which frustrated those who were secretly ready to go to battle.

When Judas had received the sop from Jesus, they looked at each other intently. Judas had set his teeth on edge, and if anyone had taken notice, they would have seen the muscles in his cheeks flex, almost uncontrollably. There was a look of arrogance in his eyes, like he knew something that no one else knew. His heavy, bushy black eyebrows remained fixed and rigid.

Before Jesus let go of the bread that had been swiped through the dipping sauce, he pulled Judas toward him and said, "Is this what you really want to do, Judas?"

"Is there any other way, Jesus?" he hissed.

That recognized patented hiss filled Jesus's ears. There was no doubt that Judas was now totally under the dominance of that old serpent, the devil. He took the sop almost as if it were a prize and stuffed the whole piece into his mouth, donned a satanic grin, and pushed his way past his teacher out into the darkness of the Judean night.

Knowing that the last deed had been done that was necessary to secure his death, Jesus murmured, "Now is the Son of man glorified, and God is glorified in him such as, will manifest his perfections and show his goodness, truth, and justice. God will honor the Messiah. He will not suffer him to go without a proper attestation of his acceptance."

Thinking that Judas had left the room to buy things needed for the week of Passover or indeed to give money to the poor, the men reclined on their left elbows and continued eating the Seder meal. As they ate, Jesus took a piece of bread and held it up over his head, blessed it, broke it, and gave a piece to each one and said, "Take, eat, this is my body which is broken for you. Do this in remembrance of me." Then he took the cup of wine, and when he had given thanks, he gave it to his men and they all drank from the cup. He said to them as they drank, "This is my blood of the New Testament, which is shed for many. As often as you drink it, do it in remembrance of me. Verily I say to you, I will drink no more of the fruit of the vine until that day when I drink it new in the kingdom of God."

After all had eaten the bread and had drunk the wine as the cup was passed around to each one reclined around the table, still seated on his heels, Jesus said, "I am the genuine vine and my Father is the vinedresser. Every branch in me that bears no fruit he takes away, and every branch that bears fruit, he prunes it that it may bring forth more fruit."

Setting before them on the table was the lamb, the bread, and the fruit of the vine, the wine. How could the disciples not grasp the real significance of what was before them? As to the lamb, had not John the Baptist said when he pointed to Jesus approaching at the River Jordan, "Look, behold the Lamb of God who is taking away the sin of the world."

Now Jesus asked his men to turn their eyes from the symbols of merely physical bread and wine and see in him the reality, the fulfillment, the antitype. He had spoken of the bread as being his body and the fruit of the vine as the new covenant in his blood, and he had spoken of himself being the real vine, not the vine that produced the grapes for the communion wine, or the nation of Israel, which was represented by a vine on the coins during the Maccabean period, but Jesus Christ himself.

Just as a vinedresser cuts off the branches from the vine that bears no physical fruit, so too God the Father would cut off and cast away those individuals who bear no spiritual fruit. Of course the fruits that Jesus was discussing were good motives (according to the will of God the Father), desires, attitudes, spiritual virtues, words, deeds, everything done springing from faith, being in harmony with the law of God, and everything done for and to his glory. Those people who bear good fruit were cleansed daily by God as a vinedresser would dress his vines.

Then Jesus said, "Already you are clean (justified) because of the word that I have spoken to you. The grace of justification you have received already and your gradual cleansing (your sanctification) will continue until you reach heaven. I tell you to remain united to me by a living faith. Live a life of dependence on me, obey my doctrine, imitate my example, and constantly exercise faith in me. If you remain attached to me, I will abide with you, teach you, guide you, and comfort you. Even though you are in the kingdom of God, you cannot bear fruit unless you remain in me, the Vine. I am the Vine. Separate from me and you can do nothing.

"If a man does not abide in me, he is cast out as a mere branch. He then dries up and loses all his peace and joy. He is like an autumn tree without fruit. He is twice dead, plucked up by the roots. Such branches are gathered as in the time of harvest when I shall say to the reapers, 'Gather up first the tares and bind them into bundles and burn them.' The Son of man will send his angels, and they will gather out of his kingdom all evildoers and throw them into the furnace of fire, and they will go away into everlasting punishment. For those that abide in me, there is great promise. Heed my principles so that they become the dynamic of your life, taking complete control over you so that you both believe them and act in accordance with them. Whatever you will, it will take place for you.

"By this is my Father glorified that you bear much fruit, for the spiritual fruits that adorn the children of God reflect his own being. And so you will become my disciples more and more."

On this sacred Passover night, the most sacred night of all, Jesus recalled all his experiences with his chosen followers, beginning with the day he had called each one to discipleship. His recollection of course went back to the eternity that preceded the foundation of the world when by his sovereign good pleasure the Father had elected them for their calling and their work. He unified this all in one sentence, "I have loved you just as the Father has loved me."

Jesus was trying to bring the whole concept together for his disciples, so he added, "If you keep my precepts, you will abide in my love, just as I have kept my Father's precepts and abide in his love."

He was implying that the believer was surrounded by invisible cords of love that draw him closer and closer to his Savior. Christ's love is always first in all things. *We love him because he first loved us.*

The question to these chosen of God is, How does love manifest itself? Answer: his followers manifest their love by keeping his precepts. "If you love me, you will keep my precepts." By keeping his precepts, there is a definite result: we stay connected to his love. "If you keep my precepts, you will abide in my love, just as I have kept my Father's precepts and have abided in his love."

It is not necessary to add that the love talked about here has never been absent. God's love precedes our love; it accompanies our love, it follows our love, and in the very process of acting out this love, more love is created toward him in our hearts. Another love cycle begins so that the present one is even better than the cycle that just finished. The believer feels himself drawn ever closer to God in Christ. Christ's love is an answer to our obedience. The Son's voluntary sacrifice to the bitter death on the cross is certainly the most glorious manifestation of this obedience.

As if he were a schoolboy, Peter raised his hand to ask a question, but Jesus waved him off with a reassuring smile. No doubt Jesus was confident that his Father would show his pleasure in what he had done. He would illustrate it not by the ministry of angels, or by any other subordinate attestation, but in the miracles that would attend his death, resurrection, ascension, exaltation, and the success of the Gospel. The time in which God would bestow this honor upon his Son was at hand. His death, resurrection, and ascension were near.

With his voice starting to show signs of fatigue and dread, Jesus turned to his remaining disciples and endeavored to mitigate their grief by the most tender expressions of attachment, exhibiting to them that he was experiencing for them the deepest interest that one would display to his heirs, and without concealing the fact that he was soon to leave them, he said, "Little children, yet for a little while I will be with you. You will seek to find me, but as I have said to the Jews, I say to you, 'Where I go, you cannot come, and for a time, you must be willing to be separated from me.' But I assure you that the separation will only be temporary and that afterward you will follow me.

"I soon will be leaving you, but I am about to give to you a new commandment, a badge of discipleship you might say, by which you can be distinguished as my friends and followers and by which you might be distinguished from all others. I ask you to love one another as I have loved you. I call this a new command, not because there has never before been given a command that required men to love their fellow men, for one great precept of the law is that you should love your neighbor as yourself."

The commandment was new because never before had it been made manifest that any class or body of men should be known and distinguished by their love for one another. Certainly, the Jew was known by his external rites and by his peculiar dress, the Greek philosopher by some other mark of distinction, the military man by another, and so on. In none of these instances had *love for each other* been the distinguishing and peculiar badge by which they were to be known.

In the case of the followers of Christ, they were not to be known because of the distinctiveness of their wealth or education or fame. They were not to seek after earthly honors, they were not to wear any peculiar clothing or badges, they were to be known for their tender and constant attachment to each other. This would transcend all distinctions due to color, tribe, social strata, country of origin, or sect. Instead, they were to feel that they were all on the same level, had common wants, were all redeemed by the same blood, and eventually would all go to the same heaven.

Moreover, this command was new in the reference Jesus made to the extent to which this *love* was to be carried out. He said, "As I have loved you, you also love one another."

His love for his disciples was strong, continuous, unremitting, and unrelenting. He was about to demonstrate a *love* that transcended all by laying down his life for them. Jesus had said to them before, "Greater love has no man than this: that a man lay down his life for his friends." Implied but not yet spoken, *We ought to lay down our lives for the brothers.*

This new love was to demonstrate the strength of bond that one Christian should have for another Christian and how prepared we should be to endure trials and tribulations, to encounter conflicts and dangers, and to practice self-denial to help those for whom the Son of God was about to lay down his life. That new love for one another should be so decisive that one would be like the Savior—that all men should be able to see it and know it. This would be the one thing for which Christians would be known among all peoples: a love of tender and genuine heartfelt affections.

Peter wanted to keep Jesus with him here on earth. But if Jesus were going to depart from the company, he at least desired to go with him. He was disturbed by the remarks made by Jesus and, with uneasiness, asked him, "Lord, where are you going?"

Jesus smiled and answered, "Where I am going, Peter, you cannot follow me now, but you shall follow me afterward."

His work was nearly finished; theirs was just beginning. Only Jesus, as the sinless sacrifice for the trespasses of his chosen people, could go to the cross and die. Only he could be glorified in the presence of the Father with the glory that he possessed before his incarnation.

Being blissfully unaware of his own weaknesses and standing on his own self-reliance, Peter boasted impatiently, "Lord, why can't I follow you right now? I will lay down my life for your sake."

Jesus stared into Peter's eyes for what seemed an eternity and then responded with a question, "Will you really die for my sake, Peter?"

Evidently Jesus's words failed to register with Peter, for the overly confident disciple answered, "Jesus, how can you ask me such a question? You know that I would!"

His self-reliant exclamation was copied by the others, for they all said the same thing however, not a single one among these men that followed the Christ knew his own heart.

Jesus slowly shook his head and replied with heartfelt sadness, "Most assuredly I say to you, Peter, about three hours before daybreak when the rooster crows, you will have denied me three times."

Peter's face sagged as if all muscle control had been lost. The glimmer of life in his eyes vanished. It was replaced by tears. The air in his lungs oozed out slowly as if something had compressed his chest. He protested, he objected, he wanted to vindicate himself. Peter said to Jesus, "Though I should die with you, I will never deny you."

The other disciples added their voices in agreement.

The disciples had become greatly distressed at what Jesus had said about leaving them. Their countenance gave them away. And not unlike a mother who ministers to a child who has been injured or to one that has been lost, Jesus proceeded to administer to them such consolations for which their circumstances called.

The eleven beloved disciples remained virtually motionless as they reclined around the low table in the center of the upper room. It was only a few hours until the agony of Gethsemane and death on the cross. Jesus had broken bread and shared a cup of wine with his beloved disciples. He remained standing and said with such supreme comfort and tenderness in this hour darkened by the shadow of Judas's treachery and Peter's failure, "Let not your hearts be troubled. You believe in God, believe also in me."

What more could he have said? Jesus gave them a statement of tender and beautiful truths of his Gospel, truths fitted to allay every fear, silence every murmur, and give every needed consolation to the soul. What he said was meant to minister to their fears rather than address his own needs at the induction of his passion. Jesus addressed all their unspoken fears, anxieties, and uncertainties with supreme rhetoric, but the fear that gripped these men who loved their Lord so came flooding into their souls unabated. They were about to lose their beloved Master and friend. They were about to be left alone to face their own persecutions, trials, and tribulations. They found themselves without wealth, without outside friends, without any honor. No doubt they felt that their Lord's death would destroy all their plans, for as of yet, they had not fully understood his doctrine of suffering and death.

Seeing the dismay that permeated their very beings, Jesus continued his soothing words by saying, "In my Father's house are many mansions. Don't you know that if it were not so, I would have told you? While the road is narrow and the gate small that leads to life, don't you remember what the books written by Moses say? The number of Abraham's children is like the sand on the shore and the stars in the sky, *a great multitude that no one can number.* My beloved, I go to prepare a place for you. What you must understand, as I have tried so many times to convey to you, is that the universe is the dwelling place of my Father. All is his house. Whether on earth or in heaven, we are still in his habitation. In that vast habitation of God there are many mansions, many dwelling places. This earth is one of them. Heaven is another. Whether we are here or there, we are still in the house, in one of the mansions of the Father, in one of the habitations of his vast abode. This we ought continually to feel and to rejoice that we are permitted to occupy any part of his dwelling place. It really doesn't matter whether we are in this mansion or another. It should not be a matter of grief when we are called to pass from one part of this vast habitation of God's to another. I am indeed about to leave you, but I am only going to another part of the vast dwelling place of God. I will always be in the same universal habitation with you, still in the house of the same God, and am going for an important purpose: to prepare another abode for your eternal dwelling."

What a true comfort! The death of a follower of Christ is not to be dreaded, nor is it an event over which we should weep. The removal of Jesus from the habitation of the earth was going to be an event over which his followers now as in the future should rejoice, for he is still in the house of God and still preparing mansions of rest for his people. The One who is omnipresent, everywhere present in the house of God, is the incarnate Son of man, the Son of God, Jesus the Christ…God.

Jesus had concealed no truth from his disciples. He reminded them that they had been cherishing this hope of a future abode with God and that his death, resurrection, and ascension would guarantee it.

"If I go and prepare a place for you," Jesus said, "I will come again and receive you unto myself, that where I am, there you will be also. I am like a ladder between heaven and earth. I am the

One who will take you to heaven. To go means that I must die first. The work that I perform in heaven secures your admission into heaven and obtains for you the blessings of eternal life. Even though I am about to leave you, I will not always be absent. I will come again and will gather all my friends to myself, and you will ever be with me."

Entertaining the common notion of a temporal kingdom, and supposing still that Jesus was to be an earthly prince and leader, Thomas did not comprehend the reason why he should die. Confessing his ignorance, he asked Jesus, "Lord, we don't know where you are going, and how is it possible that we should know the way?"

It wasn't that Thomas or the others for that matter were ignorant, but it did show the difficulty of believing when the mind is cluttered with prejudice, preconceptions, and contrary opinions. There would have been no difficulty had Thomas laid aside his presuppositions and been willing to receive the truth as Jesus had plainly spoken it.

With an unending compassion, Jesus looked at the disciple who expressed the most doubt and said, "Thomas, I *am* the Way, *and* the Truth, *and* the Life. It is true that I teach the way, guide you in the way, and have dedicated for you a new and living way. But I do not merely show the way, Thomas. Don't you understand that *I am the way?* In every act, word, and attitude, I am the Mediator between God and his elect. You and all others can have access to God only by obeying my instructions, imitating my example, and depending on my merits. I am the Captain of the way, the Guide to those that are lost, the Teacher of those who are misinformed and unknowing, and the Example to all."

Jesus is the Way from God to man, and all divine blessings come down from the Father through the Son. He is also the Way from man to God. Jesus is the very embodiment of truth, truth in person. He is the final reality in contrast with the shadows that preceded him. He is the Truth because he is the dependable source of redemptive revelation, for he reveals the Father.

His truth is a living truth and takes hold of our very lives and influences us with power. It sets us apart, guides us, and sets our spirits free, free from the bondage of sin. But more importantly, he gives us life as opposed to death because he has the life within himself. He is the source and giver of life for his own. Death certainly pronounces separation from God, but life implies communion with Christ.

The way leads to God. The truth makes men free, and the life produces fellowship. Jesus is the Way because he is the Truth and the Life. When he reveals God's redemptive truth, which sets men free from the enslaving power of sin, and when he imparts the seed of life, which produces a relationship with the Father, then he, as the Way that men have chosen by the sovereign grace of God, brings them to the Father.

Jesus continued his discourse with Thomas by saying, "No one comes to the Father except through me."

He is giving a strong affirmation that he alone is the way of salvation. Since men and women are entirely dependent upon Jesus Christ for their information of redemptive truth and also for that ignition that causes that truth to come alive in their souls, it follows that no one comes to the Father but through him. To imagine and proclaim other way is to be misled and to not be cognizant of why he came. With Christ removed from the picture, there can be no redemptive truth, no everlasting life—hence, no way to God.

Then turning round and round with his arms outstretched and his palms up, Jesus said to all his hearers, "If by daily listening to me, pondering my words and works, if by means of this personal day-to-day experience you had learned to know me, you would have gained an insight into the mental reflection, into my Father also. You do not know me as fully as you would have known me had you given closer heed to all my words and admonitions. You have failed too many times to see in me the only and absolute way to the only and absolute prize of the upward call. You have failed in many ways also to see that I am the only Son of God who, because I am the Son, reveals the Father. From now on, you do know him because of these very words, for I have now clearly told you that I myself am the Way to the Father, so that there can be even less excuse for not knowing than there has been before. You have seen the Way with your own eyes, both physically and spiritually."

Not denying God's spirituality and essential invisibility, Philip, the disciple with the Greek name from Bethsaida in Galilee, the one instrumental in bringing Nathaniel to Jesus, the one to whom Jesus before had addressed the question, "How are we to buy bread cakes that all these people may eat?" said to Jesus, "Lord, show us the Father and we shall be content."

He seemed to be asking Jesus for a visible manifestation of the Father's glory, such as had been given to Moses and other believers in the desert. Apparently, he did not recognize that a far greater privilege had been given to him.

Not denying the distinction of persons in God, Jesus rebuked him, "So long a time have I been with you, and yet you have not learned to recognize me, Philip? Have I not revealed this truth again and again to you all from the beginning of my ministry more than three years ago, that the Father has become manifest in the Son? I am the Mediator sent by God and have come to speak the words and perform the works of God, that in these words and works I reveal the Father, and that this manifestation of the Father in me as Mediator rests upon the eternal relationship between the Father and myself, the only begotten Son. How can you say, 'Show us the Father?' Do you not believe that I am in the Father and the Father in me? The Father and the Son do not exist apart as human individuals do but in and through each other as moments in one divine, self-conscious life. The words that I speak to you, I do not speak of myself. The Father who dwells in me is giving me the words. I speak the mind of the Father because this is also my mind. The works of the Father are not limited to the works of the Son but include his miracles and signs. These serve to confirm faith, to strengthen it, to assist it in becoming strong. Believe me when I say that I am in the Father and the Father in me, but if not, believe me because of the works themselves.

"You waver in your faith, a faith that has never been strong. But whatever faith you do have has to be strengthened, especially now, when I am about to leave."

For this reason, Jesus exhorts his disciples, "I most solemnly assure you, you need not fear. He who believes in me and the works that I do will do also, and greater than these will he do, because I am going to the Father."

The very departure of Jesus will benefit the disciples. As a result of his departure, the disciples will perform not only works that Jesus had been doing all along in the physical realm but even greater works, miracles in the spiritual realm, namely conversion of the Gentiles.

Then a smile crossed Jesus's face. "Remember this, men," he said. "Whatever you ask for in my name, both the great works and the greater works I will do, the Father will be glorified in the Son. If you ask anything in my name, I will do it. Men, we will always have this connection. You see, these prayers in my name will be answered because they are not selfish but are in the interest of God's kingdom. They proceed from faith in accordance with God's will. A prayer done in my name will always be in harmony with all that I have revealed concerning myself. When such a prayer is answered, the Father, who has abided forever in me, will do his works in you. Hence, the Father will be glorified in the Son. For your understanding, I say to you that you must pray in my name and to me. I am the One in whose name prayer must be offered. I am the *object* of prayer, and I am the *hearer* of prayer."

Jesus placed his arm around the shoulder of John, the one whom he loved, and announced, "If with the kind of love that is both intelligent and purposeful you love me, you will accept, obey, and stand guard over the rules that I have laid down for the regulation of your inner attitudes and outer conduct."

This very night an hour earlier, Jesus had issued his "new commandment" to his chosen eleven disciples. Similar precepts had already been added: "You believe in God, believe also in me" and "Believe me for the very works' sake." Clearly, Jesus, through his implied precepts, wanted his disciples to keep believing in him, to pray in his name, and to pray to him.

Jesus implied in his statement to his disciples that the precepts must be kept if they were going to be a blessing, and that from a certain aspect, love preceded obedience.

Taking the stance of a pedagogue, Jesus went over to the corner of the upper room and sat down. The eyes of the eleven remained transfixed on him, and from his seated position, Jesus continued his instructions.

"If you keep my precepts, I will intercede to the Father after my death and my return to heaven. And as a result of my intercession in the presenting of and making your prayers efficacious before the Father in heaven, you will obtain all your blessings. He shall then give you another Paraclete, another like me, a Comforter that he may abide with you forever."

Jesus had been to his disciples a counselor, a guide, and a friend while he was with them. He had instructed them, he had put up with their prejudices and ignorance, and he had administered consolation to them in the times that they had been despondent. But he was about to leave them, and they were going to take his message to an unfriendly world. The other Comforter was to come to them as a compensation for his absence so as to teach them, aid them in their work, prepare them for the spiritual battle ahead, and advocate their cause of religion in the world in bringing sinners to repentance. Unlike Jesus who could only remain with them for a short while, the Comforter would remain with them in all places to the close of their lives. Jesus further tells his chosen that the Comforter is the Spirit of Truth whom the world cannot see because the world follows Satan's lies, lacks an organ of spiritual discernment, and fails to acknowledge the Spirit, ascribing the influences of the third person of the Holy Trinity to Beelzebub or to "new wine," who cannot receive him.

"You do know him," Jesus offered, looking from one man to another seated on the floor before him, "because he dwells by your side and will be within you on the day of Pentecost. He will enter personally into the church, that I am establishing, which will become his temple, his permanent dwelling place. The church then will become a nation of prophets, a kingdom of priests, and the body of Christ.

"My departure will not be like that of a father whose children are left orphans when he dies, but in the Spirit, I am myself coming back to you. The Spirit will reveal me, glorify me, apply my merits to the hearts of believers, and make my teachings effective in their lives. Hence when the Comforter is poured out, I return truly in the Spirit.

"I will not be with you much longer, and those that do not know me or love me will see me no more. In order to see me as I carry out my Father's victorious program in the church through the Spirit, one must be fully alive spiritually. You will be able to see and observe me, for you will be alive. You will live because I live, and because I am in my own person the Way, the Truth, and the Life, you will possess the cause of your spiritual life."

Jesus turned to Philip and said, "In that day you will recognize that I am in my Father, and you in me, and I in you."

Philip looked a little embarrassed to have asked to see the Father, but he certainly wasn't alone in his lack of understanding. It was becoming clearer, however, that those that embraced the Christ by living faith would recognize and joyfully acknowledge the closeness of the relationship between the Father and the Son. They would all certainly understand that this union was in turn the pattern for the relationship between Christ and his followers.

There can be no doubt, however, that these two relationships are not identical; there is an absolute unity of *essence,* incapable of growth between God the Father and God the Son. Between the Son and believers, however, there is an *ethical and spiritual unity* which *is* capable of growth. Nonetheless, since Christ, by means of the Spirit, actually lives in the hearts of believers, the relationship between the Father and the Son is a pattern for that relationship between Christ and believers.

The relationship between Christ and believers is so close that while he is the vine, they are the vine branches. He is the Shepherd; they are the sheep. Believers are the body of which he is the head; they are the church of which he is the chief cornerstone.

After the pronouncement aimed primarily at Philip, Jesus resumed the discourse to his followers. "He who joyfully and obediently recognizes my sovereignty, he who has my precepts and keeps them, it is he who loves me. My Father's love precedes your love, and it creates in you the eager desire to keep my precepts. Then by following our love, it rewards you for keeping them. Therefore he who loves me will be loved by my Father, and I too will love him and will manifest myself in him, and in the Spirit, we will come to him and make our home with him."

This presence is very real and can be felt for the Spirit will convict of sin, lead one to repentance, impart the assurance of salvation, bestow the peace of Jesus Christ that surpasses all understanding, admonish, and comfort. This is the way that Jesus has promised to manifest himself to his followers, but not to the world of unbelievers.

Jesus got to his feet at this moment and walked about the room. In spite of the fact that sweat stood in beads on his brow, he folded his arms and rubbed his shoulders as if he felt a chill. There was definitely a sad look on his face, and yet he talked to his disciples about the love that they shared. A contradiction of emotions flooded his soul like the run of melting snow in the springtime. Because of his human nature, the coming of his death haunted him, yet the prospects of finally defeating Satan and conquering death exhilarated him.

Walking over to the one whom he loved, Jesus took hold of John's cloak and pulled the young man to his feet. Placing his arm around his shoulder, he walked about the room step by step with John and said, "He who does not love me does not keep my words. The words, my teaching that you hear are not mine but the Father's who sent me. Remember"—he patted John's shoulders several times—"these things I have told you while still remaining with you physically. Moreover, the Helper, the Holy Spirit whom the Father will send in my name, he will prepare you for battle, for every day in this life is a spiritual battle. He will teach you everything, make all things much clearer to you, and will remind you of everything that I have said to you in order that you can perform the work of witnessing, which is your duty."

They could have left the upper room by now, but Jesus seemed to linger with his men as long as possible. Again and again, he seemed to bid them farewell; nevertheless, again and again, he remained a little longer. There was a sound of departure in his words. "These things I have told you while still remaining with you." Yet he lingered. Jesus presented a distinction between his own teaching during the period of his humiliation and his own teaching through the Spirit in the glory of his exaltation.

After having paced the entire room with his beloved disciple, Jesus removed his arm from around John's shoulder, guided him back to his seat, and held his arms at full length out to his sides. He announced, "Peace, both a legacy and a treasure I leave with you. My peace I give to you, not as the world gives, do I give to you."

The peace that Jesus gave to his disciples implied absence of a troubled heart and fearful feelings. He indicated that meaning when he said to them, "Let not your hearts any longer be troubled, neither let them be fearful. You will have absence of spiritual unrest and will have that assurance of salvation and of God's loving presence under all circumstances, which results from exercising faith in God and in his Son, and from the contemplation of his gracious promises."

Even as Jesus spoke, his disciples became more and more anxious, not calmer. Over and over, Jesus had said to them, "I go away," and, "I am coming to you." If they had advanced more in their love for their Lord, they would not have been filled with such doubts. They would have been filled with joy over the fact that Jesus was going home to be with the Father. As a reward for his work, the Man of sorrows, who was acquainted with grief, was ready to return to the One who was greater than himself, for God is ever greater than man. Jesus himself, as a man and mediator between God and man, was inferior.

Peter squirmed. James kept clearing his throat. Nathaniel got to his feet and walked to the other side of the room opposite the others. The words Jesus spoke that were meant to comfort had the opposite effect. They all wanted to interrupt and offer many questions, but honestly, there was nothing they felt comfortable in asking.

Picking up on their distress, Jesus said, "You have heard me say to you, 'I go away and am coming to you. If you loved me, you would have rejoiced that I am going to the Father, for the Father is greater than I.' I have told you before about these things happening, so when it does happen, you may believe and experience no fear."

Aware of the footsteps of Judas and the Roman soldiers, temple police, and members of the Sanhedrin (all inspired by Satan) making their way even then with swords and sticks, with lanterns and torches—as if their object were to search out and catch a dangerous criminal at large—Jesus said as a man with a broken heart, "No longer will I discuss many things with you for the prince of this world is coming, and yet he will find no guilt in me."

Much had transpired that evening. The Lord and his disciples had been in the upper room for several hours. He had washed the disciples' feet, they had eaten the Passover supper, Judas's betrayal had been predicted, the denial by Peter had been pronounced, the institution of the Lord's Supper had been launched, and the prediction that all of them would abandon him had been foretold.

Now the time of departure from the upper room had almost arrived, but Jesus had indicated that he had a few things yet to discuss with them, whether here or on the way to Gethsemane.

Implying that he would not resist his capture but go forth boldly to meet Satan's representatives and lay down his life voluntarily, Jesus announced, "In order that the world may know that I love the Father, even so I do as the Father has commanded me."

Even though they would never admit it, deep down in their hearts, these wicked men who sought Jesus's life would know that his behavior, though uncommon and strange, walking with boldness into the hands of those that hated him and for what he stood, would see that he loved the Father.

In keeping with the harmony of his expressed determination to meet the foe, Jesus pointed to those still seated on the floor and said, "Get up and let us go now."

The men rose from their reclined positions, but Jesus had more to say to them before they actually departed from the room in which they had spent the last several hours together in fellowship.

Jesus started for the door, stopped, and turned to face his beloved followers. It came to him that before his trial and crucifixion, this would be the last opportunity he would have to warn his disciples not to be like Judas but to remain steadfast in the faith, to manifest in their lives the fruits of the Holy Spirit, and to remind them that the fertility of the vine suggested spiritual fruit-bearing. Jesus leaned over and picked up the half-empty cup of wine from the table and spoke this allegory to his men, "You know, my dear friends, that I am the true vine, and my blood is the true wine that gives strength to the soul. My Father is the vinedresser. He has the care of the vineyard. He nurtures, trims, and defends the vine and of course takes great interest in its growth and welfare."

Jesus spoke in hushed tones. His breathing had become labored, and his pulse rate had increased. The blood that coursed through the veins in his neck and through those on his scalp pulsated visibly. He swallowed repeatedly to quiet the raging nausea in his stomach, and he rubbed the palms of his hands together like someone trying to keep warm. The skin on his forearms had begun to itch from frayed nerves, and he had begun to scratch them vigorously.

Rubbing his eyes as if trying to ward off sleep, Jesus said, "Every branch in me that bears no fruit my Father takes away. Every branch that does bear fruit he cleanses in order that it may bear more fruit. By faith in my word, you have already become clean because of the word that I have spoken to you. In the continuing process of bringing hearts to salvation, his Spirit invades the heart of the sinner who receives power to abide in me. The more you abide in me, the more you will experience my loving presence."

Jesus is making it ever so clear that salvation is clearly sovereign grace from start to finish; however, the responsibility of remaining in Christ is placed squarely upon the shoulders of man himself, the very place it belongs. Without response, there is no salvation. Albeit the power to act and to persevere is given by God. It is certain that when a man is truly saved by the grace of God, he maintains that salvation forever, yet God requires that man to keep on the way of salvation by his own exertion, diligence, and watchfulness.

"One cannot enter the kingdom of God without being born again from above. One who is in the kingdom cannot bear fruit without remaining attached to the vine as a branch that has been severed from the vine can bring forth no fruit. He who remains in me produces not only fruit, but much more fruit. On the other hand, those who are out of relationship with me can do virtually nothing. I have spoken these things to you that my joy may be in you, that your joy may be complete.

"Above all, keep on loving one another as I have loved you. I want you to continue to love one another with that same kind of love that I exercise when I lay down my life for all those who are truly my friends. There is no greater love than when a man lays down his life for his friends. By constantly doing my will, you obtain for yourselves the assurance that you are my friends, that is, that you will abide in my love.

"I no longer call you servants, but friends. When a superior tells his servants to do this or that, he does not give them the reason why, but with a friend, the case is different. A friend is a confidant. The task that a servant must perform for his master is often arduous, but my yoke that you have had laid upon you is easy, the burden is light."

Clearly, Jesus was telling his disciples that he was not satisfied with mere servile obedience, but his friends would be motivated by friendship when they did his bidding. Obedience would be a clear manifestation of their love.

Jesus continued with his oration. "I expressed the free, independent, spontaneous character of my love when I chose you, for you did not choose me. As the Torah says, 'Jehovah did not set his love upon you nor choose you because you were so numerous, for you were the fewest of all peoples, but because he loved you.' My Father elected you out of a world of darkness in order that you might be my followers and as such bear fruit, not merely for a period of time then stop but continuously and abidingly. Unto that purpose, you have been appointed and set apart from the world. God has given his Spirit to give you the qualifications, talents, and tools you need.

"Abiding in me is rewarded by fruit-bearing, and not only by fruit-bearing but also by answered prayer. A true disciple prays for fruits, for these fruits are pleasing to my Father. Whatsoever you ask in the Father's will and in my name, he will give it to you. I bid you to do these things in order that you may keep on loving one another."

Jesus's logic here is simple. In myself, I may see myself unlovable and be unable to love my brother, who (in my eyes) is also unlovable; but if I constantly reflect and remain in the love of Christ, all things are possible. We love him because he first loved us, and we will love one another because he first loved us. Loving one another is merely an extension of Christ's love that is shed abroad in our hearts so overwhelmingly that that love overflows into the lives of others.

Still looking like one that was in distress, Jesus changed the subject somewhat to comfort his disciples further. He said, "Remember this: if the world hates you, know that it has hated me before it hated you. Bear in mind that you are in excellent company. When people show hatred to you because you profess me, this shows that you belong to me, and that this hatred that has been present from the very beginning of my public ministry I have experienced all along. If your spirituality was of this world, the world would have affection for you for it loves its own kind. But you are not of this world, the reason not lying in you, but because out of the world of darkness, you were elected for me. Remember the word that I spoke to you: a servant is no better or greater than his master. You must not consider yourself immune to persecution. If they persecuted me, they will also persecute you. Also, those who keep my word, they will invariably keep yours as well. The fact is that the world will treat you like it has treated me. Therefore, don't be surprised when they will do all these things to you for my name's sake because they do not know the One who sent me.

"If I had not come and spoken to the people of the ancient covenant, they could have never been guilty of the great sin of rejecting me, the Son of God. But now they have no excuse for their sin. They know better. He who hates me hates my Father. I tell you the truth, the Jews may claim God as their Father, but they claim me to be demon possessed. They claim to love the Father while they hate the Son. Remember, men, the Father and the Son is one in essence, therefore, such an attitude is impossible. A person may think that he loves the Father while at the same time he hates the Son, but that person deceives himself. For whoever hates the one by necessity hates the other. They have seen the miracles that I have done and have both hated me and my Father. They do not recognize the evidential value of them. Therefore, their hatred is inexcusable. But all this happened in order that the word written in their law might be fulfilled. It is obvious that they have hated me without a cause. Regardless, God is fulfilling his plan of redemption. The hatred that these people show toward me, the Son of God, must end in my crucifixion, in order that his people might be saved. I say to you that the eternal decree is being fulfilled before your very eyes and in such a manner that the guilt must rest on man, not on God.

"When the Helper comes, whom I will send to you from the Father, even the Spirit of Truth which proceeds from the Father, in the midst of the wicked world, he will testify against the world and at the same time testify of me. Whenever you bear witness against the world, your witness will be the work of the Spirit. Whenever you, by word and example, draw others to me, this too will be the work of the Spirit. By and large, the world is hostile to me and therefore will not receive the Helper, namely the Holy Spirit. Nevertheless, from among those who are openly hostile, some will be drawn by the Father. They will leave the kingdom of darkness to live in the kingdom of everlasting light. Since you have been with me from the beginning, you must continue to testify of me regarding the things that you have seen."

Jesus could see that his chosen ones appeared like people who were in a state of shock. The look upon their collective faces revealed concern, fear, weariness, uncertainty, and confusion. Peter, who usually had something to say, was speechless. He motioned with his hands several times as if to have a lead-in to some statement, but no words came forth. John looked as if he had lost his only friend in the world. Each man garnered enough strength to look one to another for answers, but the only answer stood right there before them. This man, this God incarnate, this Teacher-Friend had all the answers. All they had to do was to listen and obey.

Seeing how perplexed they were, Jesus said, "These things, the things pertaining to the hatred that you will experience from the side of the world, I have spoken to you in order that you should not be caught unawares. In order to prevent the grievous disappointment, which would tend to undermine your faith, I tell you all these things ahead of their occurrence. Thus you will know that my departure and the hatred of the world were included in God's plan for your progress in salvation.

"The hatred of the Jewish leaders will be so fierce upon you that they will expel you from the synagogues. You will be cut off from their hopes and prerogatives, and you will be considered by your former friends as worse than pagans. Your worst enemies will be those people in your own households. They will even deny you the privilege of an honorable burial. Worse still, they will actually kill you and consider what they have done as a meritorious act, thinking that their deed was offered in the service of God."

From the time of their youth, Jews had been taught that there is only one true God and that they should worship him only. But Jesus claimed to be God as well. The Jews therefore considered recognizing Jesus as God or equal with God as blasphemy, punishable by death. They were convinced that they ought to do many things contrary to the name of Jesus of Nazareth. And certainly, the value of this was considered a dogma among the people of Israel: "Whoever sheds the blood of the wicked is equal to one who brings a sacrifice."

The hostile Jews had created their own God, different from the One of the Torah. The true God that was revealed in Jesus the Christ they did not serve. In spite of all the signs, they refused to acknowledge both the Sender and the Sent. There is no doubt that when one rejects the Son, he rejects the Father as well, and of course the opposite is true.

The time had arrived when there could be no further delay. Jesus left the upper room with his eleven faithful disciples following in his shadow. Feeling the conviction of Jesus's sermon on being a servant, Peter was the last to leave the room. Holding the door for all to leave, he pulled the heavy wooden door closed behind him and knew down deep inside that after this night nothing would ever be the same.

⋄⇌⇋⋄

It was springtime. The shepherds had returned to the fields where their sheep grazed lazily in the fields, and the people stayed out in the streets talking and walking to a much later hour. The spirit of the people had become excited during the Passover week at the advent of the Messiah. He had entered the city riding on a donkey, an event that had been prophesied for hundreds of years. In spite of the high the people were experiencing, things were not right. Satan was afoot and, at this very moment, was directing Judas to do his dirty deed of betrayal. Even as the door to the upper room came to rest against the jambs, Judas was in the midst of the Sanhedrin, collecting his thirty pieces of silver and receiving his instructions on how he should identify Jesus with a kiss.

Springtime or not, the night air was eerily chilly. The breeze that came up from the valley below was crisp, and it sent chills clear to the bones of the disciples as they tried to keep pace with their beloved Teacher. The moon had wrapped itself in a mask of clouds like some participant in a masquerade. Outside the Horse Gate of the eastern wall of the city, between Jerusalem and the Garden of Gethsemane, lay the Kidron Valley, which on this night spread over itself a thick blanket of fog that protected the modesty of the small creek that passed through it.

Destiny loomed ahead, preordained souls waited for their redemption, and Satan yearned for his victory. God was in his heaven, but all was not right with the world. The script had been written, the players had taken their positions on the stage, and Jesus, with sweat on his brow, experienced some kind of unfamiliar nausea at the prospects of giving his life for a people that seemingly did not care. But the people for whom he was about to sacrifice his life, a humanity that had been set aside as a love gift from the foundation of the world, a humanity that awaited the ultimate act that would ever be acted out, moved about the city like nothing was out of the ordinary. However, there was about to take place a scene that would forevermore change the course of history, forevermore change the face of mankind.

"Hurry, Mary, They Have Arrested Jesus"

I HAD STAYED for the last couple of weeks with Andrew's sister in the heart of Jerusalem. I wanted to stay close to the heart of what was taking place and yet at the same time be far enough away from Jesus that I would not be hurt again by his lack of attention. I just didn't understand his position! On the one hand, he said he loved me, but the love he mentioned was always some "agape, sacrificial" love of the Father. Ever since that day when I ran into him in the city of Magdala, I had loved him with a love that I personally felt was an enduring love, an everlasting love, a love that burned its way from the bosom of one person into the other.

I lay awake for hours on my mat trying to figure out what in the world it was that I had done wrong. This man Jesus, whom they call the Christ, had captured my heart and my desires. He had placed in my stomach a sickening longing that I could neither overcome nor forget nor pretend never existed.

"Oh, my God! My heart aches so! Can't you do something?" I begged. "I love this man who claims to be your Son! I love him so, and yet I don't know how to love him at all."

I got up from my bed and ventured outside into the night, hoping to receive some revelation. The air was brisk. I pulled my cloak tight around my neck and hugged my own shoulders tightly to stay warm. I gazed up into the sky overhead to see the billions upon billions of stars that hung suspended from the black canopy. The words of Yahweh came rushing into my head: "And I will make thy seed as the dust of the earth. Look now toward heaven and count the stars. If you are able to number them, so shall your seed be."

Andrew's sister was awake as well. She came up behind me and put her tiny hand upon my shoulder and asked, "Mary, you can't sleep either?"

"No," I responded. "This Jesus has me tied up in knots."

She laughed and said, "I understand that is true of everyone with whom he comes in contact."

"Well, I can tell you one thing, Anna," I responded. "He may think he can overwhelm everyone, but that does not include me! You know I just hate him! I hate him I tell you! How dare he take me for granted! Who does he think he is anyway?"

I dropped to my knees and cried like some spoiled child whose plans had been frustrated. I threw my head back, thrust my hands toward heaven, and screamed, "All my life! All my life I have waited for a prince to come to my rescue! Oh, where is that prince tonight? Is there no one for me?"

At this point, I could say no more. I simply cried until there were no more tears, until my head became so clogged that I could no longer breathe, until my heart ached so that I thought I would die.

Anna knelt down beside me and put her arm around my shoulder. She twisted and twirled the ringlets of my hair with her other hand. Whispering in my ear, she said softly, "Scheee, don't cry so! Things will work out, you'll see. Everything will be all right. Scheee! Just let it go, Mary. Please, just let it go."

Somehow, her soothing voice did calm me somewhat, or perhaps I was just about cried out! My nose was running, my eyes were stinging, my shoulders were heaving up and down, and all was not right with the world.

Anna got to her feet and pulled me to mine and said, "Mary, we need to go to bed and try to get some sleep. Who knows, Jesus may send for you in the morning. All this moaning and groaning will have been for nothing."

"How can you say that, Anna?" I asked, "You lost your husband, and Andrew said that you cried and wouldn't eat for days on end."

Anna cut me a terse look and replied, "Don't you even compare losing a husband with never getting the one you want! There is no comparison!"

I capped my hand over my mouth and said, "Forgive me, Anna. Of course you are right. I would never presume that they were even close to being comparable. I know the heartache that I feel can only be a fraction of what you must have felt when Cleo died. All I'm saying is that it really does hurt."

The ice in Anna's eyes melted. She took both my hands in hers and said, "I'm sorry to have reacted the way I did. Of course your pain is great. It's just that…it hasn't been that long and I miss him so!"

"I'm so sorry, Anna," I replied. I put my arms around her shoulders and walked her back into the house. We removed our outer garments and lay down on straw mats that had been placed side by side on the floor.

After having said good night to each other, we lay there on our mats, staring at the ceiling, counting the hours until the rooster would crow.

After what had seemed hours, someone came to the front door and pounded on it. A man's voice screamed, "Anna, Mary, open the door! Open the door, it's me, John!"

As quickly as possible, Anna and I covered ourselves and ran to open the door. Anna yanked it open. John fell forward inside onto his knees. His face was red, and the cloak he wore was soaked through and through. Gasping for each and every breath, John snorted, "They've…they've arrested…they've taken…Jesus!"

"John, slow down. Try to get your breath!" I admonished.

He remained on all fours for a couple of minutes, pushing his torso down toward the floor and then arching it upward, taking in volumes of air to alleviate the wheezing and burning sensation in his lungs.

Finally, John was able to speak clearly; however, he babbled so that he ran all his words together.

Again, I admonished him, "John, slow down and tell us what has happened!"

Without waiting for him to begin again, Anna grabbed his face, turned it toward her, and asked, "John, has something happened to Jesus?"

John could see the fear-stricken look on my face. He took both Anna's and my hands into his and said very slowly, "They have arrested Jesus!"

I was struck dumb for the moment, but Anna blurted out, "What? They have arrested Jesus? Who has arrested him, and why?"

Before John could answer, I answered for him, "The Pharisees! Because he just would not leave them alone. I told him that this would happen, but he just would not listen! He kept right on pushing and challenging them and claiming to be the Son of God until…I told him!"

"Enough!" John shouted. "Now's not the time to be judgmental or to point fingers!"

Anna interrupted us and asked, "What happened, John?"

"Jesus had just prayed a farewell prayer for us," he replied. "I did not understand all that he said, but it was beautiful! He asked the Father to keep us during that time when he could not, for that short while when we were going to be out of his protection. He asked God to sanctify us through his truth before sending us out into the world like he had sent him into the world. And he asked the Father to love us as he had always loved him and as he himself loved us."

John looked first at me and then at Anna and said, "I speak the truth. His prayer made the hairs on my arms and on the back of my neck stand on end."

"Then what happened?" I asked impatiently.

"Well," John continued, "when we had sung a hymn, we left the upper room where we had just celebrated Passover and the ordinances of the bread and the cup that Jesus had just given to us."

"What are those?" Anna asked.

"Never mind that now," John answered. "We went out through the Horse Gate, crossed the Kidron brook that is running red and thick with the blood of all the animals that were sacrificed today and went up the Mount of Olives into the Garden of Gethsemane. Jesus told us to sit down and rest. He was going a stone's throw farther to pray. But after we had all sat down, it was as if he had changed his mind and said to Peter, my brother, and me, 'I want you three to go with me.'

"Then it became somewhat mysterious. His whole attitude changed to the dark and gloomy side and he said to us, 'My soul is exceedingly sorrowful, even unto death. Please stay with me and watch with me.'

"Well, the three of us said, 'Of course, Lord, whatever you ask!'

"Then he went a little ways beyond us and fell down prostrate upon the ground and started praying. We could just barely hear what he was saying, 'Abba, Father, all things are possible unto you. If it be possible, let this cup pass from me. Nevertheless, not what I will but what you will.'

"He must have remained down like that for some time, for when he returned to us—and I'm ashamed to say—he found the three of us asleep. He woke us up and rebuked us saying, 'What! You couldn't watch with me for a mere hour?' Then he said to us, 'Watch and pray, lest you enter into temptation. I know that your spirits are ready, but your flesh is weak.'

"He again left us to go and pray, and I at least heard him say, 'O my Father, if this cup may not pass away from me, except I drink it, your will be done.'

"He said this the last time he prayed, but this time it's like his emphasis changed. Before he had emphasized that he would like for what he had to do be taken away from him, but now he stressed that his Father's will be done."

John stopped talking for a moment, as if he were reflecting on what he had just said. He squinted his eyes and furrowed his brow and said, "I tell you both, it's like Jesus, by his own very painful and distressing experience, was fully understanding what it meant to be obedient and was intent on revealing this obedience to us in a progressively glorious manner.

"Somewhere between those last words and when he came again to arouse us, he said that he had come a second time and that we were fast asleep, so he returned to his prayers and left us alone. Then he said to us, 'I let you sleep because you needed the rest, but it is enough. The hour has come when the Son of man will be betrayed into the hands of sinners.' Then he said, 'Get up. Let us be going, for lo, the one that betrays me is close by.'

"Even as he spoke, Judas came with a great number of palace soldiers that included men from the chief priests and elders of the people, all with lanterns and torches, with their swords and staves drawn."

"Wait," I interrupted. "Judas who was leading them?"

"Judas Iscariot," John answered.

"Judas Iscariot!" I said bewildered. "How can that be? I thought he was with you and the others."

"Well, he was," John replied, "but before Jesus instituted the ordinance of the bread and the cup in the upper room, he said one of us would betray him. Since I was seated right beside Jesus, Peter, who was seated across the table from us, mouthed to me to ask Jesus who it was that would betray him. So I leaned back against Jesus's chest and asked him. Jesus replied, 'The person to whom he handed the first bread dipped in bitter herbs.' Jesus handed it to Judas and said, 'Do quickly what you have to do!'

"Judas took the sop and ate it. He got up and brushed right past Jesus as he exited the room. I guess I must have been naïve or didn't want to believe it. I just couldn't imagine that Jesus meant that Judas was really going to turn his back on him and us. I suppose the rest of the disciples thought that Judas was leaving to give some of our money to the poor or buy what we needed for tomorrow, because no one said a word about his departure or any more about someone being a traitor. It's as if the very thought of it passed from our minds."

"Then what happened, John?" I asked.

"I think Judas must have made a bargain with the Sanhedrin not only to identify Jesus, but was being paid to do it. The way he acted, I think he must have said that the one whom he kissed on the cheek would be the one they wanted.

"As soon as Jesus saw Judas coming with his throng of followers, he went before us and stood his ground. Judas said, 'Master, Master,' and leaned into Jesus and kissed him on both cheeks.

"Jesus looked Judas coldly in the eyes and, without even flinching, said to him, 'Judas, do you betray the Son of man with a kiss?'

"Judas didn't answer Jesus. He stepped to the side, and Jesus asked those that followed him, 'Whom do you seek?'

"They answered, 'Jesus of Nazareth.'

"Jesus responded, 'I am he.'

"As soon as he had said, 'I am he,' they stumbled around as if drunk on wine and fell to the ground on their faces."

"They did what?" Anna asked.

"They fell down and, for a minute, were like dead men. Those from the chief priest screamed at the men on the ground to get to their feet and take Jesus. But Jesus asked them again, 'Whom do you seek?'

"Again, they answered, 'Jesus of Nazareth.'

"Jesus said to them, 'I have told you that I am he.' But this time they remained standing. He then said to them, 'If you seek me, let these men go their way.'

"Several of us standing nearest to Jesus said to him, 'Lord, shall we smite them with the sword?'

"I think we knew his answer would be no, because of what he had been teaching us. But Simon Peter, who reacts without counting the cost, drew his short sword from underneath his cloak and smote a servant to the high priest, a man called Malchus, cutting off his right ear. Like a cat, Jesus quickly placed himself between the soldiers and Peter. He pushed Peter's sword down with his hand, and said, 'Put away your sword, Peter. Shall I not drink the cup which the Father has given me to drink?'"

"Then what happened?" I implored.

"An amazing thing happened," John responded. "Jesus reached over and touched the bleeding head of the man whose ear had been cut off and healed him instantly. There was no trace of a wound. The man was made whole again. However, that had absolutely no effect on those who had come to arrest him!

"Jesus turned to address the chief priests, the captains of the temple, and the elders who had all come out to collect him, and said, 'Do you come out at night as against a thief, with swords and staves? When I was among you daily in the temple, you stretched forth no hand against me. So we can say that this is your hour. Let us not forget, it is also the hour of the power of darkness.'

"Then the band, the captains, and the officers of the Jews took Jesus, bound him, and took him first to Annas. But I heard that he was going to send Jesus to his son-in-law, Caiaphas, the high priest."

"Why are they taking Jesus to the high priest and the members of the Sanhedrin at two hours before daybreak?" I asked. "Are they planning to do away with Jesus under the cover of darkness?"

"That is why I came for you, Mary," John said. "That is why I came for you. I thought you might want to put aside your personal hurt and come with me to Caiaphas."

"I don't know if I should or if I really want to," I said angrily. "You know, John, Jesus ignored my feelings for him totally. Why should I go to him now?"

"I hate to say this, Mary," John answered, "but this is not the time to be thinking of yourself. This is serious! He has been saying that he came to die and this may be it."

I stood there frozen like a limestone stalagmite on the floor of a cave. I didn't know quite what to do. I loved this man so, but he would not return that love or, for that matter, listen to my warnings. My heart ached for him and at the same time ached because he rejected me. "All right, John," I answered. "I'm coming, not as much for him as for you and the others."

"Hurry then, Mary!" John exclaimed.

He held the door for me, and we were off running through the dark streets of Jerusalem like wild animals. I must admit it made me feel very uncomfortable running through dark alleyways again like I had once done.

Running for the Cross

ABOUT AN HOUR before daybreak, we got to the courtyard of the palace of Caiaphas. John knew the young man who kept the door to the palace. He spoke to him briefly out of earshot of the guards about allowing us to go inside the gate to the courtyard. He hesitated but then opened the gate for us to enter.

We warmed ourselves by a fire kindled with coals glowing red in the midst of the hall while we waited for some word that might be forthcoming. John looked up from rubbing his hands together over the open flames and noticed that Peter was crouching against the wall outside the entrance gate.

He whispered to me, "There's Peter! I don't think they will let him in. I'm going over to see what I can do."

"Okay," I said softly, "but please be careful."

"Don't worry, Mary," John answered. "I'll be right back."

John walked over to the young man who was the keeper of the gate and asked him if he could be let outside for just a minute or two. Evidently, it would not be a problem; John went out the gate to Peter. From where I stood, I could see them discussing something, and in a few moments, John returned with Peter. He had evidently persuaded the keeper of the gate to let Peter come inside with him.

As Peter passed by a damsel who stood talking to the gatekeeper, she asked him, "Are you not also one of the arrested man's disciples?"

Peter never turned his face toward her but answered over his shoulder, "I am not one of his!"

John flashed him a questioning look but never said a word. They both came back to the fire where I stood. John asked Peter where the others were, but Peter mumbled that he had no idea. He said that he had followed Jesus and the soldiers to this place.

There were other servants and soldiers of lesser rank standing by the fire, warming their hands as well. One of them said to Peter, "Are you not one of his disciples?"

Peter looked squarely in the man's face and growled, "I am not!"

A servant door to the palace opened, and one of the servant girls came out to tell her friends what she had heard inside the chamber where the Galilean man was being questioned.

"Tell us what's happening?" the other servants said to the maid as she approached them.

"Well," she answers, "Caiaphas has assembled all the chief priests and the elders and the scribes. The chief priests and all the council are asking if anyone can be a witness against the Galilean, this man from Nazareth, so they can put him to death. But so far, they have found none. It seems as though the testimony of the witnesses are false, for their witness against him does not agree."

"That's it? They can't find anyone to testify against him?" another asked.

"No, no!" the maid responded. "As far as I can tell, all of them are telling lies. There's this one witness who came forward and said, 'We heard him say, "I will destroy this temple that is made with hands, and within three days, I will build another made without hands.'" But none of the witnesses agree with one another. So then the high priest stands up and asked this Jesus, 'Do you answer nothing? What do you say to these witnesses against you?' But this prophet from Galilee held his peace and said not a word. By this time, Caiaphas was becoming a little perturbed. He snapped at Jesus, 'Are you the Christ, the Son of the Blessed?'

"This time Jesus answered and said, 'I Am. You shall see the Son of man sitting on the right hand of power and coming in the clouds of heaven.'

"Can you believe he used the divine title for himself that Daniel used for the Messiah in the Torah?" the maid queried.

"Then Caiaphas tore his mantel and said, 'Why do we need any further witnesses? I told you that it was expedient that one man should die for the people. You have heard his blasphemy! What think you?'

"Everyone in the chamber started shouting, 'Put him to death! Put him to death!' Some began to spit on him, to cover his face with pieces of cloth, and to strike him on the head and shoulders with reeds. They made fun of him, asking, 'Prophesy, tell us who is it that hits you?' And then they would slap him with open palms."

While we had been eavesdropping on the maid's report, another man came close to warm his hands and said to Peter, "Surely you are one of them, you sound like a Galilean. Your accent is from there."

To our horror, Peter began to curse and to swear, saying, "Damn you! I do not know this man of whom you speak! I would not follow such a one!"

Before the venomous words had cleared his lips, the cock crowed, and Peter recalled what Jesus had said to him, "Before the cock crows, you shall have denied me three times."

Suddenly, the great doors to the palace flung open, and Jesus, bound hand and foot, was brought out. Crusted areas of blood were in his hairline where handfuls of hair had forcefully been yanked out. There was a purplish swelling starting to rise under his left eye, and his garments were soiled from the spittle that had been mixed with dirt from the floor. Because his feet had been bound together, Jesus had to shuffle his feet and was unable to move as fast as they wanted him to.

He passed by us just a couple of feet away. The last and final denial had just left Peter's lips. He stood there being forced to stare directly into the eyes of Jesus, the one he had been given special revelation by God to proclaim that Jesus is the Son of God, the Messiah. Peter's neck became so frozen in place that he was unable to turn his head, and his eyes became so fixed that he was unable to close them. Tears welled up in his eyes as he met the fixed gaze of his Lord. Peter wanted to break and run, but the question is, Where can one hide from the all-seeing eyes of the Lord?

Peter or James or John could not stay awake, stand watch, and pray with Jesus for the short time that he had asked them; neither would they stand with him while he was being brought to the place where he would have to drink the cup.

The first man, Adam, was created from dust. Dust over time with wind and water will form a rock. Simon had been given the name Peter, meaning "rock," by Jesus after he had made the great confession that Jesus was the Christ, the Son of the living God. But now the rock had just crumbled back into dust. Peter slumped right before our very eyes into a clump of base humanity, sobbing for all he was worth.

Jesus was led by the palace guards out the front gate of the palace compound. We stood motionless for a time, not wanting to draw attention to ourselves. My throat went completely dry, and my tongue clung to the roof of my mouth. For the first time the chill of the night air got to me. I started to shake a little at first and then I shook violently. John ignored me as if in a trance. He leaned forward and touched Peter's shoulder and started to say something that would console him, but the moment Peter felt the warmth of John's hand on his shoulder, he jerked away. He sprung to his feet, stared at us with empty hollow eyes, and ran out the gate into the darkness. We could hear him screaming as he ran away, "What have I done to my Lord? He knows me too well! Oh, woe is me! I am undone!" And he was gone.

I grabbed the arm of one of the guards who led Jesus out and asked him, "Where are you taking the Galilean?"

He looked at me sternly for having touched him but replied, "This Man was condemned to death by the Sanhedrin, but they don't have the authority to put him to death, so they are taking him to Pilate, the governor." He wrenched his arm out of my grasp and hurried to catch up with the others.

John looked at me desperately and said, "We must follow them, Mary. Quick! Let's go to the governor's house."

I just stood there. My feet were attached to the ground as firmly as a planted tree. The courtyard and everyone in it were spinning around me. Stars overhead were being sucked into a vortex that left a black canopy over my head. I started to enter a void that would take me far away from here, but I felt my arm being tugged at voraciously. John kept shaking me and yelling at me, "Mary, Mary! Wake up! We have to hurry!"

"I don't want to," I exclaimed. "I can't do this anymore. They are going to kill him, and there's nothing I can do to stop it. He wouldn't listen to me, he wouldn't love me."

"You can't mean that, Mary," John barked. "Jesus loves you more than you could ever imagine! You just don't understand!"

"Oh, you're right about that, John," I shot back. "I've done everything short of throwing myself at him. I could not have been more obvious about my love for him, but he was all about you and the other disciples. Since you are the ones that are important to him, you go."

I dropped to my knees and started to cry uncontrollably. My heart was breaking. The Pharisees and Sadducees were going to kill Jesus. The man who saved me from evil spirits, the man who claims to have saved me for eternity, the man whom I loved so very much, I would never be able to see or talk to again.

John reached down and pulled me to my feet, put his arms around me, and held me firmly against him. He kept saying softly to me, "Don't cry. Please don't cry. Mary, you don't understand now, but you will, I promise. By and by you will understand. You may not think that you ever want to see Jesus again, but believe me, you will never forgive yourself if you don't come with me to the governor's palace."

Holding back more tears from cascading down my face, I reluctantly agreed to go with John.

When we arrived at the gate of the governor's palace, Jesus had already been taken inside to face Pilate. One of the guards at the gate who had heard Jesus preach the sermon on the Mount and who was sympathetic to his cause told us when we arrived at the palace that we could not be admitted, but he would keep us apprised of what was happening.

The events inside were relayed by way of a series of servants and guards to the guard at the gate and then to us. First he reported, "Jesus is standing before the governor, and the governor has just asked him, 'Why have you been brought to me before I have finished my sleep? What have you done?'

"The chief priests and elders are answering the governor, making their accusations against the Galilean. They are saying, 'We found this fellow perverting the nation and forbidding anyone to give tribute to Caesar, saying that he himself is the Christ, a king!'"

"Well, what did he say?" I implored impatiently.

"Be still," answered the guard. "I'll tell you when I know."

Offended, I pulled my head back in resentment. "We're just anxious to know what they're doing," I replied with indignation.

"Jesus spoke not a word as to their charges, so Pilate has asked him, 'Do you hear how many things they witness against you? *Are you the king of the Jews?*'

"Jesus has again said nothing. Pilate looks astonished. He turns to face Jesus's accusers and says, 'I find no fault in this man. Take him and judge him according to your law.'

"Now they are frantically complaining that he stirs up the people and teaches throughout all Jewry, beginning from Galilee to this place. They are saying that it is not lawful for *them* to put a man to death.

"Pilate has just given them an unconcerned look. He's returning to the judgment hall. He's called for Jesus to be brought before him again. He is asking Jesus a second time, 'Are you the king of the Jews?'

"Jesus finally says something to Pilate very strange. 'Do you ask this question on your own, or have others told you about me?'

"That's not the wisest thing he could have said to the Roman governor! Now Pilate looks angry and screams at Jesus, 'Am I a Jew? Your own nation and the chief priests have delivered you to me. Just what have you done anyway?'

"Jesus turns to face Pilate as he walks around him and says, 'My kingdom is not of this world.'

"My kingdom is not of this world," mimicked Pilate. "What does that mean?"

The guard gets more information and continues, "The Galilean continues, 'If my kingdom were of this world, then would my servants fight that I might not be delivered to the Jewish leaders and those they cater to. But that's not a problem since my kingdom is not here.'

"Pilate has stopped pacing. He has stopped right in front of Jesus. He asked Jesus, 'Are you a king then?'

"Jesus answers him, 'You say that I am a king. To this end was I born, and for this cause I came into the world that I should bear witness unto the truth. Everyone that is of the truth hears my voice.'

"That seemed to have gotten Pilate's attention! He's got his nose right in Jesus's face and is yelling, 'What is truth, Jesus? Would you recognize it if you saw it?'

"He's coming out again to the Jews."

"He's coming out again?" John asked.

"Yeah, yeah!' the guard replied. "The Jews won't go inside his chambers because it would defile them, and they wouldn't be able to partake of Passover."

"Of course," John said. "What are they doing now?"

The guard smiled and answered, "Pilate has said to the chief priests and the Pharisees and the scribes, 'I find in him no fault at all. Besides, isn't this man a Galilean?'

"One of the chief priests answered, 'Yes, but…'"

The guard laughed a hardy laugh and answered our questioning looks. "Pilate screamed at the chief priest who admitted that Jesus was indeed a Galilean and told him that Jesus belonged under Herod's jurisdiction and to get him out of his hall. 'Herod is in town for your Passover,' Pilate has just said. 'Take this Galilean to him.'"

The door to the hall of Pilate's palace burst open and out marched the entourage with Jesus in tow. They were now on their way to the palace of King Herod. We thanked the guard for keeping us informed and fell in behind the procession. Beams of morning sun exploded into our eyes as the Sanhedrin guards, the chief priests, the Pharisees, and the scribes dragged Jesus to Herod's palace and into his presence. We waited outside the great doors that were left slightly ajar by the guards so they could hear what was going on inside.

When Herod saw Jesus, he was as excited as a child with a new toy. Jesus was still bound hand and foot. He stood staring down at the floor. "I'm so excited to see you, Jesus," Herod said. "I have desired to meet you for such a long time. I have heard so many marvelous things about you. Do something miraculous for me, Jesus. Perform some of your miracles for me. Do something, Jesus!" He pointed to a silver bowl of water sitting on a table next to a clay pot that was lavishly filled with all kinds of exotic foods and commanded, "Turn this bowl of water into wine, or better still, walk across the water in my wonderful Roman bath. Here!" He grabbed the midget court jester by the shoulder and pushed him down in front of Jesus and scoffed, "Make this little man as tall as me." He ran to his throne and grabbed his royal staff and mockingly said, "Here, Jesus, turn this staff into a snake like Moses did before the Pharaoh."

Jesus never flinched or moved. He stood there as if deaf and dumb. Dressed in all his finery, Herod paraded around him, mocking and being pompous, but Jesus never looked up from the floor.

Herod questioned Jesus for several minutes, but Jesus said not a word. Finally, Herod stopped in front of him, bent down slightly just below Jesus's chin, peered up into his face, and said, "What? Can't you speak, Jesus?" He walked away from Jesus a couple of feet, pointed to those that had brought him in, and said with childish mocking, "Have these big bad men scared you so badly you can't speak?" Then he whirled around and screamed into Jesus's face, "Don't tell me they have performed some miracle here that has shut you up!"

Then the chief priests and scribes stood before their king and, with venom in their voices, accused Jesus of many crimes. Herod waved them off and instructed one of his servants to bring him a gorgeous royal robe from his closet. When he had been handed the robe, he placed it around Jesus's shoulders, pointed at him, and said tauntingly, "Well, this is certainly a sight for sore eyes. And I thought that I was your king. I guess I was mistaken." Then he pointed to the door and screamed to the top of his lungs, "Get this imposter out of here! Get him out of my sight! Take this king of the Jews back to Pilate and let him deal with this false king, this sad excuse for the Messiah!"

By now it was midmorning and the soldiers, the scribes, the Pharisees, and the chief priests dragged Jesus, staggering because of his bindings, back to see Pilate. Pilate's personal guard came into his chamber and said, "They have brought the Galilean back to you, my lord."

"Oh, for the sake of the gods!" he complained. "What do they want of me now?" He got up from enjoying his morning meal and went out to the Jewish mob and Jesus, and asked, "What? Your King Herod can't do your bidding? What is it you want of me?"

Knowing that they had delivered Jesus to him because of envy, before they had a chance to answer, Pilate said, "I tell you what! During the feast of Passover, your governor is wont to release to the people one of the prisoners whom they request. We have in our prison a notable prisoner, a murderer by the name of Jesus Barabbas. So I ask you, which Jesus will you have me release unto you, Jesus Barabbas or Jesus whom they call the Christ?"

Pilate turned around and returned to his judgment seat before anyone had a chance to respond. The handmaiden to Pilate's wife came to him and said, "Your wife implores you to have nothing to do with this one they call Jesus the Christ, for he is just. She suffered many things last night in her dreams about him and begs you to let him go."

The handmaiden left the hall. With one leg hanging over an arm of his chair, Pilate lay back in his oversized royal judgment chair. He was brought back to reality when the multitude outside the open great front hall started screaming for the release of Barabbas. The chief priests and elders had persuaded the multitude that they should ask for Barabbas and destroy Jesus.

Taking the moment out of the hands of Pilate, the high priest said to him, "Do you hear the people? They are asking for Barabbas."

Shaking his head as if he could not believe what he was hearing, the governor instructed his guards to fetch Barabbas from his cell beneath the palace. After Barabbas had been brought forward, he was stationed beside Jesus at the top of the stairs that led down to the courtyard below. Pointing first to Jesus Barabbas and then to Jesus the Christ, Pilate yelled over the cacophony of sounds coming from the multitudes standing in the courtyard before his palace, "Which of these two men will you that I release to you?"

Some of the crowd yelled, "Jesus the Christ," but others countered with "Jesus Barabbas!"

A shouting match ensued, and soon those who had been provoked to request Barabbas overcame those wanting their Messiah released. Finally, only a handful were shouting, "Release Jesus the Christ!"

"What shall I do with this man called Jesus the Christ?" Pilate then asked.

The crowd shouted, "Crucify him!"

John and I were in the crowd near a large marble column that supported the porch. It covered the top three steps of the cascade of steps that lead to the great hall of judgment. We were among the few that shouted, "Release Jesus the Christ!" When we realized that those wanting the murderer Barabbas released had triumphed, we could only stare at each other in disbelief.

"You…you know, John," I stammered, "I warned him repeatedly that he was going too far, that they would end up killing him if he didn't stop pointing his finger at those in authority. To think I loved him so!"

"What are you saying, Mary?" John asked. "You know that you love him still. Don't be weak and turn on him like all these others."

"I am not turning my back on him. He turned his back on me," I said with venom. "We could have had a beautiful life together, but no, he had to push and push and preach this new Gospel about the love of God. What about my love, John? Why couldn't he have just returned my love and have loved me like a real man loves a woman? I hate him. I just hate him!"

Tears started streaming down my face; I ran away from John into the thick of the crowd. I was blinded by my hurt and was irrationally shaken. I knew that I was being pushed by the spirit of Satan; I just could not help myself.

It was strange though. As I struggled to get through the mob, I knew that John was shouting to me and reaching out to stop me from running away. However, it was not his eyes that I felt looking at me or his hand that reached out to me. I stopped for a moment, turned, and looked back at the two prisoners standing side by side upon the platform, a platform representing the final stage of one of their lives. Jesus Barabbas was jumping up and down and throwing kisses to the crowd; Jesus of Nazareth stood motionless. His eyes looked so sad, and yet they still maintained the power to pierce to the depths of one's soul. I felt him looking straight at me. Then something from outside reminded me that he had rejected my love; it was time to reject him. As a final gesture, from over my right shoulder I flipped my wrist, turned, and walked away slowly.

As I exited the scene, I heard the governor shout to the crowd, "Why would you want me to crucify this man? What evil has he done?"

But the multitude cried out that much more, "Let him be crucified!"

When Pilate realized that there was nothing that he could do to persuade them and that good sense was not going to prevail, he ordered his manservant to bring a basin and a jug of water to the front of the great hall where he, Barabbas, and Jesus stood before the yelling mob below. When the basin and water had been brought to him, he placed the bowl on a pedestal, held his hands over it, and instructed a manservant to pour the water from the jug. As the water splashed over his hands he rubbed them together before the multitude and said, "I am innocent of the blood of this just person. You do what you must do to him."

He took a white linen towel and dried his hands and looked out upon the crowd for their reply. The consensus was shouted back to him by one of the chief priests, "His blood be on us and on our children!"

Pilate thought to himself, *You all are such fools! Here comes along one who has been preaching love your neighbor and a turn-the-other-cheek doctrine, and you want him killed. Just like this man said, "Hypocrites! What fools you are!" Let it be upon your heads then!* He turned to his guards and instructed them, "Release the man called

Jesus Barabbas and take Jesus of Nazareth and scourge him. After that, turn him over to the soldiers to be crucified!"

Pilate's soldiers remained motionless. They stared at their commander way too long. They normally enjoyed being cruel to the Jews. They normally took delight in scourging them near unto death. But this man, this Jesus of Nazareth, he was different.

The commander of the legion came close to Pilate and whispered, "This is what you want, sire?"

Pilate recoiled and answered brashly, "Do as you are told!"

The few soldiers that were guards to the governor took Jesus into the common hall. They gathered together the whole band of soldiers that had gone out the night before to arrest Jesus in the Garden of Gethsemane. They stripped Jesus of all his clothing and placed upon his shoulders a scarlet robe and on his head a crown that they had been plated out of three-inch thorns. They took a reed that had been gathered from the riverbed of the River Jordan and made Jesus hold it in his right hand. They bowed at the knee before him and mocked him, saying, "Hail, king of the Jews."

They spit on him and took other reeds and beat him over the head. When they had tired of their sport, they removed Jesus's "royal" robe and led him naked to the rear of the governor's palace. There they tied his hands to a wooden pole that had been planted four feet into the ground and commenced to scourge him.

The customary scourging was thirty-nine lashes using a leather whip consisting of three heads, each laced with fragments of broken bones and pieces of jagged copper from the shop of the smithy. With each flick of the wrist, the three cattails of leather laced with these jagged pieces of bone and copper ripped and tore at the flesh of the one being scourged. By the time the thirty-nine lashes had been delivered to their mark, the back of the torso, back of the neck, and back of the arms and legs would be a bloody, unrecognizable grotesque pile of mangled carnage. The whip's tips would rip and tear at the flesh until the white of the bone of the ribs would be exposed and the odor of ripped bowels permeate the air. Crucifixion was just a ceremony after this, a place to hang the body until the birds of the air would be filled. Most of the people who were scourged in this fashion usually were reconciled with death before the first nail was struck.

But Jesus, this man from Galilee, this Nazarene who called himself the Son of man, the Son of God, still had breath in his lungs and blood in his veins after the beating of a lifetime. The three-inch thorns in the crown on his head had been pressed down into his skull from the beatings with the reeds. Both his eyes were swollen nearly shut from the many fists that had their slugfest, and blood poured from his every orifice. The left nostril had been sliced wide open with a fragment of copper that was pulled through as the whip's tail had been retrieved. Flesh hung in clumps from the exposed white ribs on his back and on the sides of his torso. Both his ears had been shredded.

The purple robe was once again placed on his shoulders, and Jesus was led back into the great hall to the top of the stairs. He could barely stand. Pilate gazed upon him momentarily with a certain amount of respect and a certain amount of empathy, and standing off to the side so as not to be smeared with the blood of the Christ, he pointed to him and said, "Behold the man!"

Regardless of the fact that Jesus as a man would probably succumb to death from the scourging at any moment, the chief priests and officers who saw him, cried out, "Crucify him, crucify him!"

Once again, Pilate shouted down to the mob below, "You take him and crucify him, for I have found no fault in him."

The leaders of the Jews answered him with a shout, "We have a law, and by our law, he ought to die because he made himself the Son of God. Do not forget, Governor, if you let this man go, you are no friend of Caesar's, for whoever makes himself a king is no friend of Caesar's."

Upon hearing this, Pilate was disgusted but fearful. He said to the yelling crowd, "Behold your king!"

Again they cried out, "Away with him, away with him, crucify him!"

Pilate yelled down to them, "Shall I crucify your king?"

The leaders of the Jews and the chief priests shouted back, "We have no king but Caesar!"

At this, Pilate had his last to do with this whole mess. He flipped his wrist toward Jesus and said, "Take him away! Crucify this innocent man if you must! You have cried for his blood. Now drink it till you drown in it!"

As the soldiers led him away, it was a certainty that Jesus would not be able to carry the crossbeam of his cross as was prescribed by Roman law. Standing by the alleyway that led from the courtyard of the governor's palace was a man from Cyrene by the name of Simon. He had brought his two sons to Jerusalem for the feast of the Passover, and as Jesus passed by them with the crossbeam upon his shoulders, he stumbled and crashed down upon the ground, the heavy wooden crossbeam lying squarely across him. One of the Roman soldiers grabbed Simon by the arm and screamed at him, "Pick it up, you'll carry this man's burden!"

Startled, Simon started stammering, "But…but…but…"

"Pick it up I said," bellowed the soldier. "Do as I say or you'll be carrying your own cross!"

"Yes, sir!" Simon submitted meekly. He reached down, helped Jesus back to his feet, picked up the cross, and placed it partly on his shoulders and partly on Jesus's. Together they started off toward the place called Golgotha, the hill of the skull, where criminals against the rule of Rome were punished with crucifixion. The struggle for Simon was fierce, for he carried the bulk of the weight of the crossbeam on his own shoulders and, with one arm around the waist of Jesus, supported half of his weight as well.

As they passed by, I was on the street leaning up against one of the buildings that lined the street where Jesus and Simon stumbled along. I could see on the opposite side of the street John and Jesus's mother moving slowly alongside as the procession made its way to Golgotha. With his arm around Mother Mary's waist, John half supported her as they moved slowly along. She appeared so weak from her wailing that one could see that she could hardly stand on her own two feet.

When Jesus, bloody from head to toe, beaten beyond recognition and Simon, the one conscripted to help carry his cross, were directly in front of me, I could no longer restrain myself. Like a tide going out, the pull on my emotions drained everything that was within me and tugged at my emotions. With my heart aching so badly that I could hardly breathe or speak, I garnered enough strength to run over to Jesus. Squatting down before him, I screamed into his face, "Why? All you had to do was stop provoking these people! I told you this is what would happen! But no, you couldn't just go away with me! Don't you understand, Jesus? I loved you!"

Turning his head so that he might see me through his left eye, the lesser swollen of the two, a drop of blood fell from the corner of his eye onto the top of my foot. I felt it. I saw it. That drop of blood was like the dividing line between the tide going out and the tide coming in. It hit so hard it felt as if a stone had been dropped on the top of my foot.

All time stopped. The yelling, the chanting, the conversations, the sound of sandals upon the stones, the groaning, the wailing—all sounds rushed into a total vacuum of silence. All movement slowed to a pace slower than that of a snail's. Birds stopped in midair, the Roman soldier's whips came down across Jesus's back as if they were flimsy, and the second drop of blood that cascaded down onto my foot splashed like a rock dropping into a pit of thick mud.

Jesus mumbled to me something that I could not comprehend. I shouted into his face, "What did you say?"

His chest moved in convulsions. He tried to moisten his lips that were crusted over with his own blood. After sucking in as much air as he could and swallowing the blood that had pooled in the back of his throat, he said in a voice that was just above a whisper, "This blood is…this blood is for…" and then he gave way and went down to the ground on his face.

I reached down, placed my open hand under his cheek, and lifted up his head that seemed to weigh a ton. Blood and water ran down the back of my arm. I turned his face toward me and then shouted into it, "What are you trying to say, Jesus?" Then I screamed into his ear. "What are you trying to say?"

I saw tears mixed with blood trickle down from the corners of his eyes. His face had lost most all semblances of life. Then suddenly, with the plethora of clanging bells, Jesus said clearly to me, "Mary, this blood is for you. I shed this blood to cleanse all those to be redeemed from all their sins."

As if I had been flattened by a giant wave of an incoming tide, I fell backward onto the rock-paved street. Like a crab running across the beach back to the ocean, I scrambled backward on my hands and feet to the wall that I had been leaning against prior to Jesus's approach. I glared at the man on his knees under the cross. He was no longer recognizable as even being human, but his words ricocheted around between the convolutions in my brain like a rubber ball bouncing between the walls of a hallway.

I saw Simon help Jesus once again to his feet and encourage him to move forward. The cacophony of sounds in the street returned with a vengeance, and they were all directed at me. Barely able to breathe, I gasped for each breath, and I fought off my desire to enter into darkness. Pushing my back flat up against the wall, I drew in the air as deeply as I could and then exhaled it until there was nothing left. I covered both my ears with my hands in an effort to block the noises that were deafening.

My ears began to ache so badly that I cried out in anguish, "Stop it! Stop it!"

The sounds in the street escalated to such a pitch that I truly felt that my head might explode. I fell forward onto my knees and cried out, "O God, help me! Help me!"

Then I realized that people were looking at me, trying to figure out what in the world might be wrong with me. At that moment, I had stopped caring what people thought. Everything that had seemed out of control, everything that had been out of sync started to come into focus. As the incoming waves of tears lapped over my consciousness, the tears that had stung and clouded my eyes now washed the confusion away. At a distance, I could still see Jesus and Simon struggling together to carry the crossbeam on which Jesus was to be hung. Like someone with a physical affliction, I struggled to my feet, struggled against the incoming rush of human emotion, against the overwhelming desire to run away. I stretched out my hand toward my Lord and screamed as loudly as possible, Jesus!"

Like an ocean wave that crashes into the back of an unsuspecting wader, my mind was jolted into a realism that before I had never had to confront. For the first time in my life, I knew who I was and to whom I belonged. A thousand oil lamps had been ignited all at the same time.

The waves of doubt that had been pulling me back I was now able to resist. I stretched forth my right hand to touch Jesus, who appeared at my fingertips, but it was just an illusion. He was too far away. My hand trembled like a hand with palsy as I reached for him. "My God," I screamed! "I know who you are! I now understand! I know what you meant when you said, 'I love you.'"

I pushed away from my safe wall and shouted the words that I had struggled so hard not to say, "My Lord and my God!"

Like a tide going out, the undertow of uncertainty tugged on me, but my feet started to move, and I knew beyond a shadow of a doubt that I wanted to be a servant! I wanted to be *his* servant! I had come to realize that his love overshadowed my petty little desires. I cried out as loudly as I could, "My Lord and my God, forgive me! I have sinned against you, and I have sinned against heaven."

With my right hand still outstretched as far as I could extend it, I found that I was running—*running for the cross!*

Epilogue

RUNNING FOR THE Cross! Are you running for the cross, or are you running from it? For the better part of her life, Mary Magdalene was in hot pursuit of love and happiness, but without Christ, both were just an illusion. Living life in this manner is akin to what the preacher in Ecclesiastes tried to tell us. When we pursue fulfillment through pleasure, wine, great works, wealth, aesthetic and artistic pleasures, and fame, all of these fail to bring lasting satisfaction.

Solomon, the wisest man who ever lived, tried to tell us that setting your heart on knowledge in the absence of knowing God is like grasping for the wind. Relying on our own wisdom brings much grief, and whenever we increase it, sorrows increase. When we consider ourselves wise and pursue love (in the absence of the love of Christ), not recognizing what true sacrificial love is and what it entails, it all amounts to vanity and vexation of the spirit.

In his wisdom, Solomon also said that we can certainly enjoy love and life if we enjoy them as God's gifts. In fourteen pairs of antithetical actions, (Ecclesiates 3:2-8) Solomon tells us that God has a sovereign design behind every one. One of these, of course, is that there is a time to love and a time to hate (or not to love).

Like Mary of Magdala, we charge headlong in the pursuit of love, a love that is temporal, one we think we need to fulfill a longing that we cannot identify. When Jesus showed her compassion, caring, and love, Mary mistakenly thought that his love was the love that would satisfy her romantic desires. It wasn't until Jesus had been falsely accused of sedition, beaten nearly to death, and was on his way to be crucified that Mary was confronted with real agape love—a love that gives and a love that sacrifices. Her first love was for the man, her ultimate love, was for her Savior.

If your search for love has not ended and your search for fulfillment has not netted results, perhaps you are searching in the wrong places and for the wrong kind of love. Look to Jesus. He cares for you in a way no one else can. He loves you so much that he gave his life for you. If you are running on empty, do what Mary Magdalene did: run for the Cross.